LIGHT AT THE TOP
OF THE STAIRS

Light at the Top of the Stairs

By
Dorothy Martin

MOODY PRESS
•
CHICAGO

Seventh Printing, 1981

ISBN: 0-8024-4748-1

Printed in the United States of America

Contents

Part I

ESCAPE TO REALITY

1

Monday and Problems

CONNIE SLAMMED THE DOOR behind her, cutting off the sound of Betty whining and the smell of burned toast. Mornings were horrible any time you had to go to school. But when there was nothing to eat and it was almost as cold inside the house as outside, it wasn't even worth getting up. She huddled into her jacket, her thin body tense against the bitterness of the air.

The wind swept in from the lake over thin sheets of ice which already covered the water curving along the shoreline. She stood at the corner shivering, waiting for the light to change, and looked down the avenue. The store buildings were still shuttered in the cold November morning, giving them a ghost-town look. The snow was late this year, and there was nothing to cover the ugly outlines of the business part of town that sprawled along the edge of the lake, nor the dirt-blackened building toward which she moved reluctantly.

Other kids hurried past her, heads ducked against the wind, intent only on getting into the warmth of the building. Connie walked alone, her thoughts somber. She didn't belong to any of the groups in school and knew she never would. It was something you pretended you didn't care about and never admitted even to yourself how desperately it hurt to be left out. It was easier to act as though you wanted to be a loner. That way you covered up the crummy place you lived in, and the fact that you couldn't go anywhere because you didn't have money to spend or decent clothes to wear. Even the thin friendship she'd formed last year with Pat and Janet was becoming more uncertain. She didn't know what was the matter with them. Sometimes they knew you and sometimes they didn't. Of course there were others who were loners too. Like Agnes. But who wanted to be seen with a creep like her?

On a dismal, depressing day which had begun with an empty stomach and undone assignments, it was easy to slip into familiar daydreams—to be a famous actress, mobbed by people wanting her autograph—to be stretched out in the warm sun beside her private swimming pool with wide green lawns and a black iron fence shutting her off—to move through stores ordering anything she wanted without bothering to ask the price.

While her mind imagined impossible pictures, her feet automatically carried her up the worn steps of the building, through the heavy doors, into the pushing crowds, and up to her locker on the third floor. Then cold fury brought reality back as she flipped the combination and pulled the locker door open to the sliver of space left her from Agnes' heavy coat and warm scarf.

Fat old Agnes and her fat old clothes! There ought to be a law against anyone having her as a locker partner.

She yanked off her jacket and scarf, cramming them onto a hook and ignoring Agnes' sweater and mittens that fell to the floor of the locker. Rummaging in the clutter on the shelf, she dug out the math book for first period. How she hated the stuff! It was bad enough to have it in school, but they expected you to lug the book home and work on it at night too. Nuts to them!

She managed to get through class without having to go to the board. Teachers always pretended this was to help you when they were really just showing you up as a dummy. How did they think it helped you to stand in front of the class wearing your sister's old skirt, knowing the holes in the heels of your socks showed? And to know that everyone was laughing at you for being stupid!

When the bell rang, Connie was the first one out of the

room, and her steps quickened as she went to home ec. Her stomach was clamoring for something, even tapioca pudding. But after a quick glance around the room, she sat down at her table gloomily. Today was just going to be talk—no cooking. To take her mind off her hunger she stared moodily across the table at Agnes, whose greasy hair and pimply face showed how little she cared about her looks. Connie stared at the roll of fat bulging over the top of Agnes' skirt and automatically tightened her stomach muscles and sat straighter.

That's one good thing about not having enough to eat, she thought grimly. *At least your stomach stays flat.* She opened her purse in her lap and sneaked a quick look in the mirror, glad for the smooth reflection that stared back at her. But she frowned at how pale she was and moistened her lips with the tip of her tongue, wishing she'd had enough nerve to sneak some good lipstick from Myrna instead of putting on the cheap stuff she had that wore off right away.

By the time third period was over, Connie was so hungry that she wished she had eaten the cornflakes and canned milk she'd gagged at the thought of. It didn't help any to sit and stare at the menu she'd written down in her home ec notebook. *Whoever has orange juice and scrambled eggs and bacon and popovers and hot chocolate for breakfast anyway,* she thought crossly.

She was lucky she'd been smart enough to get out to the kitchen in time to get the last two slices of bread for lunch. Betty had been mad that there was only the crust left for toast, when she should have been glad she had that much. It wasn't *her* fault it got stuck in the toaster and burned before Betty could pry it out. Besides, Betty was lucky. Grade school kids got a free hot lunch at school. And if Myrna had planned on taking a lunch it was her tough luck that there wasn't anything left. Anyway, she could always con some guy at school into buying her something.

Connie looked at the clock. Ten minutes to go until

she could eat. Lunch was nothing to get excited about when she had only a peanut butter sandwich, but at least she had the apple, too, that she'd hidden last night so Betty wouldn't find it.

Then a vision of the heavy lunch sack she had seen on the shelf in the locker crowded out the discussion of the US constitution. Her mouth watered at the thought of the food that must be in it. She swallowed and pressed her arm across her stomach to quiet the noise it made.

Sudden inspiration hit her, and as soon as class was over she shoved through the next row to walk out the door with Agnes.

"Hey, how about saving me a place in the cafeteria?"

Agnes blinked. "You want to eat with me?"

"Sure. You go save the places and I'll get the lunches. No sense both of us tearing up to third and then all the way down to the basement. Hurry up!"

She turned without waiting for an answer and pushed through the lunch crowds up to the locker, reached for Agnes' sack and opened it. "Just as I thought," she muttered. One—two—three—*five* sandwiches plus cake and a banana. And a candy bar. Connie partly unwrapped one of the sandwiches. Good! Tuna. She loved it. She wanted to cram it down right then but made herself stick it in her purse. She put the cake in her sack and went down to the lunch room. Stopping just inside the door, she looked around and saw Agnes standing across the room waving her arms, but pretended not to notice. The milk line was short, so she didn't have to wait long and went over to dump her books on the table beside Pat and Janet.

'Boy, am I starved!" She unwrapped her peanut butter sandwich and bit into it ravenously.

From behind her Agnes said breathlessly, "Hey, Connie! I've been waving like mad. I saved seats over there."

"Oh, really? I thought you'd disappeared. Look, since I'm already sitting here I'll just stay. Here's your lunch."

As Agnes reached for it, Pat said, "You mean you're running errands for Agnes?"

"Just trying to be helpful," Connie shrugged.

"Did you say thank you?" Janet asked solemnly, looking sternly at Agnes.

Agnes looked from one to the other uncertainly and then down at her sack, while her lips trembled. "Well, uh, thanks," she said and turned slowly away.

Connie shrugged. "Anytime."

"How come you did something nice for fat Agnes?" Pat asked.

Connie looked at her coolly. "Just helping her out."

"I'll bet!"

The second sandwich and the cake helped fill her up and got her through the afternoon, though she regretted she hadn't taken the candy bar to eat on the way home. She got to the locker after school just as Agnes slammed it shut and turned to face her.

"Oh—I—I didn't know you were here or I wouldn't have shut it," Agnes stammered through the folds of the crimson wool scarf she had wrapped around her head and neck.

"Doesn't matter," Connie shrugged and flipped the combination swiftly, wondering if Agnes would mention the missing sandwich. The dumb kid! Her mother probably fixed her lunch for her.

"You going right home?"

"Sure."

"I'll walk with you," Agnes offered timidly.

"I'm walking with Pat and Jan."

She yanked the door open and pulled on her jacket, her back to Agnes. After a moment she could hear her footsteps echoing down the hall.

Connie hurried downstairs to catch up with Pat and Janet, but they hadn't waited for her. She walked home, shivering in the bite of the wind, feeling lonesome and depressed. The memories of the weekend quarrels with

Myrna, the thought of a whole week of school just beginning, the coat she wanted—needed—and couldn't have,
a little bit of shame at having taken Agnes' sandwich,
all pressed down on her. The gray clouds hanging heavy
in the winter sky matched her dark mood.

She tripped on a piece of the broken sidewalk in front
of the house and felt the rip widen along the sole of her
shoe.

"Great!" she muttered. "All I need right now is to
have my shoe fall apart."

She went down the four steps to the basement apartment. At least she'd beaten Betty home, so she wouldn't
have anything to tattle about when Ma got home from
work.

She pulled the mail out of the box and went in, slamming the outside door. At the sound, Mrs. Brewster
stuck her head out from her open door at the top of the
stairs. "Hi, Connie. Did you bring in your mail?" Then
seeing the letters in Connie's hand, she asked, "There
isn't one for me mixed in with yours, is there?"

"I don't see any for you."

"Nuts!" She came out and sat down at the top of the
stairs. "As you can guess I didn't get my letter from
Mike, and I thought maybe the mailman got it mixed in
with yours. I've been itching all afternoon to go through
your mail."

"Why didn't you?"

"I wouldn't dare!" She turned quickly to put one foot
against the wall, so that her leg formed a barrier to the
stairs for Kevin who came toddling out. "Mike used to
carry mail, and he always lectured me about what happened to people who fooled around with the US mail.
What would Kevin do if I went to jail?" She grinned
down at Connie who smiled back.

Mrs. Brewster was cute. She was only twenty, and she was
crazy about Mike and Kevin and always found something to
laugh about. She and Kevin had moved in upstairs right after
her husband had gone overseas with the Army, and

she had started counting the days on the calendar until he got back. The first time Connie had stayed with Kevin she had seen the huge calendar Mrs. Brewster had made and taped to the bedroom wall. Every day she crossed out one more. Myrna thought she was nuts to sit home waiting for Mike when she could go out and have fun, and she had tried a couple of times to fix up a double date. Connie remembered and envied the way Mrs. Brewster had told Myrna off. When you were that old and were married and had your own baby you could say things to people you couldn't when you were just in the eighth grade and knew you'd get slapped.

Connie watched as Mrs. Brewster scooped Kevin up and held him dangling and squealing with delight over her head. "Ugh! He's sopping. I've got to change him." She stood up and looked down at Connie. "Don't worry if you hear someone walking around up here all night. It'll just be me pacing the floor and worrying about Mike." She grinned again and disappeared, and Connie pushed open the door to their apartment.

She turned on the television and slouched on the sofa, her books and jacket in a heap beside her. The set needed adjusting, and while she was twisting the knobs Betty came in, her cheeks red with the cold, and her nose running as usual.

Connie looked at her. "I've got bad news."

"What?"

"Ma's gone."

"Where?"

"To the hospital. She has to have an operation. A bad operation," she added, watching Betty's face to see how far she ought to go.

"She isn't either," Betty retorted, her voice unsure. Then she stared at the sad look on Connie's face and repeated, "She isn't either." And then, "You're just fooling. Aren't you?"

Connie shook her head mournfully. "She might even die."

Betty stared back, her lips trembling. Finally tears

welled up in her eyes and Connie said hastily, "OK, so
I'm joking. Don't bawl!"

"That wasn't a nice joke. I'm going to tell."

"What a big baby! Have to tell Ma everything. When
are you going to grow up?"

"Not ever if I have to be like you."

"OK, beat it and let me watch this program. Go on
out and play."

"I don't want to. It's too cold out."

"Well, go someplace just so it's away from me."

"I'm going to read my lib'ary book. It's about *nice*
people."

Connie lost track of time and sat up with a jerk when
the door slammed and her mother yelled, "Turn that
thing down! You can hear it clear outside."

"It isn't loud."

"Then you're going deaf," and her mother snapped
the television off as she went to the kitchen with a sack
of groceries.

"Hey, it isn't over!"

"Well, it had better be," her mother answered grimly.
"You're supposed to get the house cleaned up first and
then laze around. I can't work all day and then come home
and work here too. When are you going to start doing a
little something around here?"

Connie got up and went to the kitchen without answering. Anything she said would be wrong with Ma in that
mood. She opened the refrigerator to see if she could
figure out what to fix for supper without asking, but it
was as empty as she knew it would be. The bag of groceries stood on the kitchen table and she looked in.

"Are we having these pork chops for supper?" she
called to her mother, who came out of the bedroom
tying her robe, her cigarette sticking against her moist
lips.

"Yeah, and fry some potatoes to go with them. I only
got one apiece because they cost too much. Then they're
nothing but bone and fat. The stores gyp you every way

they can." She shuffled through the mail Connie had left on the table by the sofa.

"Bills! And the louse is behind on alimony as usual."

The description of her father was so usual for this time of the month that Connie only half-heard the words. His check never came on time, and she couldn't figure out why Ma always expected it to. Her memories of him were of times when he was fun and times when you hid from his drunken rages. In some ways life had been easier since he walked out six years ago. But as she sliced potatoes into the frying pan, Connie could only think of the ways life was worse.

"Did Myrna go to school today?"

Connie didn't look around at her mother as she answered, "I left before she did."

"She was still in bed when I went," Betty said as she came into the kitchen and added a plaintive, "I don't feel good. When do we eat?"

"Well, if you want to eat do a little work. Set the table," Connie ordered.

"For Myrna too?"

"No, stupid, she's working."

"How should I know?" Betty scowled back, as she wiped her nose with the back of her hand and coughed.

"Because she's been working after school for two months. Don't you ever pay attention?"

Betty coughed without answering, and her mother said, "I told you you'd get sick playing outside yesterday with just a sweater on."

"Well, I didn't want to wear Connie's old coat. It's too big."

"Of course it's too big. I wore it myself last year. Ugh! I hated it!"

"Beggars can't be choosers," her mother snapped back.

"I don't intend to be a beggar all my life," Connie said grimly, flopping the potatoes over in the grease in the skillet.

"Well, good for you," her mother mocked. "Let me

know your secret." Then she laughed harshly. "I'll tell you the secret—don't get married and have kids. Stay single and look out for yourself."

Connie was silent. She'd heard Ma regret so many times that she had ever gotten married that it didn't bother her anymore. But as she turned around to put the food on the table, she glimpsed Betty staring at her mother with trembling lips.

"Do you wish you didn't have us?"

"Sometimes." Then as Betty burst into tears and ran into the living room, she exclaimed, "For crying out loud, what's the matter with her?"

"I wouldn't know," Connie said coldly while rage boiled inside her. Betty was a brat and a runny-nosed nuisance, but that didn't mean she had to be hurt like that. Ma was always saying thoughtless things depending on how she felt, and she never seemed to understand that they hurt a person. Betty was too young to understand that sometimes she meant them and sometimes she didn't. *But young as she is she might as well learn that nothing is fair in this world and that you have to look after yourself because no one else is going to,* Connie thought grimly.

She stalked into the living room where Betty was crumpled in a heap on the sofa. "Wipe your nose and come eat," she said shortly.

"I'm not hungry," Betty answered, her face hidden in the crook of her arm.

"Good. Then I can eat your chop."

"I don't care."

"OK." Connie went back to the kitchen. "She's not coming."

Her mother was shaking salt over her food and shrugged. "If she's hungry, she'll eat."

Connie sat down with her plate and they ate silently. When her mother finished she shoved her plate back, lighted a cigarette, and looked across the table at Connie.

"How many times has Myrna missed school so far this month?"

"I don't know."

"Don't you ever walk to school the same time she does?"

"Not usually. She's always late. I'm only late sometimes."

"Don't you ever talk to each other? I thought sisters were supposed to tell each other secrets and all that stuff."

"I thought mothers and daughters were supposed to—"

Her mother reached over and grabbed her arm. "Don't you get smart with me, young lady. Not unless you want a smack across the face."

Connie sat motionless until her mother released her arm and leaned back in her chair. "Myrna doesn't tell me anything," she said finally, in an expressionless voice.

"Don't you ask her any questions?"

"If I did, she'd tell me it was none of my business."

How could she tell Ma that there were things about Myrna she didn't want to know, things she didn't want to talk to her about? She remembered the day last month when she had gotten sick in school and had to come home early, and Myrna was there. She'd heard voices in the living room; and when she had rattled the locked door, Myrna had called quickly, "Wait a minute."

When she finally had opened the door she was alone, but Connie was sure someone else had been there. All Myrna had said was that they must have eaten something that made them both sick at the same time. But she had made Connie promise that she wouldn't tell Ma she'd been home, because she wanted to work that evening. Then she had looked at Connie with that expression Connie hated and had started talking.

She closed her mind hard now against the memory of the horrible things Myrna had tried to tell her that day. She stood up abruptly.

"Betty didn't eat anything after all."

"Give it to me then. No sense in wasting it."

Connie stuck a fork in the meat and carried it over to her mother's plate and then went into where Betty lay,

one foot hanging over the edge of the sofa and her arms
thrown out in a curiously defensive way. Connie looked
at her flushed cheeks, and then put her hand on Betty's
forehead.

"She sure feels hot," she called back over her shoulder.

"They always do with a cold," her mother answered.
"Wake her up and tell her to get to bed."

"But she hasn't eaten anything."

"Well, they always say, starve a cold and feed a fever.
So she's got both so it won't matter which you do."

Connie shook Betty's shoulder; and she roused saying
hoarsely, "I wanna go to bed."

"OK, come on." Connie walked with her into the bedroom and pulled the blanket and sheet back on the cot
in the corner. She knew her kindness was mostly a
reaction to her mother's indifference, and yet she did
feel sorry for Betty who moved so listlessly and was so
strangely obedient. She must be sick not to be bratty.
She helped her undress, and Betty flopped limply onto
the cot while Connie pulled the blanket over her and
tucked it under the thin mattress. The window shade was
rattling, and she pulled it up a little, pushing in the
wads of newspaper that stuffed the cracks along the
bottom of the window sill.

She went back to the living room where she had dumped
her books when she came home. Her mother had the television on and without looking around said, "Get the
dishes done before you do anything else. Otherwise
they'll still be there in the morning and the kitchen
will be a mess."

Connie went out silently to the mess that had been
there all day from the morning's cereal bowls, the canned
milk dried into a scum. She slammed the dishes around
just enough to let off steam without getting her mother
mad, and finally stuck the greasy frying pan into the
oven out of sight. She'd be the one to have to wash it
anyway, and tomorrow was as good as today for that job.

When she went back to the living room, much as she

wanted to watch the program her mother had on, she silently picked up her books and went out to study at the kitchen table. Nothing could make her stay in the living room with her mother, absolutely nothing. She opened the math book and started reading. But the problems, always hard, were harder when snatches of the program were mixed in with the instructions that didn't make sense. She tried science but that was worse, and finally she slammed her book shut with the assignment undone. How could you do the experiments at home when you didn't have stuff to work with? And nobody who cared if you needed help?

"See what Betty is yelling about," her mother called sharply from the front room; and Connie went to the bedroom door.

"I'm thirsty," Betty said, her voice thick and hoarse.

"OK, I'll get you a drink," and she got a cup of water from the kitchen sink. Betty's hand was hot as Connie held it to steady the cup while Betty drank greedily and then sank back on the pillow.

Connie went to the bedroom door. "She sure is hot," she said, looking back over her shoulder at the thin form lying so quietly.

Her mother got up and impatiently pushed past her to lean over Betty. "Well, she went back to sleep again in a hurry anyway," she said turning away. "If she wakes up in the night, give her a couple of aspirin. All kids get fevers but they usually survive. You had plenty of them when you were a kid. When I think of the nights I lost sleep with you! You and Betty both were puny kids. Myrna was the only healthy one in the bunch."

Anybody would be who looks after themselves as much as Myrna does. Nobody is more important to Myrna than Myrna. She's selfish, selfish, selfish! I hate her, Connie's thoughts ran on relentlessly. And the echo of that feeling was in her eyes as she watched her mother come back from the refrigerator with a can of beer and settle down in front of the television.

Connie looked at her and felt the depression of the afternoon settle in her again. She wondered if Ma had ever felt this way, so alone—and lost—and desperate for answers to questions.

She sat down on the edge of the chair across from the couch.

"Ma."

"What?" Then as Connie didn't answer, she looked at her sharply, "What do you want?"

"I want to ask you something."

"Well, what?" Then she added impatiently, "If it's clothes, the answer is no. I can't even afford to buy some for myself. If you want something you'll have to get some babysitting jobs."

"It's not that—" she began and stopped as her mother turned back to the program.

"Ma," she said desperately and cringed as her mother turned on her.

"Will you stop yapping at me? I'm trying to watch this program. I've worked like a dog all day, so I think I deserve a chance to rest without you pestering me."

Connie went into the bedroom and undressed quickly, shaking with the cold and with anger, and pulled on her pajamas. Then she turned on the light and used some of Myrna's face cream. The words in the health book stood in front of her as a reminder about the importance of "soap and water for proper cleansing of the skin," but she made a face at the thought. Even thinking of washing in cold water made her shiver. *And I'm not going out to the kitchen to heat some and have to look at Ma and her beer!*

After using the cream she looked carefully at the crowded dresser top. No matter what a mess Myrna left things in or how many jars of cream and bottles of lotion were on the dresser, she always seemed to know exactly where each one had been left and how much was in it. Connie had learned to use only a little at a time, dipping from the same place Myrna had last used, and putting the jar back in the exact spot it had been. She'd had enough slaps to know that it didn't pay to get caught using any of Myrna's stuff.

She set the alarm and crawled into bed, shivering from the wind that was blowing harder and whistling in through the cracks around the newspaper. The dumb old health books talked about putting the window up at night for fresh air, when all she asked for was a warm room to sleep in.

It was really stupid of her to go to bed before Myrna got home from her job, because she always barged in and turned on the light and slammed stuff around without caring about anyone else. She was quiet only when she sneaked in, trying to keep Ma from knowing what time she got in. Maybe this would be one of those times. Anyway, by going to bed she could be alone and shut out the ugliness of the world. She stared into the dark, thinking over the day and hating the thought of tomorrow and all the days ahead. And hating Ma's not caring.

Betty stirred restlessly on her cot and coughed. Connie pulled the blanket up over her ears to shut out the sound of the television and the whine of the wind. She let her mind picture the dreams of the future until they lulled her to sleep.

Sometime in the darkness she was wakened by the sound of voices in a loud argument, and knew that Myrna was home and that she and Ma were having their nightly battle. The anger in their voices made the words indistinct even though they were yelling at each other. Connie tried to raise up enough to see the time. The crack across the face of the clock fooled her sometimes but it looked like one-thirty. Betty had thrown her blanket off but she was asleep, and Connie couldn't make herself go over and cover her. She should because Myrna wouldn't think of it. But instead she pulled the pillow over her head and pressed it against her ears to shut out the voices, and fell asleep.

2

Tuesday and More Problems

CONNIE TURNED OVER restlessly, feeling the ache in her legs from having slept doubled up to keep warm. The house was cold, and Myrna had rolled over, dragging the blanket with her. Connie yanked it back and burrowed under the part that was warm from Myrna's body, pulling the pillow close around her neck to shut out the cold drafts. Then she opened her eyes enough to squint at the clock.

Oh, no! Seven-thirty! Myrna must have shut off the alarm before she went to bed, a nice little trick she used as an excuse for being late for school. But it meant Connie would be late too unless she rushed, and school just wasn't worth it. She just wasn't going to get up in a cold house when she didn't have anything that was decent to wear, and her math and science would only get big, fat zeroes.

Connie closed her eyes again and curled up where her body had warmed the bed. Then a hoarse cough from Betty's bed jolted her up on one elbow.

"You still sick?" she demanded.

When Betty didn't answer, Connie got up, groped for the sweater she had left on the chair when she undressed, and hugged it around her shoulders, leaning over to feel Betty.

"Yow! She feels hot. I wonder if Ma's gone to work," she muttered and went to look.

The other bedroom was empty, and a coffee cup with ground-out cigarette butts stood on the dresser among the clutter that was her mother's. Connie leaned down and pulled out the heater her mother hid under the bed when she wasn't using it, took it back to the bedroom and plugged it in, standing close and shivering more than ever in anticipation of the heat. If Betty were really sick, she would have an excuse to stay home and take care of her. She leaned over Betty again. Yes, she was feverish. As she pulled the blanket over her shoulders, Betty's library book thudded to the floor from the foot of the bed.

"What are you doing?" Myrna's voice was heavy with sleep as she raised on one elbow and looked at Connie and then turned to see the time. "Rats! I just got in bed and it's already time to get up."

"You'd better hurry too or you'll be late." The room was beginning to warm up, but Connie still clutched the sweater around her arms as she stood close to the heater.

"What about you?" Myrna mumbled. "You're not exactly fit to be seen. Why don't you get yourself some decent pajamas?"

"As long as I have to wear your old junk I'll never look decent. And anyway, I'm not going to school today."

"How come?"

"Betty's sick and I'm staying home with her."

"You get dressed and go," Myrna ordered. "I'll stay."

"A lot of good you'd do her. You'd just go back to sleep and wouldn't know if she died. Besides, Ma asked me just last night how many days you'd missed so far this month."

Myrna jerked around. "What'd you tell her?"

Connie shrugged. "I told her I didn't know. Why should I care about you?"

"Yeah, well, just keep on staying out of my business." Myrna yawned widely, stretched, and sat up. "Fix me some coffee while I get dressed."

Connie started to say, "Fix it yourself." But she was afraid Myrna would still insist on being the one to stay home, so she went to the kitchen and put a pan of water on to heat. There wasn't much coffee left in the jar, and she carefully measured out a spoonful, waited for the water to boil, filled the cup, and yelled, "Do you want sugar?"

"No! Just hurry it up, will you?"

"Did you get paid last night?" Connie asked as she put the cup down on the dresser beside Myrna's pile of rollers.

"So what if I did?" Myrna's face was rigid with the cream mask she used every morning, and the words came out through stiff lips.

"I don't think Ma left any money and I might have to buy something today."

"Like what?"

"Well, something for Betty—like milk or something."

"Just let her sleep."

"Sure, but if she wakes up she's got to eat."

"Isn't there anything out there?"

"There wasn't much yesterday. Nothing even for lunches." The memory of Agnes' sackful made her mouth water even now.

"Didn't Ma shop on the way home from work? She had a new carton of cigarettes."

"She got stuff for supper but we ate that."

"Well, open a can of soup or beans or something." Then at the sight of Connie's stubborn face she said impatiently, "Oh, all right! Here's a dollar. But if you don't have to get Betty anything, I want it back. I work too hard for that lousy paycheck to give it away. I'm not supposed to have to buy the groceries around here anyway."

Connie took the money and went out to the kitchen so she wouldn't have to watch Myrna put on her makeup, hating the way she did it with such total concentration. Now that the bedroom was warm from the heater, the rest of the house seemed colder than ever and she shivered looking for something to eat. There were a few crackers left in the box and she ate them hungrily as she wandered through the house, hugging her sweater around her and wishing Myrna would hurry up and leave.

It was eight-thirty when she finally came out of the bedroom still drying her nail polish.

"Hey, where'd you get that sweater?" Connie looked enviously at the soft brown wool turtleneck.

Myrna shrugged. "Where do you usually get clothes, dopey?"

"Where'd you get the money to buy it? I bet that cost twenty dollars. And I've never seen that jumper before either."

"I work, remember?"

"Did you buy them yesterday?"

"Look, what is this? The third degree or something? Yes, I got them last night. On my supper break. I ate a hot dog on the run standing up so I'd have time to shop. Satisfied?"

"Can I have your green sweater then?" Connie couldn't keep the eagerness out of her voice, but Myrna snapped back, "No, you can not. And don't go trying it on either."

Connie made a face behind Myrna's back as she went out the door and yelled, "You've got too much perfume on."

She went into the bedroom, yanked open the dresser drawer, rummaged for the green sweater and pulled it on over her pajama top, looking at herself in the mirror. That shade really did things for her blond hair. She leaned forward to peer at herself closely. It even showed up the green in her eyes. She nodded at herself with satisfaction. It would be easy to wear it to school on days Myrna worked and got home late. If she could keep Betty from tattling.

Betty whimpered then, and Connie went over and stood looking down at her. Then she sat down on the edge of the cot as Betty opened her eyes and looked around.

"How do you feel?"

"I hurt."

"Where?"

"My stomach."

"Do you want something to eat?"

Betty shook her head. "I'm thirsty."

Connie frowned. What was it their health teacher said was good for sickness? Orange juice they didn't have. No milk either. "Want some cocoa?"

Betty shook her head with her eyes closed.

"I can make some with hot water and put some canned milk in it," Connie coaxed, but Betty turned her head away.

"Well, do you want a drink of water?"

Betty nodded.

Connie stopped to take off the green sweater. If Betty remembered anything at all later on this would be it, and she'd be sure to tattle. There was no sense in getting Myrna mad. She stopped to look at Betty again.

Ma said to give her aspirin. I wonder if we have any.

She went to her mother's room and pulled open drawers. All the bottles there were unlabelled and Connie frowned at them, wondering how she could tell if some were aspirin. She knew her mother took sleeping pills, and she didn't dare give Betty anything she wasn't sure of. The memory of the frightening scene last winter when her mother had accidentally taken too many pills was still vivid in her mind and was a grim reminder of what happened when you were careless with them. She stood for a minute and then dumped the pills back in the bottle and tightened the cap. Maybe she could run upstairs to Mrs. Brewster later on and see if she had aspirin.

Connie went back to the bedroom with a cup of water, but Betty had fallen asleep curled up in a tight heap. Connie stood in front of the heater. The warmth of the room made her feel relaxed and drowsy. She decided there was no use in her staying awake either. If Betty cried she would hear her. She was sound asleep when the repeated ringing of the phone roused her, and she sat up groggily.

"I won't answer. Nobody knows anyone is here," she muttered and slumped down again. But when the phone kept on ringing and Betty whimpered and half raised up, Connie got up and padded out to the kitchen.

"Hello?"

"Mrs. Hamilton?"

"No. She's working."

The voice sharpened as it asked, "Who is this? Is this Myrna Hamilton?"

"No, Connie."

"This is the school office calling to find out why Myrna is absent. Why aren't you in school?"

"I'm staying home to take care of my sister. She's sick."

"How old is she?" The voice plainly showed doubt, and Connie felt the need to convince it she was telling the truth.

"She's in third grade and she's sick and my mother had to go to work so I'm staying home with her. Myrna left for school," she added, wondering where she had gone.

"Where does your mother work?"

Connie hesitated. She didn't want to be caught in the middle of a mess between Myrna and Ma. They would probably call Ma at work to ask questions, and she'd be mad at Myrna, and Myrna would take it out on her.

"She's not supposed to get calls at work," she finally blurted.

There was silence for a moment, and Connie could hear voices talking. "Very well. Please tell your mother that Myrna has missed eighteen days of school since September and has only brought excuses for six of them. It would be well if your mother could come in for a conference some-time soon."

"I'll tell her," Connie promised earnestly and laughed as she put down the receiver. The thought of Ma bothering to go to school for a conference with a teacher was a scream. She'd sure blow up at Myrna though, if she found out about her missing so much.

"I hope I'm around when she hears about it," she muttered, "but *I'm* sure not going to be the one to tell her."

She went back and looked down at Betty, who lay on her side with her knees drawn up against her stomach. Connie frowned as she looked at her skinniness. Her thin face ended in a sharply pointed chin, and her shoulder blades were narrow ridges under her torn pajama top. Maybe Betty was sicker than she realized. Maybe she ought to call Ma. But knowing how much Ma hated home problems, and how impatient she would be at being bothered with them at work, Connie decided against it.

She could hear Kevin crying upstairs, so she knew Mrs. Brewster was home. She pulled on jeans and a sweatshirt and went up.

"Come in," Mrs. Brewster yelled in answer to her knock, and as Connie opened the door she looked around with a laugh. "Hi. My little angel has been screaming ever since he got up, as you've probably heard." Then she looked at Connie sharply. "Aren't you supposed to be in school, or is this one of those teachers' days off?"

"No, I stayed home with Betty. She's sick."

"That's too bad. What's the matter? Chickenpox? Measles?"

"No, she's had those. I guess it's just a cold but she looks pretty sick. Do you have some aspirin I could borrow?"

"Sure. But only give her one. Two at the most." She went into the bathroom and came back in a minute.

"Sorry, I'm all out. Look, why don't you go to the drugstore and get me a bottle, and you can have some for your trouble."

"Well, OK, if you really need them."

"I do. But mostly I need some cigarettes. You can get me a carton at the same time."

"I'll have to have a note or something. At least I do when I get them for Ma."

"Oh, yeah, I forgot. Look, I'll call the drugstore. I've bought so much medicine there for Kevin I practically own the place. I'll tell him you're coming in. He knows

my voice because I've ordered stuff lots of times. Here—
five dollars should cover it."

As Connie went down for her jacket, Mrs. Brewster
leaned over the railing to call, "Leave the door open and
I'll open mine. That way I'll hear if Betty calls out or
cries."

The sight of the kids pouring out of school for lunch,
as she passed it on the way to the drugstore, reminded
her that she hadn't eaten anything but the crackers, and
a wave of hunger cramped her stomach at the thought of
food. *I'll buy a candy bar at the drugstore to keep my
stomach from growling,* she decided.

When she went to the counter with the bottle of
aspirin and the candy, she said, "Mrs. Brewster wants
a carton of cigarettes."

The druggist looked at her sourly. "Yeah?"

"She said she'd call so you would know it was all
right."

"Well, she hasn't. And anyway, how do I know it
wouldn't be your sister trying a dodge to get them for
herself?"

"My sister doesn't smoke," Connie answered coldly,
knowing it wasn't true.

"She's tried this before," the druggist persisted. "Though
usually she pretends they're for your mother."

The phone rang, and Connie said, "That's Mrs. Brewster
now, I bet."

He looked at her with his lips folded in a thin, tight
line and then went to the phone. When he came back he
threw a carton of cigarettes on the counter and rang up
the sale without saying anything.

Connie paid him and turned away fuming. Talk about
suspicious people! She stopped at the magazine rack and
leafed through a couple, watching the druggist. When he
turned away to fill a prescription, she slipped a candy
bar into her pocket. This one was for Betty, poor kid.
She needed something to cheer her up. Besides, he had
no business being so suspicious and acting so nasty.

She hurried home to get in out of the biting wind, banging the door behind her. Mrs. Brewster was standing in the living room looking worried.

"You know, Connie, I think you ought to call your mother. Betty really looks sick. The way she's lying all doubled up like that, I'll bet she has appendicitis."

"Really?" Connie dumped her jacket in a chair and went in to look at Betty. "Is that the way you can tell appendicitis?"

"That's one way."

"But—Ma'll be mad if I call her and then it turns out there's nothing the matter with her but a cold."

"I'd sure want to be called if it were my kid."

Yeah, but you're not Ma, Connie said silently. She looked at Betty again. "Well, all she can do is get mad," she said finally, and went to dial the restaurant where her mother was a waitress and asked for her.

"She can't come now. She's taking orders," the man who answered barked.

"Will you tell her to call home as soon as she can?"

"Look, we're busy. She's got no time to make personal phone calls."

"But my little sister is sick," Connie begged. "Real sick. I don't know what to do for her."

"OK," the voice growled. "Hang on a minute."

Connie could hear the hum of voices and the clatter of dishes in the background, and then her mother said, "Well? What do you want?"

"It's Betty—" she began but her mother interrupted.

"Keep her in bed and give her some aspirin or something. Give her a couple of my sleeping pills so she'll stay asleep."

Her voice was loud and penetrating, and Mrs. Brewster motioned for the phone. Connie handed it to her and stood close to hear.

"Look, Mrs. Hamilton. You've got a sick kid here. It looks to me like it could be serious."

"She wasn't that sick when I left this morning." Connie

could hear her mother's sharp, accusing tone. "What's going on there?"

"The thing that's going on is that Betty is a sick girl."

"Now listen, I've had more experience with sick kids than you have—"

"OK, but I can tell by looking at her that she ought to be in the hospital."

"On what? Hospitals cost money."

"So do funerals," Mrs. Brewster snapped back.

Connie listened, admiring Mrs. Brewster's nerve but frightened at her words. She went in to stare down at Betty and listen to her shallow breathing.

"No, she's not my kid," she heard Mrs. Brewster answer something Ma said. "But you can't leave it all to Connie and then blame her if something goes wrong . . . Tell him you have to leave, that it's an emergency . . . Tell him if Betty dies it's his fault. That'll scare him . . . What? . . . Sure, you can call the police or the fire department or something. They'll take her to the hospital."

She banged the receiver down and turned to Connie. "Your mother's coming home. What time is it anyway?"

Connie went to the bedroom door and looked in at the clock. "A little after one." She was suddenly shivering and felt lightheaded and giddy.

Mrs. Brewster looked at her sympathetically. "You've sure had it rough today. You look kind of sick yourself. Have you eaten anything?"

"Not very much." Connie's teeth chattered as she answered, and Mrs. Brewster went out to the kitchen. Connie could hear her banging cupboard doors and muttering, and then she came back to the living room. "How about taking some soup off my hands? I fixed Kevin some but he didn't want it. He's fussy today— cutting teeth, I guess."

"I hate to bother you."

"No bother. You stay here with Betty in case she wakes

up. Kevin is sound asleep in his crib so he's safe. I'll
fix the soup and bring it down. Be right back."

Connie sat on the couch and waited, unable to stop
shivering, trying to figure out the emotions churning
inside her. She dreaded her mother's coming, knowing
how mad she would be at the trouble this was causing.
She was scared about Betty, and somewhere in the
back of her mind was the telephone call from school
about Myrna. She didn't care about Myrna's missing
school or the trouble she would be in because of it,
but she hated the yelling that would take place between
her and Ma. Her stomach always hurt when she heard
them, and then when Betty cried in fright, she wanted
to scream at them to stop. But she never did because
she knew they would both turn on her.

She looked around as Mrs. Brewster came down
carrying a tray with a bowl of soup and a sandwich.
"Sorry I didn't have enough milk on hand, but I brought
some tea. OK?"

Connie nodded weakly. The smell of the soup made
her feel more lightheaded than ever.

"How long does it take your mother to get home?"
Mrs. Brewster had gone in to look at Betty and came
back as she asked the question.

"Oh, I guess about a half hour. Something like that.
If she doesn't have to wait too long for a bus."

"I'll stay and keep you company until she gets here,
unless Kevin wakes up. I'm kind of jittery myself waiting for the mailman." She sat down across from Connie,
her feet tucked under her, and lit a cigarette, leafing
through one of Myrna's movie magazines. But the sound
of the mailman shoving letters in the box brought her
out of the chair and to the door.

"I brought yours in too," she said as she tore a thick
letter open with a sigh of relief. "At least I can sleep
tonight." She sat down and curled her feet under her
again, lost in the letter.

Connie ate hungrily thinking only of the food, until

Mrs. Brewster exclaimed, "For crying out loud!" And then, "Mike, you dope!" She shook her head with a smile on her lips and reread the letter again. Finally she looked over at Connie with a helpless shake of her head. "Did you ever meet Mike?"

Connie shook her head and Mrs. Brewster said with a laugh, "Then I can't explain him to you. He's the most terrific person—" She stopped and began again. "You've seen his picture so you know how good looking he is. And he's a life-of-the-party type, you know? And for him to get mixed up with something like this—" she broke off and reread a couple of pages.

"What is it?" Connie asked curiously.

"Oh, he's met up with some kind of a religious nut. A chaplain."

"What's that?"

"Umm, sort of like a priest."

"Oh, yeah. I've seen them on TV. But I didn't know they were ever soldiers."

"They're not really. I mean, they don't do any fighting. They just go around and say prayers over the guys that get killed. But this one and Mike have gotten to be real good friends. They've been talking and Mike says he sees how wrong his life has been up to now. He says he won't be the same person when he gets back."

She laughed again and shrugged her shoulders in a helpless gesture. "But I *liked* him the way he was. I don't *want* him any different."

She reread the letter again and then folded it and put it back in the envelope and looked at Connie soberly. "Well, I'm not going to worry about it. I'm for anything that helps him get through that mess over there and makes it easier for him to stand all the killing. The thing that's hardest for him is seeing all the orphans— all those poor little kids with no one to take care of them. I guess it gets to him because he misses Kevin so much. He'll get over the religious bit when he gets home."

She stood up and looked out the window. "Here comes your mother. I'll beat it so she won't think I'm too nosy a neighbor. Let me know what happens." She picked up the tray and ran upstairs.

Connie watched nervously as her mother came in, shrugging off her coat with a quick, impatient motion, walked over to Betty's cot and leaned over her, feeling her forehead with her hand. Then she straightened up quickly and turned to Connie, a frown creasing her face.

"You should have called me sooner," she said sharply. "She wasn't this sick when I went to work."

Connie wanted to ask, "How do you know she wasn't? I bet you didn't even look at her before you left, didn't even think of her." But aloud she only said, "She got worse after I got up."

Her mother picked up the phone book and flipped through the pages.

"Are you calling the police?"

"No. The welfare office. Somebody at work said that was the thing to do. They're supposed to help with emergencies."

Her voice was scornful as she answered and dialed a number. Then, in response to the voice at the other end of the line, hers changed to a soft, helpless tone. She explained the situation and asked, "Is there someway you could help me get my little girl to the hospital? She is very sick, and I have no car and can't afford an ambulance."

She listened, nodding her head as she wrote down a number and said, "Thank you very much for your help," and hung up. She dialed again, talking to Connie around a cigarette. "We hit them at just the right time. Ordinarily I'll bet they would have told me to go fly a kite. But someone in the office goofed a couple of weeks ago and didn't give permission for a kid to go to the hospital and it almost died. The newspapers got hold of the story and played it up big, and now they're afraid not to help. So I'm supposed to call an ambulance, and the welfare office will pay the bill!"

"Can I go with you?" Connie asked as her mother put down the phone and reached for her coat.

She shrugged. "If you want to bother. We'll probably have to sit around and wait a long time and come home on the bus."

"Will they keep Betty there?"

"They'll have to. I don't know what to do for her here."

Connie hurried into the bedroom to take off her jeans and pull on a skirt and blouse, looking anxiously at Betty who was moaning pitifully.

"I hurt. My stomach hurts."

"We're going to get you all fixed up," she tried to say reassuringly. Then she went to the bedroom door. "What do we do about dressing her? She's just got her old pajamas on."

"Leave her. They'll wrap her in a blanket."

"Should I leave a note for Myrna?"

"What for?"

"Well, what if she comes home and wonders where we are?"

"Isn't she working today?" her mother asked sharply.

"Sometimes she doesn't on Tuesday."

"Well, she can get herself something to eat. If there's nothing here she can go to the store. She's got money. She's big enough to take care of herself. Anyway, it's only two o'clock. We should be home in time for supper." She turned to look out the window. "Here's the ambulance now."

3

A Hospital and Kindness

THE AMBULANCE RIDE was a blur of swift motion until it turned onto a side street and stopped in front of the emergency door. Betty was lifted out quickly and taken into the hospital as Connie and her mother followed. Connie watched then as Betty was wheeled away on a stretcher, her eyes wide with fright. Mrs. Hamilton followed behind the stretcher with a nurse, while another one showed Connie where the waiting room was. She sat nervously on the edge of a chair until her mother came, angry lines etching her forehead.

"How is she?"

"How should I know? I'm only her mother. They don't tell you anything. Just ask a lot of fool questions and then shove some papers at you to sign."

She drew quick short puffs on her cigarette, oblivious to the curious stares of those sitting near.

"What were they doing to her?"

"I don't know," she answered impatiently. "When they started taking blood, I left. If I'd stayed, I'd have passed out."

Then she got up abruptly, her heels making sharp clicking sounds on the bare floor, and went to the desk to ask impatiently, "How come nobody comes to tell me anything? What's going on anyway?"

The nurse at the desk looked at her and asked calmly, "What is your name?"

"Mrs. Hamilton. And my little daughter was brought into emergency terribly sick, and I've been sitting here not knowing what's happening to her. It's been fifteen minutes at least. Why doesn't someone tell me something?"

Her voice was loud and demanding, and Connie cringed in embarrassment, conscious of the people listening. The nurse said crisply, "I can assure you, Mrs. Hamilton, as soon as there is any news they will tell you. I know it's hard to wait, but at this point that's all you can do."

Connie watched her mother turn away impatiently and walk toward the door leading into the hall. She came back then and sat down, taking a mirror and a lipstick from her purse. What she had worn when they came was left on the cigarette butts in the ashtray beside her. She stuck the lipstick back and examined her face, smoothing out the wrinkles between her eyes.

"Nothing worse than sitting around waiting," she sputtered, and tapped her red-tipped fingers in stacatto rhythm on her purse. She looked at Connie. "You hungry?"

"Sort of. But I had some soup."

"Well, I didn't. I was just going to eat when you called, and naturally I hurried right home."

"Naturally," Connie echoed. She had to fight to keep the mockery from showing in her voice, and was afraid Ma had guessed how she felt from the sharp way she looked at her. She watched as her mother got up abruptly and went to the desk again. "I suppose you don't know how long it will be until there is some news?"

"No, I have no idea. It could be any minute or it could be an hour depending on what your daughter needs."

Mrs. Hamilton's impatience was plain. "Is there anyplace around here to eat?"

"We have a cafeteria downstairs that is open to the public."

"Oh. Here in the hospital?"

The receptionist nodded. "Through that door and down the stairs. You'll see a sign."

Mrs. Hamilton turned and came back to Connie. "I'm going to get something to eat."

Connie straightened up. "What—what if they come and—and say something?"

"I'll be right back."

"But what if she's worse?" Connie asked in panic.

"My starving to death won't keep her from getting worse, will it? I'm not going to the moon, you know. I'll be right back."

Connie listened to her mother's heels click across the floor and watched as she disappeared from sight through the revolving outside door. Then it hit her. Ma wasn't going down to the cafeteria. She was going out someplace to eat. Connie hurried to the window and saw her mother go down the steps to the side-walk, turn the corner and disappear from sight. She went back and sat down, feeling terribly alone and afraid. They hadn't talked during the time they had sat together, but at least there had been two of them. She sat tensely on the edge of the chair until she caught the curious gaze of the woman across from her, and forced herself to lean back and relax. Picking up a magazine, she flipped through it, not really seeing anything. Her eyes slid to the clock again. It had been two-thirty when Ma left. Give her thirty minutes—no, forty-five at least to get coffee and a sandwich. She couldn't count on her being back before three-thirty. And maybe not then if she went to a bar instead of a restaurant.

Connie tried to make herself think calmly. If they came and told her that Betty—that something had happened to Betty and Ma wasn't back, how could she find her? She couldn't. Well, the next thing would be to call Myrna. No, she wasn't even sure of the name of the place Myrna worked. Well, she'd have to call Mrs.

Brewster. She rummaged through her purse. No money. Then she remembered the change from Mrs. Brewster's five dollars and reached into her jacket pocket. There wasn't any money, but her fingers touched the candy bar she had taken for Betty, and she drew her hand out quickly. Her throat was choked with sudden tears that welled up, and she clenched her teeth to keep them back. She could eat the candy if she got hungry. There was no use saving it until Betty got better; it would be stale by then.

Her eyes went against her will, to the clock. Only ten minutes had gone by since Ma left, but it seemed like an hour. To make the time pass, she watched the people who were coming and going from the afternoon visiting hours. She wondered about them—who they were, what they were like, what kind of a house they were going to, what was wrong with the people they were visiting. Some of them stared at her as they passed, and she wondered what they saw when they looked at her.

They're probably thinking what a messy kid I am, she thought bitterly and stared down angrily at her scuffed shoes and the worn jacket she had shoved down in a corner of the chair. She hated being poor—*hated* never having nice clothes, never being in style, never being sure of anything. Why did it have to be *her* father who ran out on the family so they had to live in a dump and be partly on welfare? Why did she have to have a mother who didn't care about her kids and told them so whenever she felt like it?

The waiting room began to empty slowly. An attendant came through cleaning ashtrays and straightening the magazines. Connie watched a nurse come down the hall and stop at the desk and say something to the woman there who nodded at Connie. She sat up straight, clutching her purse, as the nurse came over to her.

"Is your mother down in the cafeteria?"

"No. She went out for coffee. She should be right

back." Connie looked around at the clock. Almost four o'clock! *Where is Ma anyway,* she wondered in panic.

"Is-is something the matter?"

"No. It's just that we need your mother's permission to do surgery."

"What's the matter with Betty?"

"She needs her appendix out. It's quite a routine operation. We've done all the necessary tests, but we have to have your mother's permission to do the surgery."

"She won't care—"

"We have to have a signed paper though."

"She said she had signed some," Connie began, and the nurse nodded.

"Yes, there were several to sign giving us permission to treat your sister. But she has to sign one to say we can go ahead and operate."

"She should be here," Connie repeated helplessly. But inside she could only think of the uncertainty she always had to count on with her mother.

"You're sure she's not in the cafeteria?"

Connie nodded at the door. "She went out that way. Unless you can go around to the cafeteria from there—"

The nurse shook her head with a quick "Well, there's no use looking there for her." She went back to the desk, said something to the woman there, and disappeared down the hall.

Connie walked over and leaned forward to peer out the window into the early cold darkness. Neon lights winked off and on, and horns honked incessantly regardless of the Hospital—Quiet signs. Several of the signs advertised food but Connie was sure now that her mother had gone out for more than a sandwich. She'd gone to be with people. People like herself who hated responsibility, hated being tied down, hated feeling trapped by sick kids. Ma might not even remember that Betty was in the hospital until she woke up tomorrow morning.

Connie turned and walked over to the receptionist.

"Can't they go ahead and operate anyway? In case my mother doesn't get back in time?"

"They have to have the permission of an adult to operate on a child. It doesn't have to be your mother. Is there someone else? Can we reach your fath—" She stopped as Connie shook her head. "Well, is there someone we can at least talk to? An uncle or aunt?"

"There's my sister."

"How old is she?"

"Sixteen. Almost seventeen."

"Umm—she can't give permission. But where is she now?"

Connie hesitated and then said, "Home."

"What's your phone number? I'll call her and ask her to come down, and maybe she will know where your mother might have gone."

Connie watched as the receptionist dialed and listened to the phone ring in what Connie knew would be an empty house. After a few moments she put the phone down and frowned at Connie. "She isn't there. There isn't anyone else we can call?"

Connie shook her head, and the fright she was beginning to feel looked out of her eyes.

The receptionist smiled at her reassuringly. "Don't worry. They'll work something out."

"Is it—is it a dangerous operation?"

"Oh, no! Lots of people have it. She'll have to stay in the hospital four or five days, but then she can finish getting well at home." Then she said casually, "Does your mother work?"

Connie started to answer automatically, "At the Three Coins restaurant," but as she saw the receptionist's pen move she shifted the words to "At the Bijou restaurant. She's the cashier there."

She didn't know if there was such a restaurant, and probably the hospital was supposed to know where her mother worked. But at least she couldn't be blamed for giving out any information. She had long ago learned that her mother didn't want anyone told anything. You only gave information if you were sure you wouldn't get in trouble over it.

Connie stood at the desk for a moment until she was conscious of the receptionist's eyes on her battered purse and frayed blouse. She turned away resentfully and walked over to peer out the window again. It was silly of her to hope, and yet there was a bare chance that Ma would suddenly remember that she was supposed to be at the hospital. The sound of footsteps made her turn again, and she saw the nurse back talking to the receptionist. They both looked at Connie and then the receptionist dialed a number, talked a moment, and handed the phone to the nurse. Connie was sure it had something to do with Betty, and wished she had stayed by the desk so she could hear.

She watched as the nurse went back along the hall without looking in her direction, and then hurried over to the desk.

"Are they going to operate?"

"Yes." The receptionist looked at Connie and then away and added, "We called the welfare office and then got a court order giving permission. It—we do it often," she finished.

But Connie turned away feeling the bitterness of being an object of pity.

She sat down in a big chair in a corner of the deserted lounge. From there she could see both the door and the desk before anyone at either place saw her. She slipped out of her shoes, drew her feet up under her, and leaned her head back against the cushions of the wing chair. The hands of the clock pointed to five, and only an occasional person came through the room. The lamp on the table by the chair came on automatically, warming her with its soft glow, and Connie relaxed in the quiet. The only thing that bothered her was the empty feeling in her stomach, but she couldn't bring herself to eat Betty's candy bar. Not yet.

The next thing she knew the nurse was shaking her shoulder, and she sat up with a start, staring blankly around her.

"Your sister is all right," the nurse said. As Connie stared up at her she repeated, "Your sister came through the operation all right. She's asleep now and won't feel like seeing anyone until tomorrow."

Connie sat up and searched for her shoes, sliding her feet into them as quickly as she could. Then she stood up but sat down abruptly. She was so hungry she felt weak. Then panic hit her as she realized she was all alone and didn't even have enough money for bus fare. Whatever had made her stick the dollar from Myrna under the mattress on her side of the bed instead of putting it in her purse! And it was dumb of her not to have kept Mrs. Brewster's change in her jacket pocket. She knew the nurse was looking at her curiously so she made herself stand up slowly, and groped behind her for her jacket.

"Your mother didn't come back."

"No—I—I guess n-not. But I was sleeping."

"How are you going to get home?"

"Well, I—" she stopped. It was hard to think. Her head felt heavy and stupid.

"Where do you live?"

"I have to take the bus," Connie answered evasively.

"Do you have money?"

Connie started to say yes, then stopped. She didn't, and it would be foolish not to admit it. She shook her head wordlessly. The nurse frowned at her for a moment and then asked, "Have you eaten anything? Since you came to the hospital, I mean?"

She tightened her arms across her empty stomach and shook her head again. The nurse looked up at the clock and Connie's eyes followed. Almost seven o'clock already.

"Look. I go off duty at seven. Wait for me here and we'll get some supper, and then I'll see that you get home." She started to walk away and then turned. "Unless you think you should stay here and wait for your mother? I wouldn't want her to come back and wonder what had happened to you." But her voice was angry and said plainly that she doubted her mother would show up.

Connie said stiffly, "My mother trusts me to take care of myself." It wasn't a defense of her mother. She wouldn't admit to this stranger that she had been forgotten.

The nurse went away, and Connie sat down on the edge of the chair again, clutching her jacket and mittens and purse. The room was filling with people coming for visiting hours, and she looked every time the door spun around, hoping it would bring her mother. She got up once in panic and went over to the door, but stopped at the sight of the blackness and bitterness of the night, knowing she couldn't possibly walk all the way home.

Then the nurse came toward her. "OK, let's go," she said briskly. "My car is in the parking lot in back." She led the way down a corridor and out a side door. Connie shivered and bent over against the cold wind that hit them as they went around the corner of the building into the open space of the parking lot. She stopped as the nurse gestured toward a Volkswagen. "Here we are." She unlocked the door for Connie to get in before going around to the driver's side.

"We'll stop at a good hamburger place near here," she said as she started the engine. "That all right with you?"

Connie nodded, her teeth chattering and her shoulders shaking in the cold of the car. She tried to relax her muscles to keep from shivering but shook in spite of the effort.

The car moved through the heavy evening traffic away from the hospital area. "I hope we're going somewhat in the direction of your home, but if not it won't matter."

Connie peered out the window, looking for something familiar. "I live on Tenth Street. And Third Avenue."

"Oh, that won't be too far from where we're going." The nurse pulled into a parking place outside the restaurant and turned off the engine. As they got out of the car, she looked across the top of it at Connie. "Will there be someone at home expecting you? Should you call and let anyone know where you are?"

Connie shook her head.

"Your sister?"

Connie shook her head again, wishing she would stop asking so many prying questions. But as she followed the nurse through the door into the warm restaurant she added, "My sister usually works in the evening."

"I see. You mean she has an after-school job?"

"Yes."

"What kind is it?"

"She works in a hamburger place. The kind that takes outside orders. She's a carhop."

"Not in this weather, I hope," the nurse laughed. Then she said, "Order anything you want. This place gives quick service and the food is good."

While they waited for their food, facing each other in the booth, Connie saw the nurse's clean hands and short scrubbed nails. She quickly shoved hers on to her lap, conscious of how grubby they were and how chipped the nail polish. She was suddenly aware too that she hadn't been to the bathroom in a long time and looked around for the rest room sign.

She stood up abruptly. "I'm going to the bathroom."

"OK, but hurry so your food won't get cold. They bring it pretty fast."

Connie pushed open the swinging door of the rest room and faced herself immediately in the mirrors over the washbowls.

"Crummy!" she said, staring back at the reflection of her tangled hair and pale face. She was glad that she hadn't experimented with any of Myrna's eye shadow and liner that morning, or she would really have looked like a wreck now with no chance for repairs in the meantime. Before she went back out, she combed her hair and put on lipstick. Then she lathered soap generously on her hands and held them under the hot water faucet, scratching off as much of the nail polish as she could. When she finally went out, the waitress was putting the hamburgers and fries on the table, and the nurse was looking around anxiously.

Connie slid into the booth, her mouth watering at the sight and the smell of the food. She shook salt liberally over the fries and poured catsup in a heap on the side of her plate and ate greedily, not looking up or stopping until they were gone, and she had gulped down the large coke.

"Want another?"

She nodded, feeling as though the hole in her stomach would never be filled. But after the waitress brought the second order, she came back and laid down the check. Connie swallowed the huge bite she had taken and put the hamburger down.

"I don't have any money," she said, suddenly afraid that the nurse had only planned to pay for the first order.

"That's all right. It's on me. Just enjoy it." The nurse leaned back, sipping her coffee and not talking. She didn't seem to be looking at her, but Connie felt uneasy and awkward anyway. Now that her first ravenous hunger was satisfied, she was able to eat more slowly and take smaller bites. When she finished and shook her head no in answer to the question about dessert, the nurse stood up.

"I'd better get you home then. You've got school tomorrow, I suppose. And maybe homework yet tonight?"

"No. I stayed home from school because of my sister, so I don't have any homework."

She gave directions for her house and then sat silently during the brief ride, feeling warmer and more relaxed, and glad that the nurse didn't ask any more questions. The house was dark when they pulled up in front of it, and Connie wondered if Ma might have wandered home even though it was early.

"It looks as though someone is home."

Connie peered out the window. "No. That light is in the upstairs apartment. We live down." She gestured to the steps leading to the basement.

"Do you want me to come in with you while you get lights on?"

"No," Connie answered quickly. "I'll be all right. I always have a key." She climbed out of the car and then leaned down to look in. "Thanks for the ride. And thanks for the supper."

"You're welcome. I'm on duty this week from eleven to seven, so if you come to the hospital with your mother maybe I'll see you. If I know you're waiting in the lounge I can at least come out and say hi."

"Oh." Connie was startled to realize that she hadn't given Betty a thought in the last hour. And she wondered, what if her mother didn't plan to visit Betty?

"My mother works all day. She may not be able to come in the afternoon. The place she works is kind of mean about giving people time off for things. Can I see her?"

The nurse shook her head. "I'm sorry. The hospital rules don't allow anyone under sixteen to visit patients. But there are evening visiting hours so your mother won't have to take time off."

"Oh. Well, she'll come then. Thanks again," and Connie turned away and went down the steps, fumbling in her purse for the key. She could tell from the sound of the motor that the car had not pulled away, and, looking back over her shoulder, saw the nurse leaning over the wheel to peer out the window. She didn't drive off until Connie had gone in and turned on the light in the living room.

She looked first into her mother's room to see if she had come in and gone to bed, forgetting about Betty. But she wasn't there. There was a tap on the door and Mrs. Brewster said, "Mrs. Hamilton?"

"No, it's me," Connie called back and opened the door.

"How's Betty?"

"She had an operation like you thought. But she's OK."

"Poor kid. I was worried about her. I guess when you have one of your own you notice other kids. I suppose your mother is staying with her?"

She looked quickly around as she asked, and Connie said, "Yes."

She knew from the expression on Mrs. Brewster's face that she didn't believe her. But all she said was, "Look, do you want to sleep upstairs? I mean with your mother and Betty gone and Myrna—" she stopped, fumbling for words and finally finished. "With Myrna working late you'll be kind of lonely here."

Connie shook her head. "No, I'd better stay here." She couldn't admit even to Mrs. Brewster that Ma might come stumbling home and need help and that someone had to be there to give it to her.

"OK. But if you change your mind, come on up. Or yell or pound on the ceiling if you need me."

As she closed the door, Connie was suddenly aware of how achingly tired she was. It wasn't even nine o'clock, but she struggled out of her clothes and into her pajamas. She was too tired even to bother using Myrna's cold cream, but ran cold water in the kitchen sink and splashed it on her face and hands, and quickly brushed her teeth.

The problem now was how to stay awake until Ma came home. She debated lying down on the couch but decided the house was too cold for that. So she went to bed and pulled the blankets over her, taking the extra one from Betty's bed. If she left the light on, she wouldn't sleep so soundly that she wouldn't hear **Ma** come in.

The sounds from Mrs. Brewster's television gradually stilled her racing thoughts and lulled her to sleep. Then loud voices from the living room roused her, and she raised up enough to see that it was almost two o'clock. *I did go to sleep after all,* she thought. She got up and pulled her sweater around her to stand shivering in the bedroom door. Her mother and Myrna were glaring at each other.

"You don't even care that your poor little sister is sick," her mother was saying as she swayed on her feet, her hair rumpled and her makeup blurred.

"Well, what could I do for her? I had to go to school. And Connie was here. No use in both of us staying home."

Connie wanted to shout at her that she hadn't gone to school. But she only watched and listened and shivered.

"Had to take the poor kid to the hospital. Can't take care of her here."

"Yeah, and where have you been since you took her?" Myrna sneered. "You don't look like the mother of a sick kid."

Mrs. Hamilton had suddenly collapsed into a chair, her arms hanging limply over the sides; and Myrna looked at her scornfully. Then she turned to Connie. "How is Betty? What's the matter with her?"

"She had to have her appendix out."

"Oh, great! Now all we'll hear about is how much *that* cost! And I was going to hit Ma tomorrow for fifty bucks—" she caught herself and looked at Connie. "Don't you rat on me," she said threateningly.

"I couldn't care less about you and what you do," Connie answered coldly, hating the sight of Myrna in her too-short, too-tight skirt and her piled hair and her black-circled eyes. "I'm going back to bed."

"No, you don't. Not until you help me get her to bed,"

and Myrna gestured at their mother, who had fallen asleep and was breathing heavily.

Silently Connie walked over and helped half-lift and half-pull her mother out of the chair and guide her stumbling feet to the bedroom as she roused a little. Myrna dumped her down and Connie took off her shoes, tugged the blankets out from under her, and pulled them over her shoulders.

She stood looking down at her mother for a moment, a confusion of emotions mixed up inside her. But it was too late and she was too tired to sort them out. She closed the door and went back to the bedroom where Myrna had wiggled out of her jumper and sweater and was standing in her slip carefully putting cream on her face. The thought of sharing the same bed with her was suddenly more than Connie could stand. She wouldn't even stay in the same room. She took the blanket that belonged on Betty's cot, grabbed her pillow and her jacket and went out to the couch. Even the lumps and sagging springs were better than Myrna's presence.

Connie crawled under the blanket and lay staring into the darkness. She could hear her mother's heavy breathing even through the closed door, and the noises Myrna made in the bedroom opening and closing drawers. How she hated her life!

4

For God So Loved?

CONNIE STARED DOWN at the mimeographed math paper. If only she had known there was going to be a test she would at least have tried to study. It wasn't fair to give one without telling you in advance. She stared at the problems, but it was hard to concentrate on them when her mind kept going over the events of yesterday. And the scene last night. And her mother's bad temper this morning because Myrna refused to get up, claiming she didn't feel well.

"You say *you're* sick whenever you want to," Myrna had snapped back at her mother's demand that she get up and go to school. Connie had hurried out the door shutting off her mother's reply, wanting only to get away from the shouting, hateful words they flung at each other.

She was still mad too at the persistent questions Agnes had asked when they met at the locker. "Where were you yesterday? Did you know you missed a big science test?" And then, looking over Connie's shoulder, she asked, "What are you doing? Are you writing your own excuse?" Her sharp, indrawn breath and horrified eyes had been the last straw.

"Shut up and mind your own business!" she had snapped and watched Agnes turn away with her eyes blinking back hurt tears.

Of course she wrote her own excuse. How else would she get one? Dumb fat Agnes!

Connie looked over at her now, hating the placid way she was doing the math problems, breathing noisily with the tip of her tongue showing at the corner of her mouth as she concentrated. Connie looked around. Even Janet and Pat seemed to know what they were doing, which meant that the problems couldn't be too hard. But she stared down at the sheet that to her was just a mimeographed blur of scratches.

There was absolutely no sense in trying to figure them out by herself when, by shifting slightly, she could see the paper on the desk ahead of her. Allen usually had the right answers, and she had discovered that even if she missed some of the steps in working the problems because she couldn't see them all, if the final answer was right Mr. Lawson usually gave some

credit. And that was more than she would get if she
tried working them by herself.

When the bell rang, she scribbled the answer to the
next to the last problem and quit, scrawling her name
across the top of the paper before passing it to the
front.

The rest of the morning was long, and Connie watched
the minutes drag by until lunch hour.

"I'm buying today," she said as she joined Pat and
Janet outside the history room. She felt rich since Mrs.
Brewster hadn't asked for her change, and Myrna
hadn't demanded her dollar back.

"Loan me some, will you?" Pat begged.

Connie shook her head. "I'd never get it back."

"Honest you will. I'm dying for a coke."

"Get milk. It's cheaper."

"Yech—milk!"

Connie grabbed a tray and slid in line, moving ahead
gradually and slipping ahead of someone whenever
possible. She wanted the meat and potatoes and gravy
that were on the menu, and sometimes they ran out
before the end of the line. Standing on tiptoe, she
craned her neck to look. Good. There was enough
until she got through the line at least. She gave her
order and watched as the food was ladled out.

"Wait a minute! He got more than I did," she fumed,
pointing to the boy ahead of her and refusing to take
the plate that was held out.

"He's bigger than you are," the woman answered.
"We always give the boys more because they eat more.
You girls only leave half of what you get anyway. Here,
take it."

"I'm paying as much as he is."

"Sure, but you won't eat it all and it will just be
wasted," the woman retorted impatiently.

"What's it to you? Anyway, I won't either leave any.
I pay as much as he does so I get as much as he does."
Connie's voice was loud and demanding and stubborn

as she stood defiantly with her arms folded. The other women behind the steam counter came over to listen and one of them said, "She's got a right to it. Give it to her. She's paying for it."

The woman shrugged, added another piece of meat and a spoonful of potatoes and gravy and held the plate out again. "Hope you choke on it," she glowered, and Connie made a face at her as she reached for the plate and a roll at the same time. She took one and then deftly slid another under the strap of her purse, casually laid the napkin over it and paid for the meal. As she squeezed in beside Pat, she exclaimed, "How'd you get two rolls?"

"How do you think?" Connie retorted.

"You sure know how to look out for yourself."

Connie shrugged. "Why not? Nobody else is going to. Look, I'm going downtown to bum around after school for a while. Want to come?"

"I can't," Janet said. "Got a babysitting job."

"I'll go," Pat agreed. "You going to buy something?"

"What with? A dollar?"

"A dollar! You've got a dollar and you wouldn't lend me thirty-five cents for a coke? Some friend you are."

"I'll give you some candy when we go downtown," Connie promised, remembering the bar in her pocket. Then she said casually, "I had supper in a restaurant last night."

The girls looked at her. "You? How come? What'd you do—wash dishes to pay for it?"

"I was invited," Connie answered coldly.

Pat snickered. "What's his name?"

And Janet added, "One of your sister's ex-boyfriends?"

Connie glared at them, seeing the looks they exchanged. "What do you mean by that?"

Her voice was so deadly that Janet said hastily, "Nothing."

"It's just that her sister is jealous because Myrna has more dates than she does," Pat added. But Connie had seen the nudge Pat had given Janet and knew there was more to it than that. Lately they always seemed to be hinting at things they knew—things about Myrna. Maybe it was just jealousy. She had gotten to know Janet because her sister and Myrna had run around in the same group until they had a fight about something.

"Betty had to go to the hospital in an ambulance yesterday and have her appendix out."

"Tough. But who took *you* out to eat? The ambulance driver?" and they leaned against each other in laughter.

Connie stood up, accidentally knocking Pat's purse on the floor and somehow not quite clearing Janet's head with the tray, as she turned to put it on the counter. "Sorry," she said, staring back at them and watching as they bent to pick up Pat's stuff.

"You did that on purpose," Janet protested.

"Well, wouldn't you have?"

"Not to a friend."

"I don't consider people friends who mock me."

"Oh, come off it, Connie. We were just having fun."

"I wasn't."

She picked up her books and walked out without looking back at them. *Even your supposed friends weren't really friends when you came right down to it,* she thought bitterly. Pat and Janet probably had problems at home too, but at least they had fathers as well as mothers. And their mothers worked just to buy things they wanted and not because they had to. And if their mothers yelled at them, they at least cared about their kids.

She walked upstairs, making herself think back to her eighth birthday—the day her father had called it quits and walked out. The terrible months that followed had never dimmed in her memory. Ma had been angry and bitter and had started drinking. When she had had too much she loudly blamed them for his leaving, saying he did it because there were too many kids around always wanting something and always yapping at him. Maybe it wasn't only Ma's fault that everything was in such a mess, but it certainly wasn't theirs. They didn't ask to be born!

And Myrna was getting more—she stopped, not even wanting to think of the mess of Myrna's life. Everything seemed to be gradually slipping downhill, and she had the feeling that some day they would be completely swallowed up by the trouble that hung over them.

But not me, she thought grimly, as she endured science, waiting for the final bell to ring. *There has to be a way out. I'm not always going to live in a run-down basement apartment with cold water and no heat and no food.* Myrna and Ma could look out for themselves. And Betty—even though she was a whiny, runny-nosed brat—she at least deserved a chance. *But I come first,* she promised herself.

She was still feeling grim when she and Pat walked downtown and looked longingly at the clothes in the windows. "Let's go in and try something on," Pat urged.

They flipped along the clothes on the racks, taking off an armful. As they headed toward the dressing rooms, a clerk came toward them. "How many do you have there?"

Pat shifted her notebook and load of books and answered, "I've got four. She has three."

"Are you just looking or are you seriously interested in buying?"

"Oh, buying," Connie assured her seriously. "We've got this big thing coming up at school, and we need just the right outfit for it."

"Very well," and the clerk watched them move away.

Pat exploded with laughter when they got in the dressing room and pulled the curtain. "What a witch! You were great, Connie. Did you see her trying to memorize what we were wearing and what we were carrying? She expects us to try to walk out with a couple."

Then she held one of the dresses up against her.

"Mmm, you know—I *could* get away with this one. It would fit right under my skirt and sweater."

"No, you couldn't," Connie answered, twisting to see her reflection in the mirror. "You're already tagged as a poor kid looking for something for nothing. To get away with one, you've got to walk in a store and act like money doesn't mean a thing to you. Then no one thinks you have to steal, and they don't suspect you. I'll bet she's standing out there now waiting to search us when we come out."

Pat peeked through the curtains and giggled. "You're right. She's standing in the doorway pretending not to look in our direction. Well, let's give her something to get excited about. Let's act as though we were taking something and trying to hide it from her. Then when she accuses us we can—"

"No." Connie was still absorbed in trying on the clothes she had brought in.

"Why not? It would be fun to show her up."

Connie shook her head impatiently. "That's dumb. Then they mark you down in their files and never forget you. And you end up without anything to show for it. Except the dumb thing you thought was fun."

"I'd just like the satisfaction of getting the old bag's goat."

"Go ahead. But wait until I've cleared out. And don't expect me to stick up for you when you get in a mess."

Pat wilted under Connie's opposition, but she was indignant at her for smiling at the clerk and thanking her and helping to put the dresses back on the racks.

"What'd you want to softsoap her for?"

"It might be useful someday," Connie answered absently. "Maybe I'll want a job there sometime. I can get a job in about a year and a half. You get twenty percent off stuff when you work there."

"I didn't know that."

"Sure. Myrna found out when she applied for a job this summer."

"How come she isn't working there then, when she's so crazy about clothes?"

"Because she likes the one she's got better," Connie answered shortly. It wasn't the job, Connie knew, but the people she waited on that she liked better. No guys ever came to a dress shop. But she didn't intend to tell Pat that.

They walked along the street, shoving through the hurrying crowds. As they passed a drugstore, a low, long whistle made them both turn, and Pat giggled at the small knot of boys lounging near the door. She slowed her steps and glanced in their direction, but Connie grabbed her arm impatiently.

"Come on, Pat!"

"It doesn't hurt to be a little bit friendly," she protested.

"Do you know them?" Connie demanded.

"No—but you never know—" she hesitated and then asked, "Do you want to do something Saturday night?"

"What?"

"Oh —" Pat was evasive. "Just bum around with Janet and me. We came down to the show last Saturday and met a couple of guys from high school. We had a blast. We went and got something to eat and fooled around, and then they took us home. Want to come next time?"

"Maybe. It depends." Then she said abruptly, "Let's go into the dime store. I'm freezing. And I want to look at the lipsticks."

They wandered around through the store, their mouths watering as they passed the candy counter. "Which reminds me. Where's my candy?" Pat demanded.

"In my pocket." But instead of reaching for it, Connie asked, "Have you got any money?"

Pat looked at her suspiciously and didn't answer.

"I know you tried to borrow from me for a coke, **but I figured that was just because** you didn't want to spend your own money. But if you've got a quarter, I've got one, and we can buy one of those long hot dogs and split it.''

"OK," Pat agreed. "I'm starved."

They stood at the counter while they ate, watching the crowds surging past them. When they finished, Pat looked longingly at the rows of hot dogs. "I could eat six more like that."

"Me too. Let's go so we can't smell them anymore."

When they got outside, Pat exclaimed, "Yow, it's dark! It must be later than I thought. I've got to get home or my mother will kill me."

Connie shivered in the cold, wishing she had mended her mittens last night, and doubled her fingers into the palms of her hands. She held her books and notebook tight against her and said crossly, "Why did we do such a dumb thing? It's such a long way home. We'll be frozen stiff before we get there."

"Let's take the bus," Pat urged.

Connie looked at her. "The bus? Are you crazy? You can't con the driver into letting us ride for free."

"I've got some money," Pat said recklessly.

"Sure, and you couldn't buy yourself a coke—"

"Well, it's not mine really but I can use it temporarily. Especially for an emergency like this."

"You going to pay for me too?"

"Sure."

"You going to want it back?"

Pat was shivering as she shook her head. "No, I'll treat. Then maybe next time you'll loan me something when I need it."

They stood on the corner braced against the wind and stamping their feet on the sidewalk as they waited for the bus. The first one was crowded and passed them up. The next one was packed too but it stopped and they managed to squeeze on. They dropped in their fares and gradually inched toward the back, but had to stand. Pat leaned down to look at the clock

on one of the stores as they passed it and groaned
as she straightened up. "Five-thirty already! Will
my mother ever be mad!"

I'll be lucky if mine is home, Connie thought. *Or
maybe I'll be lucky if she isn't.*

As they swayed with the motion of the bus, Connie's
eyes strayed to the placards of ads along the side
opposite her. She poked Pat. "Look at that one,"
she laughed.

Pat laughed too as she read it. "I should get one
like that and hold it up in front of my dad. He smokes
like a furnace. Hey, what's that one for—that one
with the little black dot in the corner?"

"I don't know. You'd think they'd explain it. Maybe
there's another installment that they save for the
next time you ride the bus." They both giggled, and
then Connie looked at the next one, and the smile
faded and her face hardened. The only thing on it
was a cradle in one corner and a cross in the opposite
corner with the words "For God So Loved" connecting
the two pictures.

God? Love? What a laugh!

The bus gradually emptied enough for them both
to find seats but not together, and Connie was glad.
She was too tired to talk. She stared out the window,
hating the reflection of herself in it. Her hair was a
mess, and her shoulders were stooped, and her cheeks
were hollow. She looked like something nobody wanted,
and she felt miserable and hungry and tired. And
unloved. Her mind jerked resentfully at this reminder
of the ad, and she made herself blank it out of her
thoughts.

Pat got off two stops before she did. "See you
tomorrow," and Connie nodded back, glad she didn't
have as far to walk from the bus stop as Pat did.

But even the half block she had to go seemed long
as she got off, ducking her head against the wind, and
ran, hugging her books close for shelter and gasping

for breath. She could see a light in the living room
which meant Ma must be home. The television was
blaring as she pushed open the outside door and
stumbled over one of Kevin's toys in the dark hall.
She kicked it out of the way and opened the door to
the apartment. Her mother looked at her from where
she sat on the couch.

"Where've *you* been?"

"Downtown with Pat."

"I wanted you to go to the store and get something
for supper. I didn't know you were going to be so
late."

"I'll go now. What do you want?"

"I don't know. A couple of TV dinners I guess."

Connie dumped her books on a chair and looked
at her mother, trying to guess her mood. She seemed
reasonably peaceful so she asked, "Are you going to
the hospital tonight?"

"I suppose so. Someone has to." She exhaled smoke
as she answered, and then looked around sharply.
"If you don't step it up there won't be time for me
to do anything."

"Where's the money?"

Her mother reached for her purse and gave her two
dollars.

"What if they don't have any of the eighty-nine-cent
kind?"

"Get wieners then or meat pies or something. I
had a big meal this noon so I'm not hungry."

Connie turned toward the door and then stopped.
"We don't have any bread for breakfast or lunches
or anything."

"Oh, all right! Here's five more dollars. Get some
cheese or something and you can make a sandwich out of
it. Hurry it up, will you?"

Connie ran the block and a half to the small corner
grocery store. It was warm inside, and things smelled
good. She walked past the meat counter staring at

the display of cold meats and trying to figure out
how much a couple of slices would cost. She finally
got a small hunk of bologna, a couple of slices of
cheese, bread, two bananas, and the TV dinners and
raced home.

She hurried out to the kitchen, hoping Ma had put
the oven on, but she hadn't. Connie lit it and got
the dinners ready to go in. She didn't want to study,
but it was something to fill the time while the dinners
baked, and it was warm in the kitchen. Science was
easy for a change, and she skimmed over the spelling
words for tomorrow's test, eating a slice of the bologna
slowly to make it last.

They ate a silent meal with Connie thinking that
the best thing about TV dinners was that there were
no dishes to wash. Her mother leaned back when she
was through, lighting a cigarette and making no effort
to change out of her robe and slippers. Connie got
up and began to clear the table with a quick glance
at the clock. Ma could only stay with Betty until
eight-thirty and it was already after seven. By the
time she got ready and took a bus over, she'd only
have about a half hour to visit. But that would probably
be long enough. What would she and Betty talk about
all that time anyway? She took another furtive glance
at the clock.

"What are you so itchy about?" her mother asked
abruptly.

"I was just thinking—visiting hours are over at
eight-thirty."

"So?"

"You said you were going."

"I was. But you were late coming home."

Connie knew it wouldn't be wise to point out that
she could have had supper ready. Instead she said,
"Won't Betty be expecting someone to come and
see her?"

"Look, she's my kid, isn't she? Just quit worrying

about her, will you? She's getting along all right. I
called the hospital while you were at the store, and
they said everything was fine, that she's a real good
patient and doesn't cause any trouble. In fact, she
just lies in bed real good and quiet and does just
what they tell her to. What could I do for her if I
went over in this cold? Sit and hold her hand?"

"So you're not going?"

"So I'm not going. Not tonight. It's too cold out.
She's warm and comfortable. Besides, there are other
kids in the same room so she's got plenty of company.
And other kids' parents will be there. She can watch
them. Maybe I'll get there tomorrow."

For God So Loved. The thought strangled Connie as
she finished clearing the table. She couldn't stand
to look at her mother. Love! Where was there any of
it in this house?

5

An Unwelcome Visitor

"WAIT FOR ME, you guys," Connie called as she saw Pat
and Janet slam their locker door shut and start down the
hall. She reached in to grab her jacket and mittens, shoving ahead of Agnes who had just opened the locker.

"We can't," Pat called back over her shoulder
while Janet hurried her along toward the stairway.

"Where are you going? I'll walk with you. I don't
have to hurry home for anything—"

Pat said something in answer but it was lost in the
noise of the hall, and Janet didn't even look back.

Connie stopped to grab her books. That Janet. She
could never wait a minute for anyone. *If only I'd
hurried,* she scolded herself angrily.

"I can walk with you," Agnes offered but Connie interrupted, shaking her head, her lips tight. "No, thanks. I'm going to catch up with them."

She pushed through the crowded halls to the stairs and hurried down. It would be quicker to go out the side door than the front, and she could catch up with them before they'd gone very far. Then she could find out what the big rush was. She shoved the door open with her shoulder and backed through. As she turned around on the top step, she saw the girls standing at the curb. But before she could yell at them to wait, a car came along the street and stopped. She watched as Janet ran around and got in beside the boy who was driving, while Pat jumped in the back seat beside another boy who put his arm around her. Then the car pulled away, its tires squealing.

Connie stared down the street long after the car had disappeared from sight. They had to be high school guys at least to be driving. Maybe they were the ones Pat said they'd met last Saturday. She turned toward home, dragging her feet through the snow, feeling alone and anxious. Her friendship with Pat and Janet would be thinner than ever, now that they had crossed the magic boundary into the world of boyfriends and dates. It was a world she longed for and yet dreaded. How could you know whether the world held good or evil? If it was like Myrna's, she didn't want to belong to it. And how could you know until you got into it?

Every year seems to get worse, she thought despondently. When you're young like Betty things don't bother you, you don't ask questions that don't seem to have answers. The older you get, the more you wonder about things, and the more mixed up everything gets. *If I just had someone to talk to!*

Someday when she was rich, when she was famous—and the comforting dreams into which her mind slipped took her home through the cold, unaware of Agnes a block behind.

When she pushed open the outside door, Mrs. Brewster was sitting at the top of the stairs waiting for her.

"Hi, Connie. Could you watch Kevin for a little while?"

"Sure. When?"

"Right away if you can. There's a terrific sale on downtown, and I'd love to go down and snatch something away from someone else, even if I don't need it." She grinned down at Connie. "I might even find something to surprise Mike when he comes home."

"Let me dump my stuff and I'll be right up."

"You could take him down there when he wakes up if you want to."

"No, it's warmer upstairs. I'll come up."

She went in and dumped notebook, books, jacket, and mittens in the usual place on the couch. Myrna hadn't made the bed, naturally, and in contrast to its tumbled mess which she could see through the open bedroom door, Betty's cot with its folded blanket across the foot looked stark. Connie turned quickly and went into the kitchen, staring grimly at the open jar of instant coffee and the can of evaporated milk in the clutter of cups and spoons and an opened loaf of bread. Myrna had apparently fixed herself some breakfast for a change.

"Clean, really clean people," she muttered, and left it to go upstairs. One thing about Mrs. Brewster, her house was clean, even if it was always littered with Kevin's toys. You could always tell where he had been by the trail he left behind him.

"Come on in," Mrs. Brewster called from the bedroom. "Cold out, I suppose."

Connie nodded. "Like always. Hmm, your perfume smells good."

Mrs. Brewster sniffed. "Can you tell I have some on? I can't. I guess I use it so much I'm too used to it. It's Mike's favorite, so I wear it a lot to keep him handy."

Connie looked around the bedroom at the pictures

of Mike, of Mike and Mrs. Brewster, of Mike and Kevin, of the three of them together. "You've got lots of reminders," she said, "plus all the letters you get from him."

"He's really good at writing. I wouldn't have believed it." Mrs. Brewster brushed her short curly hair as she talked, and Connie stood watching and admiring her slim figure in slacks and sweater. "The one I got today was about ten pages long. Of course, half of them were about this religious kick he's on, but they're still Mike."

"He still talks about it, huh?" Connie turned to look at the big colored picture of him on top of the television out of Kevin's reach. She knew from what Mrs. Brewster had said that he had been a terrific football player in high school. Personally she thought he looked like a movie star with his black hair and blue eyes and that smile. Why did anybody with all that need religion?

"Yeah, more than ever. He's even given up smoking. Mike of all people! He's been smoking since he was about twelve. I didn't think even cancer scares would stop him, and now he's quit just like that," and she snapped her fingers. "Just overnight practically."

"What's smoking got to do with religion?"

"Nothing I guess. But this chaplain doesn't smoke, so Mike quit. Now I don't know whether to try to stop or wait and see if he starts again when he gets home." She reached for a cigarette and then put it back. "Maybe I'd better practice a little bit even though Mike's never told me to stop. Mostly he talks about God and how He loves people. Things like that. He's really swallowed it all. At least temporarily."

"What if he still believes it when he gets back? Will you, too?"

"Look, what's good enough for Mike is good enough for me," Mrs. Brewster answered firmly. "I think it's just a crutch he needs for now while he's over

there. But if it's for real? That's OK too. I'll go along
with him."

Kevin whimpered in his room and she grabbed her
coat with a quick, "Give him some juice and a cracker.
And get yourself something to eat too. Be back about
five."

Connie got Kevin out of his crib, ignoring his cries
for his mother, and gave him a graham cracker. She
could tell his diaper was wet but decided to leave
it for a while. If she changed him now, she'd have to
do it again in an hour, so she might as well wait and
do it only once. She got herself milk and a piece of
cake and hunted through the television schedule.
Most of the afternoon movies were love stories, but
she finally found one that was a comedy. She settled
down to watch, surrounding Kevin with a barricade
of toys and making sure the door was shut tight.

Gradually she became aware of a thumping sound
and jumped to look around for Kevin. He was safe
under the kitchen table methodically tearing pages
out of his mother's latest movie magazine. But the
pounding noise was repeated, and it finally dawned
on her that someone was knocking on the downstairs
door. She opened the door and looked out over the
stairway banister and saw the person standing before
their apartment.

That's what I want to look like someday, she thought
as one quick glance took in the woman's shining
hair, the black coat with a ring of brown fur for a
collar, and the black, heeled boots. As she turned to
look up the stairs Connie's first reaction was, *Now
there's someone who knows how to use makeup.
Myrna ought to take a lesson.*

Then the woman smiled. "Hello. I'm looking for
Mrs. Hamilton."

"She isn't home."

"Do you know when she'll be back?"

Connie looked at her silently for a moment and then went down a couple of steps. "Why?"

"I want to see her."

"Why?"

The visitor hesitated. "Are you a neighbor?"

Connie shook her head. "I'm babysitting up here."

"Oh." The woman turned back then, wrote something in a looseleaf notebook, scribbled a few words on a card, slipped it under the door, and left without looking up again. As soon as the door closed behind her, Connie dashed back into the kitchen, grabbed a startled, crying Kevin under one arm and ran downstairs. She opened the door to the apartment and leaned down for the card and then groaned. The woman was from the welfare office! She sure didn't look like the one who had been here last.

"Yow! Now what do I do?" Connie muttered. One thing her mother had drummed into them was that you were always nice to the welfare people when they made their checkups. You smiled at them and meekly answered their prying, nosy, insulting questions. And here she had turned her away.

She leaned over the couch and pulled the curtain aside to look out the front window. The snooper must have stopped to write something else in her notebook, because she was still there, just walking up the steps to the sidewalk where her car was parked. Connie put Kevin on the floor and hurriedly pulled open the outside door.

"Hey!"

The woman turned around.

"You left before I could tell you that I'm Connie Hamilton."

She hugged her arms around herself as she stood in the cold and watched as the woman turned and came back to her.

"Oh. Well, may I come in for a minute?"

"I guess so." Connie backed away to let her through

the door. Kevin was still sitting where she had put him, and he looked up at the visitor with a smile and held up his arms.

"Well, well, who's this?"

"He belongs upstairs. I *was* babysitting there."

"When will your mother be home?"

"I'm not sure. She usually gets off work about five." There was no point in explaining that her mother might be home within a half hour or maybe not for half the night, depending on how she felt and who she was with.

"I suppose she'll be visiting your sister in the hospital this evening?"

"You know about Betty already?" The surprise in Connie's voice changed as she remembered. "Oh, because of the ambulance. I suppose you've got that written down somewhere." She couldn't help the bratty sound of her voice even if it got her a black mark in the welfare office records.

The visitor looked at her and then down at the pen poised in her fingers. She put it down. "Yes, I know about Betty." She hesitated a moment and then added, "But it's because I'm interested in her. And you too. So far you're only names to me, and I'd like to know you as people. You see, I—I'm new at this job, and I wanted to get acquainted with the people I'm supposed to work with."

Connie listened silently. This was a new way of saying she was coming to see how they spent their welfare money.

"I visited Betty this afternoon—"

"You did? In the hospital? How come?"

"Just to get acquainted. You see, your family has been assigned to me—" She stopped, looked at Connie's set face and away, biting her lip. Then she went on, "Betty's getting along fine. She's in with a lot of other children in a nice sunny room."

Connie was conscious of the dark bedroom behind

her and wished she had put the visitor in a chair where
she couldn't see directly into the bedroom at the
mess of the unmade bed and the clutter the three of
them always made.

Then the woman said, "But she really needs to have
someone come and see her."

Connie didn't answer.

"You see, the other children have visitors."

Connie looked back with an unchanging expression.
What would the woman say if she knew that Ma
thought that watching the other parents visit their
kids was all Betty needed?

"I wondered if your mother were ill and couldn't
come?"

"She works," Connie answered and knew that was
no explanation of why she didn't visit in the evening.

"I see." Then the visitor looked at her papers and
said hesitantly, "Your sister, your older one. She's
over sixteen—"

"She works too."

In the silence that lengthened between them across
the room, Connie could read the pity which she resented
in any form from anybody and tightened herself against it.

"They told my mother Betty was getting along all
right," she said defensively. "She called the hospital
and they said she was fine. She's probably getting
better food there than she would if she was home,"
she added, and the bitterness in her voice was clear.

The visitor nodded but then said slowly, "But she
needs more than food and a clean bed. She needs—love."

The word came out reluctantly and Connie stared
back at her. She had to shut her lips in a tight line
to keep from saying, "She'll get more of that, too, in
the hospital from strangers than she will at home."

She could see the visitor didn't know what to say
next and that she was trying to keep from too obviously
staring around the room. Connie wished she would
leave.

Instead she asked, "What grade are you in?"

"Eighth."

"Do you like school?"

"No."

"No favorite subjects?"

"No."

They sat looking at each other then until the woman shuffled her papers together and stood up. She looked at her watch. "Please tell your mother I plan to stop by soon and meet her and get acquainted. Perhaps I could come on a Saturday?"

Connie shrugged. "She doesn't work then usually. Besides, that's when the others usually came to check on us."

"Really, that's not why we come, my dear. It's part of the job, of course, but we—I do really want to help you."

Connie stared back, her face expressionless. She wasn't going to be taken in by that kind of talk. How could she tell this outsider how much she resented being on welfare and having to give an account to someone else for everything they thought and did and felt? How could anyone like this understand how much she hated it that her mother just took for granted that someone owed them something just because there was no father to provide for them? How could she understand what it was like to be poor, when you could tell by looking at her how easy her life was.

But remembering her mother's repeated warnings to "keep your mouth shut when those snoops come around and tell them only what will get something more for us," Connie closed her lips firmly and stared back at the pleading expression in the other's eyes.

"Good-bye, then. I'll come by another time," and she pulled the door open and went out.

Connie walked over and peeked through the curtains and watched as the woman walked quickly through the gathering darkness toward her car. Kevin began to cry behind her, and she turned to pick him up, catching sight of Betty's empty cot. Kevin clung to her, burrowing his head against her shoulder, his sodden diaper soaking through his playsuit and wetting her arm. She stood rocking him gently back and forth, staring somberly at Betty's cot as the words "She needs—love" repeated themselves in her ears.

If you didn't have love, how could you give it? she wondered, and turned to climb the stairs slowly with the burden of Kevin heavy in her arms, and a heavier burden pressing her from inside.

6

Myrna and a Decision

CONNIE WAS IN THE KITCHEN when her mother came in, and she knew from the moment of silence that Ma had seen the card on top of the television and had stopped to read it.

"What's she doing snooping around for now? This isn't the time she's supposed to check up!" Mrs. Hamilton stood in the doorway looking at Connie suspiciously. "What did she want? What did she ask? What did you tell her?"

"Nothing."

Her mother made a threatening gesture. "What do you mean nothing? I asked you more than one question."

"Well, she didn't ask very much and I didn't tell her very much."

"What did she come for then?"

"Because of Betty."

"Betty! What's she got to do with it?"

"The welfare office found out that no one **had** visited her—"

''For crying out loud! How do you like that? Just because I get a lousy one hundred bucks a month from them does that give them the right to stick their nose into all my affairs? Can't a person have any privacy? So what's it to them if she has any visitors or not?''

Connie was silent, and her mother glared at her. "So what'd you tell the nosy old bag?"

The memory of the green wool suit under the rich-looking coat with its fur collar, the leather gloves, the scent of expensive perfume swam before her, and the contrast with Ma's description almost made Connie laugh out loud. She managed to turn it into a cough to keep from getting slapped.

"Well?" her mother demanded.

"I just said you worked and that anyway Betty was being taken care of."

Mrs. Hamilton shrugged out of her coat as she listened, rummaged for a cigarette, and sat down by the table. "When are they going to send her home?"

"I don't know."

"Haven't they called or anything?"

"Not while I've been here."

Mrs. Hamilton got up. "Hurry with supper, will you?"

Whatever else she said was lost as she went into her bedroom and closed the door. Connie had fried hamburger and opened a can of corn by the time her mother came out in her robe, her hair in rollers and her face creamed.

"Got any coffee?"

"The water's on," Connie answered as she scraped out a teaspoonful and waited for the water to boil. She looked in the jar. "I had to borrow some coffee from Mrs. Brewster yesterday and now it's almost gone. There's only enough left for one more cup."

"Get some tomorrow when you go to the store. Get some other kind of meat too. I'm sick of hamburger."

Connie sat down and they ate silently. When her mother finished, she lit her cigarette and smoked, watching Connie. "You going babysitting tonight?" she asked abruptly.

"No. I stayed with Kevin this afternoon."

"How come you don't get many babysitting jobs? Myrna had a lot of them when she was your age."

"There aren't as many kids around here, I guess."

"You gonna be home then?"

Connie nodded. "Unless you want me to go with you." When her mother stared back at her, her cigarette halfway to her mouth, Connie added, "To the hospital, I mean," and knew instantly that she had made a mistake.

"Will you get off my back about going to that hospital before I belt you one? I'm not going to the hospital."

Connie retreated out of reach. "Well, you're going out and I thought—you said yesterday—"

"Yes, I'm going out. I have a date, if it's any of your business." She glared at Connie. "I suppose you think I shouldn't. I suppose you think I should stay home and cry because Betty is in the hospital. Well, I'm not going to. I have to have some fun out of life. Believe me I haven't had very much of it so far." She ground out her cigarette on her plate and went into the bedroom, slamming the door.

Connie got up and scraped the dishes and heated a pan of water. Ordinarily she knew she would have put off washing the dishes as long as possible. Now she wanted to get them clean right away and scrub the table and the stove and scour the grimy sink. If only she could get rid of all the dirt and ugliness and meanness of her life by just scouring things clean. *If only Ma*— The faster her thoughts raced, the harder she scrubbed.

Just as she finished there was a loud knock on the door, and her mother hurried out of the bedroom, fixing a dangling earring. "I'll get it," she said hastily to Connie. "Do me a favor and stay in the kitchen until I'm gone," she ordered.

She went to the door, and Connie heard it open, and a man's voice said, "Hi, doll, let me in. It's cold out there."

"I'm all ready. Sit down on the couch while I get my coat."

"Don't tie me down. I want to see what kind of a place you've got here."

His voice got closer, and Connie felt him standing in the kitchen doorway and turned to face him.

"Well, well, who's this? You didn't tell me you had a daughter—and such a pretty one," he said over his shoulder to Mrs. Hamilton while staring at Connie.

"Cut it out," she snapped back. "She's just a kid." Then Connie watched as she came close to him and smiled up into his face. "Let's go. I'm in the mood for some fun."

He looked over her head at Connie. "You leaving her all alone?"

"She's not a baby. She can look after herself. Come on," and she urged him through the living room and out to the hall. Then Connie heard her say, "Wait, I forgot something."

She hurried back to the kitchen and came close to Connie. "I promise I'll go see Betty tomorrow," she said quickly in a low voice. "I meant to go tonight, honest. But then I got this chance for a date. And I can't ask him to take me to the hospital even for a few minutes. It'll scare him off if he sees all my problems. And he may be the answer to a better life for me—for all of us."

Her eyes asked for understanding, and Connie stared back at her uncertainly. Then she nodded and watched as her mother turned away and walked to the door with a carefree, "OK. Let's go."

The man looked at Connie as she came into the living room and winked at her. She watched her mother close the door behind them, abruptly cutting off a trail of cigar smoke. She stared at the door, her

throat tight at the memory of her mother's pleading
eyes. What did she mean? Did she hope he would
marry her without knowing she had three children who
would cost money? It was obvious he hadn't known
about her so he probably didn't know there were
two more. It didn't matter to her if Ma remarried. She
had no loving memories of her father. Why shouldn't
Ma grab a husband if she could get one? But the
thought of the man's possessive eyes on her and the
familiarity of his wink made her shiver. She didn't
like him. *But so what? Ma would do what she thought
would get her something no matter what happens to
the rest of us.*

She looked at the books still in a heap on the couch
where she had left them after school, saw the torn
sleeve of her jacket and the holes in her mittens that
had been there for weeks, and then turned to flip on
the television. It was early, and the whole evening
stretched ahead of her to be filled. There would be
time to watch a program first and work later. Anyway,
nobody did homework on Friday.

She twisted the knobs to try to get a brighter picture.
The sound made a buzzing noise but she knew how to
hit the set to make it work better temporarily. This
time it didn't help, and the sound faded away completely,
although the picture grew brighter. She could hear
Mrs. Brewster's television, so she flipped the channels
until the picture she got matched the sound from
upstairs.

With the door to the hall open, she could hear the
sound better, but the cold air rushing in made her go
to the bedroom for a blanket to wrap around her.
*Maybe I could use Ma's heater—no, I guess I'd
better not.* Some of the wires were loose, and if she
fell asleep with it on and it got overheated it could
be dangerous. It had scared her the other morning
when she woke up and found it was so hot.

She curled up in a corner of the couch nearest the

door so she could hear the sound from upstairs. But she finally got up restlessly to flip the channels and pound the set. She might have known Mrs. Brewster would be watching a love story. They were her favorite kind. And Connie hated the prolonged kissing scenes in this one. There was a comedy on another channel, and she decided to try to follow it by closing the door and sitting on the floor close to the set.

The phone rang just as she got the blanket wrapped around her, and she muttered, "Nuts!" and got up to answer.

"No, she isn't here," she replied to the voice that asked for Mrs. Hamilton.

"Is this Connie?"

"Yeah."

"This is Betty's nurse. I thought I'd call and let you know how she's doing."

"Oh. How is she?"

"Doing real well."

"Is she—I mean, does she—seem lonesome?" Connie craned her neck to see the clock as she asked. Almost eight. That meant visiting hours were still going.

"Oh, so-so. I stayed and talked to her a little while tonight. She's cute."

Connie blinked. Cute? Betty? But aloud she said, "My mother is coming tomorrow."

"That's the main reason I called. The doctor says Betty can go home tomorrow—"

"Already? I didn't think she'd be well enough so soon."

"Oh, sure. There isn't much that appendix patients need after a while. Just rest for a few days. So when we get crowded here and need the beds we usually send them home."

"OK, I'll tell my mother to be there."

"She'll probably want to be here by noon. They charge for an extra day if the patient isn't checked out by one o'clock."

"I'll tell her." And Connie wondered if her mother remembered that she would have to pay a bill.

"I told Betty I was going to call you and she said to say hello."

"Oh." Connie felt awkward and stupid. She and Betty never talked except to argue, and she didn't know how to express herself to this outsider who seemed to like Betty and thought she was cute.

"Well, tell her hi," she finally said.

She put the phone down reluctantly, feeling as though she ought to have said something else, as though the nurse expected something else, but not knowing what. She went back to the television again and waited while it flickered through a couple of commercials. The picture and the sound were both better, so she curled up on the couch again under the blanket and watched a couple of programs.

She got up to switch channels, when the sound of someone fumbling at the outside door made her freeze. It was too early for Ma or Myrna to be coming home. She should have locked the door, but she was too scared now to move. She could hear a car motor running outside, and there were footsteps in the hall and whispers and heavy breathing. Then the outside door closed and after a moment the car drove away. She watched as the door to the apartment was pushed open and stared at Myrna standing in the doorway swaying on her feet, her face flushed and her eyes glazed.

She looks—she looks like Ma does sometimes, Connie thought. Only there was a difference. Myrna acted not just drunk but strange. The many warnings Ma had given Myrna about drugs flashed into her mind. Ma threatened to turn Myrna out if she got started on them, and Myrna had only laughed. "I'm not going to be that dumb," she had answered. "But if I did, what's it to you? You drink. That's as bad as drugs, so don't tell me what to do."

Now she watched as Myrna walked stiffly to a chair and lowered herself into it. She sat staring ahead of her for a few minutes, and then she began to laugh and rock herself back and forth, hugging herself with her arms. Connie turned off the television and closed the door and watched her, helpless and scared.

"Myrna? Myrna, what's the matter?" she pleaded.

But the laughter went on and on, and Connie didn't know what to do to stop it. She was scared even to touch Myrna. She wished her mother were there. and yet she was glad she wasn't. Ma would only yell at Myrna and maybe hit her, and there was no telling what Myrna might do when she was like this.

Then, as suddenly as it had started, the laughter stopped, and Myrna fell back in the chair, closed her eyes, and her head rolled to one side.

"Myrna?"

Heavy breathing was the only answer, and Connie walked over and timidly touched her on the shoulder. "I guess she's asleep," she muttered. "Now how do I get her to bed before Ma comes home?"

She didn't want to try to waken Myrna and risk getting that horrible laughter started again, and yet she couldn't possibly get her to bed alone.

In the silence there was a light tap on the door, and Mrs. Brewster said, "Connie?"

She opened the door a crack, shielding a view into the living room with her body, hating to have anyone see Myrna like this, with a trickle of saliva running down her chin and her hair all matted.

"Is something wrong?"

Connie hesitated, and Mrs. Brewster said sympathetically, "Let me help, Connie. Don't be ashamed of her."

Connie nodded without speaking, the sympathy in Mrs. Brewster's voice making her want to cry. She shifted so that Myrna could be seen. "She's sick. Can you help me get her into the bedroom?"

Mrs. Brewster came in, saying apologetically, "I was awake. I couldn't sleep. And then I heard—" she stopped and gestured at Myrna. "I thought maybe it was your—" she stopped again, embarrassed. "I thought maybe your mother wasn't home and you needed help."

She walked over and stood looking down at Myrna, her hands on her hips, and shook her head. "This kid really needs help. The trouble is she won't admit it." Then she leaned over and put a hand under Myrna's arm. "Get hold of her on the other side and I think we can manage all right."

But Connie bent over and put Myrna's right arm across her shoulder, as she and Myrna had done so often with Ma, and straightened up. "This is the easiest way."

Between them they guided Myrna's stumbling, dragging feet into the bedroom and collapsed her on the bed. Connie took off her shoes and helped Mrs. Brewster pull off her coat and then looked down at her, frowning.

"You want to leave her like this?" Mrs. Brewster asked.

"I guess so. If we can get the blankets out from under her and cover her, Ma won't know she didn't undress."

"Anyway, she's in her own bed." Connie looked at Mrs. Brewster quickly, her eyes wide at something undefined in her voice. She looked back at Connie and added gently, "I mean, at least your mother can't get mad at her for staying out late."

Then she looked around the room. "Where are you going to sleep?"

"On Betty's bed."

"When is she coming home?"

"Tomorrow."

Connie closed the bedroom door as they went out, and Mrs. Brewster sat down on the arm of a chair, hugging her robe around her. "It's cold down here. Is it always like this?"

"Usually," Connie shrugged. "Ma says it's something about how the pipes in the furnace are fixed. All the heat goes upstairs instead of spreading out. But you get used to it."

"It's just a part of life, huh?"

"Yeah. You don't like it but you live with it."

Connie sat down, pulling the blanket around her again and wishing Mrs. Brewster would stay a while but not wanting to ask her to. She was glad when she slid down off the chair arm onto the seat and put her slippered feet up, hugging her arms around her knees. Connie closed her eyes against the picture of Myrna sitting there a few minutes ago. Why did she have to have a sister like that? If Myrna were like Mrs. Brewster they could have talked about things, really talked. And she could have asked her the questions that were bottled up inside. There were things she had to know, but she couldn't ask either Ma or Myrna. Ma would be impatient and angry and maybe even laugh at her for being so dumb, and Myrna would give answers that would make her sick inside at the pictures they painted.

But maybe Mrs. Brewster wouldn't have the right answers either. Connie watched her as she sat curled up in the chair, not looking any older than Myrna. It was funny—she used a lot of makeup. Connie had experimented with it when she sat with Kevin. But Mrs. Brewster didn't look made up the way Myrna did.

"How come you moved here?" she asked curiously.

Mrs. Brewster laughed. "Because the rent is cheap. Mike wanted me in a house with other people in case Kevin got sick or I needed help. We want to buy a house when Mike comes home, so we're saving every penny we can."

"Is that why you don't go out much?"

"Who would I go with?"

"Myrna said—" Connie began and stopped, wishing she hadn't brought up the things Myrna said.

Mrs. Brewster nodded. "Yeah, I know what she says. Myrna thinks I'm nuts. But that's all right. I'm happy. I wouldn't go out with anybody but Mike."

They sat in silence, while Mrs. Brewster smoked and looked at Connie thoughtfully.

Finally Connie said, "I'm sure glad you came down. It's a good thing for me you heard the noise."

"I wasn't asleep. I guess the late movie kept me awake. I shouldn't watch war pictures because I get to thinking about Mike. And then I go crazy because I don't have anybody to talk to so I talk to myself and smoke too much and worry."

Her eyes looked off beyond Connie, and she went on as though she were really talking to herself. "A person needs somebody to talk to. I do anyway. That's one thing about Mike and me. We can talk, you know? Really talk. About anything. How we feel. What we think. What we want for Kevin. What a mess the stinking world is in. I tell you, Mike's a thinker."

She was silent and then said slowly, "I guess that's why he's so taken with this religion thing. He says it's given him answers. He says believing there's a God back of everything is the only way he can make sense out of what he's doing over there."

Connie looked down at the blanket edge she was pleating and unpleating. "He really believes it then. About God."

"All I know is that he talks about it in every letter he writes." Mrs. Brewster laughed then. "He used to write every day. Now he sometimes writes two or three times a day, whenever he has a chance. So I guess I should thank God—or something—for that."

"I can see believing in God when you're rich and you've got everything going for you. But if you live like this—" Connie's voice cracked with her pent-up feelings as she gestured around the cramped, dingy room.

Mrs. Brewster nodded sympathetically. "I know what you mean. You've got it rough. Still, Mike doesn't have everything going for him now either. He doesn't say much about it, but I listen to all the news, and I've seen war pictures. So I'm for anything that will help him get through. Even if it's religion."

"I'm going to quit school when I'm sixteen and get a job and make money. I'm not going to be poor all my life." Connie could hear the hardness in her voice and knew Mrs. Brewster had too from the way she looked at her.

"I'm not so sure about the quitting school part," she frowned in answer. She glanced at the closed bedroom door and then back to Connie. "Look, I don't want to meddle, but I'd like to help you if I could. I'm not much older than you are, and I've been through the growing up bit, and I know how easy it is to get mixed up and make mistakes."

This is my chance. Connie thought, and questions trembled on her lips but she couldn't bring herself to ask them. And then Mrs. Brewster was talking again.

"Mike and I got married the day after we graduated from high school, and I'll admit it's been rough sometimes. For him, I mean, having to support a wife and baby. Maybe if we had it to do over again, we'd wait. But we were so sure we had all the answers, and we didn't want anyone telling us what we should do."

Connie, listening, remembered her mother's sneering comment to Myrna after Mrs. Brewster had moved in that this was a "had-to" marriage. She was glad it wasn't, glad Ma was wrong.

"I know we're going to make it because we love each other and we've got Kevin to plan for and maybe there'll be other kids. I'm telling you this so you won't rush into things before you're ready for them. Like Myrna—" She stopped. "I should say all this to her or to your mother but I haven't got the nerve. Your mother should know that Myrna's on the way to getting mixed up with a bunch that plays rough and doesn't have any pity for the guy who gets hurt. It's awful to see her wreck her life when she's so young."

"You mean—drinking like this?"

Mrs. Brewster nodded. "And staying out late and dating just anybody she meets." She eyed Connie for a moment thoughtfully. "If I'm snooping, tell me. But have you ever met any of the fellows she dates?"

Connie shook her head. "But they're guys she knows from school. They usually take her to work."

Mrs. Brewster made no comment, and after a moment she got up and stretched. "I guess I'll go up. Maybe you want to go to bed even if I don't."

She walked to the door and then turned to face Connie with a slight frown, biting at her lip. "You know, even if there's nothing to this stuff Mike's been writing. Even if there isn't a God or any sense to things—" She threw out her hands in a helpless gesture. "Even if it's just a—a way of escaping from reality, if it works it's OK to try it. Don't you think?"

Connie didn't answer because she knew Mrs. Brewster was asking the question for herself. But she closed the door and walked back to pick up the blanket from the couch. She would need it on the cot. She opened the bedroom door softly and looked at Myrna in the light coming in from the living room. She lay on her back, the mascara streaked in black smudges across her cheeks.

Connie was swept with despair. You couldn't escape something like this by believing in religion, by believing in a God who was way off somewhere. You could only get out of your problems by your own efforts.

She turned on the light since Myrna was too far under to be bothered and stared at herself in the mirror. "No more daydreaming about the future," she told herself grimly. "The movie star and the fashion model business are out."

They were just escape from reality too, like Mike's religion. You had to have a goal. Get a job and save your money and look out for yourself.

She lay down on the mattress on Betty's cot, not bothering with sheets or pillowcase. She was jittery from tiredness, and her muscles jerked when she tried to make herself relax. She lay rigid, waiting for her mother to come in, and wondering if she would need help as Myrna had.

"I won't give it," she said aloud in the darkness. "I'll let her take care of herself."

7

Homecoming

A SOUND REACHED THROUGH to Connie and she sat up with a jerk, surprised to find that it was morning and that she had slept after all. She hadn't heard Ma come in. She looked around groggily, wondering what had made her wake up. Then she saw Myrna curled in a heap on the bed, her knees drawn up against herself, and her breath coming in short, quick gasps.

"What's the matter? Myrna, are you sick?"

There was only the harsh, strained breathing in answer, and Connie got up, pulling the blanket around her and went to the foot of the bed. Myrna's face was hidden in the pillow, and her arms were wrapped tightly across her stomach. "What's the matter?" Connie asked again.

"I feel rotten. But don't tell Ma."

The panic in her voice was too real to be ignored, and Connie stood watching her, frowning. Maybe she ought to tell Ma. Myrna hadn't been feeling good for quite a while and maybe there was something wrong with her. Then she remembered last night and thought, *No wonder she's sick.* Ma couldn't get mad at Myrna for drinking when she did it herself. But Connie knew she would be and would yell at her.

"Well, that's her problem," she muttered and turned away.

She hurried to dress in the cold, pulling on her jeans and sweatshirt and went out to the living room. Her mother's bedroom door was closed, and Connie went over and listened. Her heart sank at the sound of her mother's breathing. She'd heard it too many times not to know what it meant. She opened the door, not even trying to be quiet, and looked in. Her mother lay where she had fallen on the bed. She hadn't even tried to undress, hadn't even taken off her coat. And Connie wondered what time she had come home.

She leaned over and shook her mother's shoulder. "Ma. Ma! Can you hear me? Ma, wake up! We're supposed to get Betty at the hospital today."

There was no response and she shook her again. "Ma!"

She watched as her mother roused and opened her eyes to stare vacantly at her. "Wh' matter? Lemme 'lone. Wanna sleep," and she sank back on the pillow.

"Ma! You've *got* to wake up. We have to get Betty."

Her mother's head turned restlessly on the pillow. "Leave her 'lone. Safe in hospital." Her voice drifted off again into a mumble.

Connie straightened and looked at the clock. No use trying anymore now. There was still time to try again later. Maybe if Ma had another hour of sleep it would help. She realized suddenly that she was ravenous and went out to the kitchen. While she waited for water to boil for cocoa, she ate a piece of bread, staring out the window at the cold banks of snow, and sighed. Winter was such a long time of

year. It seemed as though she had spent most of her
life shivering with cold.

The water had begun to boil, and she dropped two
slices of bread into the toaster, poured the water
over the cocoa in the cup, and stirred it while waiting
for the bread to toast. She watched it closely, waiting
to grab it as soon as it was brown, since the toaster
no longer shut off automatically. The sound of footsteps made her look around, and she stood motionless,
the toast in her hands. Myrna stood in the doorway,
and Connie thought she had never seen her look so
wretched. It wasn't just that she was pale and so
thin that the skin seemed to be stretched taut over
her cheekbones. She looked sick, and Connie could
see the pulse beat in the hollow place in her throat.

Myrna groped for a chair and sank into it heavily,
putting her elbows on the table and holding her head
in both hands. And Connie felt a flare of pity for
her. "Want some coffee? There's enough for one cup."

Myrna shuddered. "No! Don't fix it. Even the smell
makes me sick!"

Connie said nothing, but put her toast on a plate
and sat down across from Myrna, her brief moment
of pity dissolved in Myrna's crossness. As she got
up to get margarine from the cupboard, Myrna said,
"Fix me a piece of toast. Plain—nothing on it." She
didn't lift her head from her hands as she barked the
order, and Connie obeyed silently.

When it was ready, Myrna tore off a small piece
and chewed it slowly. Connie watched, fascinated
by the tiny bites. Myrna waited between each bite
before taking another and finally finished the whole
slice. She sat motionless for a while before finally
shifting her position and raising her head from her
hands.

She looked across at Connie. "Never felt so rotten
in my life. It's the lousy food they serve at the joint.
They never give us time enough to eat. I had to eat

so fast last night I almost choked. And the lousy
customers expect you to run your feet off for them.
Then they're so stingy with their tips."

Connie listened but said nothing. This was the same
familiar complaint Myrna had griped ever since she
started working there. Then she saw Myrna looking
at her narrowly and instinctively shifted out of her
reach.

But when Myrna spoke she was surprisingly good-
natured. "You know that green sweater of mine you
wanted? If you still do, you can have it."

Connie gaped at her. "You mean it? I can *have*
it?" Then her own eyes narrowed. "What do I have to
do to get it?"

"Nothing."

"Yeah?" Connie looked back at her and then Myrna
shrugged.

"OK, just don't tell Ma about last night. No sense
in telling her now that it's all over. And believe me,
I'm never going to get like that again." She shuddered.
"First time I ever drank so much it made me sick."

Connie was silent, remembering other times when
Myrna had come home and acted silly and giggled
foolishly over nothing.

"Oh, yeah, and don't bother mentioning that I
didn't feel so good this morning." Myrna was so casual
in her manner that Connie looked at her suspiciously.
"I wasn't really sick anyway," Myrna went on. "Just
hungover from last night. You know, like Ma sometimes is."

Connie nodded. Myrna *had* looked like Ma last
night. Drink was certainly better than drugs—at least
Ma thought so. Connie felt her skin crawl at the way
Ma would scream if Myrna ever got hooked.

"Where is Ma anyway? Still sleeping? Or didn't she
come home last night?" The familiar I-know-something-
you-don't smirk was back, now that she was feeling

better, and Connie got up abruptly and carried her cup and plate to the sink.

"She's still in bed and we have to get her up because she has to go to the hospital today to get Betty."

"Already? She just went. They ought to keep her so we can have some peace around here."

The words made Connie mad, even though she knew she had thought them herself, and she answered angrily, "Well, she's coming anyway. And we have to get her by one or they charge for an extra day."

Myrna laughed. "Tell Ma that. That'll get her up."

"You tell her. I've already done my share."

"Do some more," Myrna said and fumbled in her pocket for a cigarette.

But Connie leaned back against the kitchen sink and folded her arms, staring back at Myrna. She had never been this defiant of her before, and she could feel her heart pounding, scared at what Myrna might do.

After a moment Myrna got up angrily. "OK! If you're going to use this as blackmail, go ahead and tell her about last night and I'll keep my sweater!"

She turned and stamped out of the kitchen, but Connie listened and heard her go into Ma's bedroom and followed. It was already ten o'clock, and Myrna was not being any more successful than she had been.

"Sa'urday and Sunday I sleep," she heard her mother say. "This is Sa'urday, so go 'way."

Myrna straightened up in disgust. "Some mother she is!" Then she suddenly doubled over and rushed to the bathroom where Connie could hear her gagging. When she came out she was white and shaking and brushed past Connie to the bedroom. "Got the flu," she said thickly, but her voice was blurred with fright, and she shut the door.

Connie followed and opened the door to see Myrna in bed with the blanket pulled up over her shaking shoulders. "You that cold?"

Myrna's teeth were chattering and she nodded weakly.

"But what'll I do? How will Betty get home?"

"It's not my business," Myrna muttered. "Close the door and go away."

There was nothing else to do and Connie obeyed. Her mother was sound asleep again, and she stood in the living room helplessly. She hated to ask Mrs. Brewster for help with both Ma and Myrna here, but she'd have to.

She went upstairs and knocked on Mrs. Brewster's door and explained the problem. Mrs. Brewster's face was grim as she listened.

"Stay with Kevin a minute, will you? Be right back." She went out, and Connie heard her clattering downstairs.

When she came back, she said briefly, "Your mother's up. Are you going along to get Betty?"

"I—I don't know." Connie walked over to the door and stood hesitating, dreading going down. "Was she—was she mad? When she got up, I mean?"

"She wasn't happy. Maybe you'd better fix her some good strong coffee. I think she needs it."

"We haven't got enough to make it strong."

"Here. I've got an extra jar. Take it. I don't like this brand anyway," she answered Connie's protests about already having borrowed so much.

Connie went down slowly, sure that her mother would be mad because she'd run to someone for help and exposed her neglect. But her mother said nothing except, "Fix me some coffee and hurry it up. You should have gotten me up sooner. If you'd told me this last night, I'd have planned to get up."

Connie knew better than to answer as she fixed the coffee and brought it into the bedroom, wondering what Mrs. Brewster had said to her.

"Is Myrna still in bed?"

Connie nodded. "She's sleeping."

She watched as her mother drank the coffee, not

bothering to dress, and thought, *It would be just like Ma to try to send Myrna in her place and then she'd find out about her being sick.* So she said quickly, "Do you want me to go with you?"

Her mother shrugged. "If I've got enough bus fare for us both."

She sat silent for a few moments after she had finished the coffee, blowing smoke thoughtfully. Then she got up and went to the phone.

"I'm going to see if I can wangle some help out of those skinflints at city hall. They owe me something, it seems to me."

She dialed, and Connie listened as she explained her need in a soft, helpless voice with many references to "my poor little girl" and "no husband to lean on in emergencies" and "have to depend on the kindness of other people."

When she finished, she banged the receiver down with a triumphant, "That did it. She fell for the whole bit, and someone is coming to take us to the hospital and bring us home."

"Who?" And Connie wondered if it would be the one who had visited.

"I don't know. Some old warhorse in the office. She was as sour as a grapefruit, but I guess my sob story worked. Someone will be here in half an hour."

Connie went to the bedroom, turned the knob of the door silently, and eased herself in without opening the door enough for her mother to see in. Myrna's eyes were closed, and the blanket was pulled tight around her ears, so Connie decided it was all right to turn on the light. Then she saw herself in the mirror and stopped in dismay. She didn't look much better than Myrna had. *My hair is a mess; everything about me is a mess,* she thought critically.

She went out to the kitchen to heat some water and scrubbed her face and neck until the skin was red. She brushed her hair, and then leaned forward to look at herself again, and frowned. She was too pale, but it was too risky to use some of Myrna's makeup with her right there, even if she was asleep. But she did slowly ease out one of Myrna's glossy lipsticks, keeping watch on her in the mirror, and used it quickly. There, that was better. At least it gave her some color.

She frowned over the question of what to wear. Probably jeans and a sweatshirt wouldn't be right. On impulse, she dug into the drawer for the green sweater. If she didn't take it right away, she'd probably never get it. The only thing to wear with it was her old brown skirt, which looked pretty crummy anyway and looked even worse when matched with the sweater.

She heard the knock on the front door and came out, closing the bedroom door behind her, and watched as her mother opened the door to the welfare visitor. Old warhorse, huh? She almost laughed out loud at the expression on her mother's face as her eyes took in the stylish red coat, the long yellow scarf wrapped around under the collar, and the furtrimmed gloves.

"Hello, I'm Ruth Nelson." She looked across at Connie and smiled. "Nice to see you again. My car is outside so we'll go whenever you're ready."

As they drove the ten blocks to the hospital, Connie listened in silence to her mother's repeated assurances of her gratitude for the ride, her delight that her little girl was better and able to come home, how worried she had been, how difficult it was to be both mother and father to three girls. She even dabbed at her eyes a few times to wipe away tears.

Connie stared out the window away from her mother. What a fake! She wondered if Miss Nelson was being taken in by it. She couldn't tell from her expression or from the murmured comments that she occasionally made in answer.

When they got to the hospital and parked, Miss Nelson said, "You're supposed to go to the cashier's window and settle the bill first. I'll go with you."

She turned to Connie. "Why don't you go and help get your sister ready? It's all right for you to go up since she's going home. Ask at the desk for the room number."

Following directions, Connie took the elevator to the children's floor and walked down the hall looking for room 218. She stopped in the doorway at the sound of laughter, and saw the children's rapt attention on the nurse who was telling a story with puppets. She saw Betty immediately and stared. The sun coming in the window behind her shone directly on her, making a glow of her blond hair. But it was the happiness on her face that stopped Connie. Her only picture of Betty was of a whiny, fussy kid, always tagging along and always wanting something she couldn't have. This pretty little girl who looked so clean and dainty and glowing wasn't the Betty they had brought to the hospital.

The story ended just then and the children clapped. Betty looked toward the door and saw Connie, and the delight slowly drained from her face as she looked at her and then past her shoulder at someone else.

"Betty, baby!" Mrs. Hamilton pushed past Connie and rushed to the bed to hug her. "How are you?"

Betty hesitated and then hugged her back, her thin arms twining around her mother's neck as she patted her hair. Then Mrs. Hamilton pulled away and looked around the room.

"My, you haven't had a chance to be lonesome, have you, with all these nice children to be with."

The nurse who had been watching moved forward now, and Connie recognized her. She spoke briskly to Mrs. Hamilton after she had smiled briefly at Connie.

"We've got Betty's things about ready." She gestured to a brown paper sack and an enormous stuffed cat.

"Now aren't you glad you came to the hospital?" Mrs. Hamilton exclaimed in a high bright voice. "Just look what you got."

Betty nodded. "*She* gave it to me," and she pointed shyly at the nurse who was retying a bow at the end of one braid. "She gave me a whole bunch of hair ribbons too."

"We're going to put you in a wheelchair and give you a ride," the nurse said briskly, and in a few minutes she was wheeling Betty down the hall with the rest of them following along. Connie was close enough to see Betty turn to look up at the nurse and heard her whisper, "You said you'd ask her."

"You're sure you don't want to ask her yourself? So she'll know you really want to go?" the nurse asked back.

Betty shook her head so hard her braids flopped. "She'd say no."

"All right. I'll ask."

Miss Nelson drove the car around to the entrance, and after Betty had been put into the front seat, the nurse looked at Mrs. Hamilton. "I'd like to come for Betty next Sunday and take her to Sunday school. She won't feel like going tomorrow, but I think she will be up to it by next Sunday."

"Sunday school?" Connie heard the hardness in her mother's voice as she repeated the words and saw the effort she made to smile and soften her voice as she gave a short laugh. "Well, I suppose if you want to bother with her and if she wants to go—"

"Oh, I *do!*" Betty broke in eagerly.

Connie, listening, thought, *She shouldn't have said that. It'll be just like Ma not to let her go just because she wants to.*

But the nurse replied, "Good. I'll call next Saturday to let you know what time I'll come for her."

She leaned down to look at Betty. "Bye. Be a good girl. I'll see you next week. Don't forget now." She said the words to Betty but straightened up and looked at Mrs. Hamilton as she spoke.

The ride home was a jumble of more ingratiating

comments by Mrs. Hamilton, an attempt at conversation by Miss Nelson, incessant chatter from Betty about the hospital, and confused thoughts in Connie's mind. She couldn't think clearly enough to talk or to follow the endless flow of words Betty was pouring out about her good time in the hospital. She was shaken by this further unexpected encounter with God. The ad on the bus—the letters from Mike—and now the nurse's interest in Sunday school. Having heard of God all her life only as a swear word, it didn't seem possible that He was real, or that people believed in Him as someone who was a person who could help you.

When they got home, Mrs. Hamilton and Miss Nelson helped Betty down the icy front steps from the side-walk, along the short walk and into the house, with Connie following carrying the sack and the cat. Miss Nelson left immediately and Connie was glad she didn't offer to stay and help get Betty into bed. The contrast between the sunny room at the hospital and the room where Betty's cot stood with its bare mattress was too great.

Mrs. Hamilton's pose of friendliness dissolved abruptly as the door closed behind Miss Nelson.

"They're getting pretty low at that office when they have to send out rich, smart-aleck little twirps to do their snooping!"

"How do you know she's rich?"

"Look at her clothes. You don't have to see the label to know where that coat came from!" She walked around the room, her eyes hard. "And that nurse! Her and her know-it-all looks."

"I liked her," Betty said.

"Well, forget about her. You've seen the last of her."

"She's going to come and get me next week." Betty stared at her mother with trembling lips.

Mrs. Hamilton snapped, "That's what she thinks."

"You promised," Betty pleaded.

"That was just to get her off my back. We're not

fooling around with any church stuff. We never have and we're never going to. We haven't got money to throw away to some church. And that's all they want."

"You promised!" Connie's voice was hard as she spoke, and she stared back at her mother even though she was trembling. Betty was crying silently, her thin shoulders bent over the huge cat on her lap. Connie was filled with such anger that she had to clench her hands until the nails dug into her palms. Maybe you could be mean to a kid who was well and bratty but not to one who was sick and helpless.

Her mother turned on her. "What's it to you?"

"You promised," Connie repeated, even though she flinched from the anger in her mother's eyes and the threat in her voice.

"Oh, all right! Stop that sniveling," she ordered Betty. "You can go once. This one time. But that's all. No more. Hear me?"

Betty nodded without looking up.

Mrs. Hamilton picked up her purse. "I'm going to the store. Get her bed made and take care of her."

"You buying food?"

"Yes, if I can find anything I can afford," her mother snapped back.

"We're out of everything," Connie persisted. How could she be sure Ma would buy the food they needed instead of spending the money on other things? Something Miss Nelson had said flashed into her mind.

"Miss Nelson said she was coming back some day next week. She said she wanted to be sure Betty was getting the food she needed to get well."

Her mother glared at her. "It seems to me you're getting too sassy for your own good."

"I'm only telling you what she said."

She watched as her mother went out, slamming the door behind her without answering.

Betty raised her head with tears still streaking her cheeks. "Do you think she'll really let me go?"

"You heard her. She said once. And that means once so don't plan on more than that. Stay there while I make your bed."

As she worked, Connie's angry thoughts raced on. There was no use getting Betty's hopes up for anything more. She'd only stuck her neck out for her this time because she felt sorry for her. It wouldn't be safe to do it again. Besides, church wasn't worth it.

She went back to Betty and picked up the paper bag. "Come on. You'd better get in bed and cover up or you'll get another cold. What do you have in here anyway?"

"Don't open it!" Betty's voice was a cry of alarm as she grabbed the sack and clutched it to her.

"Well, OK! I was just trying to help."

She turned to make the bed Myrna had left in a rumpled mess. Apparently she hadn't been so sick after all. She must have gotten up right after they left and beat it.

As she smoothed out the sheets, Connie could tell from the sounds Betty made that she had taken something out of the sack and put it under her pillow. She waited until Betty went into the bathroom and then quickly lifted the pillow and pulled out a small blue covered book with pictures and words in large print. On the outside in gold letters were the words Connie had half expected and yet dreaded to see — *God is Love*.

She shoved it back. God was following her. There seemed to be no way of escaping from Him. She looked around the shadowed room helplessly. What could anybody — even God — do for her?

8

Thursday and Despair

THAT NIGHT the bitter cold air that had kept the city icy for the past week moved east, but the warmer air brought a blinding snowstorm that closed the schools. By Wednesday the snow had stopped, and most of the streets were plowed out so that schools could open on Thursday. But many sidewalks were still clogged with snow, and Mrs. Hamilton told Betty to stay home the rest of the week. Mrs. Brewster offered to check on her during the day and see that she got something to eat at noon.

Connie reluctantly set the alarm Wednesday night, one part of her hating the thought of going back to school, the other glad to get out of the house where there was nothing to do but watch television on a set which didn't work, and listen to Betty complain how slow the days were going by.

The alarm's shrill ring sent her groping for it, and then she shook Myrna who was sleeping with the blanket pulled over her head.

"Not gonna get up," she muttered and turned over to bury her face in the pillow.

"OK, but don't blame me afterward and say I didn't wake you." She looked at Betty who had roused and was watching. "If Ma asks, tell her I tried to make Myrna get up." Then she said enviously, "You're lucky. I wish I could stay home."

"But there's nothing to do," Betty complained. "It's no fun all by myself. It was funner in the hospital," she said wistfully.

Connie went out to put water on to heat for coffee, and Betty followed. She looked like a stick figure in her too-short pajamas, and Connie said, "You've got to eat more. You're too skinny."

"I'm gonna fix four pieces of toast and eat 'em in bed."

"Sure, and then you'll have to sleep on crumbs for a couple of weeks and you'll be mad."

"No, I won't. I'll brush them on the floor."

"Watch the toast," Connie warned. "If it burns you'll have to scrape the black off and eat it anyway. I'm going to get dressed. Holler when the water boils."

She hurried to dress, deciding to wear the green sweater since Pat and Janet hadn't seen it yet. As she combed her hair she looked past her own reflection in the mirror, and then turned at the sight of Myrna, who was sitting up in bed, her arms around her knees and her head bent on her clasped hands.

"Anybody who didn't know you would think you were praying."

Myrna didn't move, and Connie demanded, "What's the matter? I suppose you're pretending to be sick again. How much longer do you think Ma's going to buy this I-must-have-the-flu bit as an excuse for not going to school?"

"Shut up." Myrna's voice was tired sounding rather than mad, and Connie shrugged. "OK. *Be* sick. But if you're staying home, don't pester Betty."

She went out to the kitchen and poured water in a cup. "Drop me in a piece of bread, will you?"

"I already did," Betty answered. "Look—I cut it the way they did at the hospital. See?"

"Fancy. Bet it doesn't taste any better."

"Yes it does. And it's easier to eat. Except they had jelly. Three kinds, and you could have all of them if you wanted."

"Big deal."

"Wish we had some jelly."

"You're lucky we've got bread."

Then at the sound of the bathroom door closing, Connie groaned. "Oh, no! There she goes and I won't stand a chance of getting in there." She went to the kitchen door and yelled, "Myrna! Hurry up. I'm going to school even if you aren't."

"If she stays home can I still go up and eat with Mrs. Brewster? I like her better. She doesn't say mean things like Myrna."

"Don't worry. Myrna's not going to pay any attention to you."

Then as she listened to the gagging sounds in the bathroom, she felt a stab of remorse at having been so mad. "I guess she really is sick," she said to Betty. "Maybe you'd better stay away from her so you don't catch whatever she has."

Myrna stumbled out looking haggard, with her arms pressed tight across her chest and burrowed into bed with a moan.

"Does she have 'pendicitis too?" Betty asked curiously. "That's the way my stomach felt like it looked."

"I don't know. Maybe. Could be." Connie looked at Myrna and frowned. Well, there was nothing she could do. Myrna was old enough to look after herself and get help if she needed it.

She pulled on her boots, muttering in disgust as one of them ripped along the sole. There was no chance of getting a new pair, so these would have to last through the long winter that still stretched ahead. She sighed gloomily and went out. The snowplows had been along the streets, banking the snow in deep piles along the curbs. By the time she got to school her feet were wet, and her shoes squeaked as she walked.

The morning dragged by as usual, and all they did in home ec was copy a list of foods that had certain kinds of vitamins.

"Why didn't they give us samples?" Connie muttered, aware of her empty stomach. Then when she went to

her locker at noon, she realized she had forgotten to
fix a lunch.

"Nuts!"

"What's the matter?"

Connie glanced briefly at Agnes. "Nothing. I just
forgot my lunch," she muttered.

"You can have some of mine," Agnes offered eagerly.

Connie started to give a curt "No thanks," and then
thought of how good the sandwiches would be. The
trouble was she couldn't take any without sitting with
Agnes and that meant Pat and Janet would mock.

"I've got enough money for a bowl of soup."

"Well, take one sandwich anyway." Agnes opened
her lunch sack. "Here."

"Well—OK—thanks." Connie took it, and then
pretended to look for something in the locker until
finally Agnes turned and walked slowly down the
hall. She couldn't make herself call, "Look, I'll sit
with you."

She waited until she was sure Agnes would be in
the lunchroom before she went down and peered in
the door and saw her across the room. Pat and Janet
were at a table near the door, laughing, and Connie
got soup and slid in beside them. "What's so funny?"

"Oh, different things. Especially people," and they
both laughed again at Pat's answer.

So they were going to be mysterious today. Connie
decided she wouldn't give them the satisfaction of
thinking she was curious. But she couldn't help seeing
the way they kept looking at each other and laughing.
Anger welled up in her, but she fought it down. If
they knew it bothered her it would make them worse.
She'd hoped they would notice the green sweater, but
they were too busy with their secret joke.

Then Janet asked, "Is Myrna in school today?"

Connie started to say, "No, she's sick," but caught
herself in time, warned by something in Janet's voice.

She gave a careless shrug, "Look, when I start keeping track of my sister, that'll be the day."

But even that was the wrong answer, she knew, when Pat said, "From what Janet's sister says someone ought to keep tabs on her."

"What's that supposed to mean?"

"Anything you want it to mean," Janet answered smoothly, as she and Pat picked up their books and purses and left.

Connie stared after them, furious. What did they think they knew about Myrna that made them act so smart? It was something they knew from Janet's sister, something they thought she knew too. If she could figure out what they were talking about, she'd know how to answer. She munched Agnes' sandwich hardly tasting it. Maybe Janet's sister had seen Myrna the other night. Maybe that was it. But so what? Everybody drank sooner or later. She'd seen the stuff in Janet's house the couple of times she'd been there. Unless they thought Myrna was on drugs—which she wasn't.

It bothered her the rest of the day and she purposely walked up to the locker slowly after school so she wouldn't have to see them. *I'll even walk with Agnes if I have to,* she decided.

But Agnes was gone too, and she walked drearily down the stairs and outside, hating the thought of the feel of wet shoes again. She had to wait for a car to turn the corner, and as it passed she looked directly into the grinning faces of Pat and Janet as they stared at her out the window. They were with the same boys they'd been with the other time, and Connie stared after the car.

She was swept with such envy and longing and despair and loneliness that she moved along the street toward home, stopping automatically at corners and detouring snowdrifts without really seeing them. Every place she turned, she seemed to be on the outside looking in at love, never having any herself. Some kinds she didn't want. Not Ma's kind. Not Myrna's. Mrs. Brewster seemed to have found the real thing with Mike. And Mike had found God was love.

Connie shivered, pushing the thought away, and turned down the steps. When she let herself in the outside door, Mrs. Brewster came out on the upstairs landing. "Betty's up here. She was kind of lonesome down there after Myrna left, so I brought her up."

"When did Myrna go? She wasn't feeling good this morning so I thought she'd be here all day."

"She left about two o'clock. Somebody came for her." Mrs. Brewster looked down the stairs and frowned, biting her lip. Connie waited but she didn't say anything more.

"Send Betty down anytime."

"She's watching a program. Leave her for a while if you want to."

Connie went into the apartment, knowing she would be smart to do her homework right away, but she hated to get started. She sat down at the kitchen table and pulled her books toward her, staring at them without opening them, seeing Pat and Janet as they had laughed at her through the car windows, and feeling again the lostness of not belonging.

She got up restlessly and looked in the refrigerator. Nothing there, of course. But at least there was still half a loaf of bread, and she put two slices in the toaster and waited, hearing Kevin's feet as he ran back and forth across the floor upstairs and Betty's laughter. *It's funny Betty never laughed like that before,* she thought. Not around home anyway. Then as she spread margarine on the toast it hit her that if she could hear Kevin that plain, it meant Mrs. Brewster could hear what went on down here. She probably knew a lot about them, especially about Ma and Myrna and their fights.

She sat down to eat the toast, staring at the worn spots in the oilcloth on the table. *They'll be holes pretty soon,* she thought idly, scratching at one. *And no wonder. We've had it ever since I can remember.*

But the toast was finished, and she sighed and brushed the crumbs to one side and opened the math book. She struggled through the problems, putting down answers whether or not they were right, and slammed the book shut. That earned her the right to watch some television while waiting for Ma to come home. There was nothing to cook, so she couldn't start supper even if she wanted to. But the phone rang as she started into the living room, and when she answered, her mother said, "Did that welfare snoop come around today?"

"No. There's no card left anyway."

"She probably won't today then. Did Myrna go to school?"

Connie hesitated and then said, "I guess so. She isn't here now."

"Does she work today?"

"I suppose."

"Well, don't you know?" Her voice was impatient and made Connie mad. "Why don't *you* know?" she asked back silently but aloud said, "Yes, she does."

"I called to tell you to find something to eat for you and Betty. I won't be home—"

"There isn't anything here. I thought you'd bring something home," Connie broke in.

"There's certainly something there you can eat!"

"I don't know what."

"Can't you fry some potatoes?"

Connie didn't answer and her mother said, "Oh, all right! I've got a couple of dollars hidden in that brown jar in my bottom dresser drawer. Just take one and get something at the store." Her voice changed then as she went on in a low, confidential tone. "I'm doing this for you and Betty. I've got a date—an important date. I may be late."

Connie wanted to beg, "Please, please don't go out

with that man!" But she didn't dare. She put down
the phone and went upstairs to tell Mrs. Brewster
she was going to the store.

But Mrs. Brewster said, "Stay and eat with me.
I'll fix us a big spaghetti supper. I'm tired of eating
a chop all alone while Kevin messes around with
chopped spinach."

"Well, if you're sure—"

"I am. It's no fun cooking only for myself. You
can brown the meat while I cut up some onions."

Connie still wasn't used to the easy friendship of
Mrs. Brewster's voice. It left her feeling unsure of
herself and uneasy. She didn't know how you talked
to someone who treated you as though you were on
a par with her. She and Myrna had never been like
this.

"Do you have any brothers and sisters?" she asked
shyly.

"Four of each."

Connie stared at her. "You mean there are eight-
nine of you? Nine kids?"

"Yup, and I'm the exact middle."

"Did you fight?"

"Oh, sure. Doesn't every family? But we got along
pretty well. You see, I grew up in a small town, and
there weren't a lot of other kids to play with. So we
did things together. Especially my sister just older than
me."

Connie had a stab of envy thinking how lucky she
would have been to have had a sister like Mrs. Brewster.

They worked in silence until Mrs. Brewster said,
"Betty learned something new at the hospital, didn't
she?"

Connie glanced around with a questioning frown.

"Hasn't she told you? The story with the little book
the nurse gave her?"

"Oh, that. I knew she had a book but she wouldn't
let me see it."

"From what she says, the nurse told her some of the same things that chaplain's been telling Mike." She gave a little laugh. "She and Mike will get along OK. They talk the same language." She looked at Connie questioningly. "She said she was going to Sunday school—"

Connie nodded. "With that nurse."

"Mike keeps telling me to find a good church and start going but I don't know any. Maybe I'll go with Betty next time if she likes it."

"Ma said she could only go this once."

Connie felt Mrs. Brewster look at her but she didn't ask any questions. After supper Connie insisted on doing the dishes while Mrs. Brewster put Kevin in bed, and Betty watched a program.

"He was worn out. I guess he likes having company," Mrs. Brewster picked up the towel to wipe the last few pieces, and Connie said, "I didn't know how much you could hear things in this house until today— until I heard Kevin and Betty playing up here."

"Yes, the walls—and floors—are pretty thin."

"I guess you know a lot about what goes on down-stairs then," Connie said slowly.

"Some of it comes up loud and clear, I'll admit."

Connie felt as though her throat were choked with so many things she wanted to say, and yet they seemed to be in such a jumble in her mind, she was afraid they wouldn't make sense if she said them. Then to her embarrassment and anger, she began to cry. She could feel the tears sliding down her cheeks and nothing she could do seemed to stop them. She was glad Mrs. Brewster went on quietly putting dishes away and didn't say anything or try to help her.

After a while, she wiped her cheeks with the back of her hand and blew her nose.

"I never cry," she said in a thick voice. "I get mad and I—I *think* things but I never cry. It doesn't help anyway."

"Oh, I think it does," Mrs. Brewster patted Connie's shoulder as she went by. "It sort of lets things out and washes away a lot of hurts. At least, that's what my mother always said."

"My mother never says things like that."

And then she was crying again, and slumped down in a chair at the table with her head on her arms. Mrs. Brewster sat down beside her and put her arm across her shoulders, patting her gently but not talking. Connie cried for all the loneliness she felt at school, all the longings she had for a nice house and for a mother who cared, for all the nameless fears and haunting questions she had carried for so long.

"I'm sorry," she said finally, her voice coming muffled and indistinct from where her face was hidden in the crook of her arm. She groped for the box of tissues Mrs. Brewster shoved toward her and blew her nose.

"I'm so mixed up," she said thickly.

"About what?"

"Oh—everything." Her voice trembled, and she swallowed hard as she blinked back the tears that threatened again. "Pat and Janet are acting so f-funny—they're my only real friends and now they're-they're going with some b-boys. Not that I care!"

She stopped, shredding the tissue. "It's just—you hear things at school—you know, kids whisper about things—and, well—if I ask Ma she gets m-mad or else tells m-me I should know s-stuff by now. And Myrna just—Myrna says things—" Tears brimmed in her eyes again, and her voice cracked.

"Look, Connie. If you want to know something, come and ask me and I'll give it to you straight. Anything you hear whispered around in school washrooms is mostly a bunch of misinformation, not the true story. I know—I've been through it myself."

Mrs. Brewster frowned, and then with a quick laugh added, "In fact, if I have a daughter I'm afraid I'll want to wrap her in cotton and put her on a shelf for safekeeping until she's grown up."

She looked thoughtfully at Connie for a moment and gathered a little pile of the shredded tissue. "As far as your mother goes, you have to remember that she's had it pretty rough—"

"She makes it rough for us!" Connie's voice was rebellious as she blurted out the words.

Mrs. Brewster nodded. "I know. I told you the walls in this place are pretty thin. But when people are hurt they usually take it out on someone else. And she's been pretty badly hurt, you know. It must be awful to have your husband leave you—to be alone with no one to love you and take care of you." Her voice was troubled.

But Connie sniffed and blinked and wiped her eyes. It was easy to be sorry for Ma if you didn't have to live with her. Just because she'd had a hard life was no excuse for her taking it out on them. And she closed her mind tight against any thought of understanding or of forgiveness.

"It won't do any good to try to sell you on how hard Myrna has had it, I suppose?"

Connie shook her head. "She hasn't had it any worse than I have," she said sulkily.

"Look, Connie, your mother's ideas about life are pretty bitter because of what happened to her. I'm not saying she was entirely right and your father entirely wrong because I don't know. But just when Myrna needed advice, the only kind your mother could give was colored by your dad leaving the way he did. So Myrna's ideas are pretty mixed up and that's why they come out the way they do when she tries to tell you things. You see?"

Connie listened and nodded, but the bitterness inside refused to understand. But she felt oddly relaxed and at peace, and finally managed a faint smile at Mrs. Brewster, who sat smoking and quietly watching her.

"Thanks. I didn't know I was going to bawl like that."

"You needed it. That's one advantage girls have—we can cry and get rid of some of these uptight feelings."

Connie thought Mrs. Brewster must be right because the tensions and pressures she'd felt the last weeks didn't seem as bad the next couple of days. She was able to get through school Friday without being bothered too much by the secrets that linked Pat and Janet in a tight twosome. Even Ma's nagging at her to clean the house on Saturday didn't bother her the way it usually did when she wanted to yell back, "Clean it yourself!"

She even felt a faint moment of pity for Myrna, who was still feeling sick, when she got up just before noon on Saturday and sat down at the kitchen table, her elbows on the table and her hands holding her head.

When Mrs. Hamilton lashed out at her for being a lazy good-for-nothing, Myrna only replied weakly, "Cut it out, will you? I'd be all right if I didn't have to have that lousy job every night. I'm tired."

"Whose fault is it you got the job—"

"Yours! If I didn't work I wouldn't have any clothes. I'd look as crummy as—as Connie does."

Connie's feeling of pity was washed away in anger, as she turned to stare pointedly at Myrna. "Apparently you didn't look in the mirror this morning."

"Keep out of this, will you?" Myrna asked without lifting her head.

Mrs. Hamilton leaned over the table and tapped her finger on it for emphasis as she said, "I'm telling you that there'll be no more of this coming in late at night. And no more of this missing school either. I'm going to see to it that you get through high school if it's the last thing you do."

The phone rang then, and she turned to answer it, her shrill, angry voice becoming softer.

Connie watched Myrna curiously as she sat motionless at the table with her eyes closed and her hands supporting her head. She was breathing rapidly and her hands trembled slightly.

Maybe Myrna really was sick and Ma wouldn't admit it because she didn't want to spend money on a doctor, she thought. Then Myrna got up slowly and went into the bedroom. She looked better when she came out dressed, with her hair combed and her makeup on.

She looked out in the kitchen where Mrs. Hamilton was still talking on the phone and motioned Connie into the living room.

"If Ma asks where I am, you don't know."

"Well, I don't, do I? You might say you're going someplace when you're really someplace else."

"You sure think you're smart." Myrna's words were the same scornful ones she always used but her voice was different—tired and helpless. She went out, and Connie pulled aside the curtain to watch her as she went up the stairs to the sidewalk.

It must be very cold out from the way Myrna held her slight figure taut and leaned into the wind. Connie frowned, somehow disturbed by the fact that Myrna's coat was not very warm. Then she shrugged and stood up. Myrna was probably only going to the bus stop. Or else she had a boyfriend with a car waiting for her down the block out of Ma's sight.

Later that afternoon she discovered her biggest job was to keep Betty quiet about Sunday school or Ma would get so tired of hearing her yap about it she wouldn't let her go.

"What do you do at Sunday school?" Betty asked after supper.

"How should I know?" Connie answered crossly. "I've never been."

"What should I wear?"

"Do you have a choice?"

The sarcasm was lost on Betty as she answered, "Sure—my green dress I wear to school or that pink one. Or do I wear jeans? Is it a place you play games?"

"Will you shut up about it? I don't know what they do. No, don't wear jeans. If you had some decent ones you could, I suppose. But yours are unravelling around the bottom. Besides they're too short. Wear—oh, wear one of your school things."

"Connie, will you put my hair in rollers tonight so it will look nice?"

"Oh, I suppose! But wash it first. It's greasy."

"The nurse washed it last week in the hospital."

"Wash it again if you want me to touch it. But I'm warning you. You don't know how to sleep on rollers. They hurt."

"I don't care. I want my hair to look like the nurse's does. I don't like braids anymore."

After Betty had gone to bed, Connie could hear her tossing restlessly on her cot and went to the open door. "You want me to take them out?"

"No! I want my hair to be curly."

But when Connie went to bed later, she laughed at the rollers Betty had taken out in her sleep and put in a careful row on the floor by the bed.

9

Sunday and More Sadness

THE ALARM JERKED Connie awake, and she leaped to stop the shrill noise. Then she sat down on the side of the bed for a couple of minutes, hating to start the day. It seemed as though the only thing she'd done the last couple of weeks was get up in answer to the alarm. Today she had to because it was the only way Betty would be ready on time. Ma certainly wouldn't get up, and Betty's going to Sunday school had become sort of a symbol. It was a victory for Betty because she was getting to do something her mother didn't want her to. And it was a victory for her because she had stood up to her mother.

The noise of the alarm hadn't wakened either Myrna or Betty, and Connie had to shake Betty awake.

"Look what you did in your sleep," and she pointed to the rollers.

"Why didn't you put 'em back in?" Betty whined, following her out to the kitchen.

"Because I didn't want to bother, that's why."

"You're mean."

"Look! I didn't get up early on Sunday because I wanted to, you know. I'm only doing it to help you."

"But I wanted my hair to be pretty!"

"Nobody will know who you are anyway, so what difference does it make?"

But Betty got out the box of cornflakes and a bowl and sat down at the kitchen table, her lips pouting and a scowl on her face.

"If you're going to be like that, I'm going back to bed and you can get yourself ready."

"OK! But next time—" Betty broke off as Connie started out of the kitchen. "All right, all right! I won't say anything more."

"You'd better not. Just get ready so you don't keep her waiting when she gets here. What's her name anyway?"

"I don't know. She didn't tell us. We just called her funny things." Betty giggled around the mouthful of cornflakes, and Connie watched her, surprised.

She's kind of cute when she smiles instead of looking mad the way she usually does, she thought.

"She told us stories out of the Bible. What's the Bible, Connie?"

"Oh, a book."

"It must be a great, great big one 'cause she knew lots of stories from it. Are they fairy stories?"

"I don't know," Connie said impatiently. "I suppose so."

"*She* said they were true."

"Well, OK! If she knows so much, don't ask me."

By keeping after her, Connie got Betty ready in time, and she was kneeling on the couch looking out the window when the car stopped in front of the house.

"Here she is!" she cried excitedly. "Hurry, get my jacket. Will she wait for me?"

"She came for you, didn't she? Don't get so worked up. Anyway, she's coming in." Connie waited until the nurse knocked and then opened the door.

"Hi," she smiled at Connie and then at Betty. "All set?"

"Do I have to wear my boots?" she complained when she looked at the nurse's feet.

"It's pretty deep out there so I think you'd better. You're so fat I couldn't possibly carry you."

Betty giggled. "It'd be OK if mine were pretty like yours," and she struggled into them, stamping her feet down to make them fit.

"Sh, you'll wake Ma."

The nurse looked from Connie to the closed bedroom doors and back again. "I wondered if you wanted to go along?"

"I'd better not." She gestured down at her jeans and sweatshirt. "It would take too long to get dressed."

"We could wait."

"Mrs. Brewster wants to go," Betty piped.

"No, she doesn't," Connie tried to shush her.

"She said she did. She said a couple of times she did."

"Well, she didn't mean Sunday school. She meant church."

"Who's Mrs. Brewster?" the nurse asked.

Connie motioned up the stairs. "Our neighbor."

"Would she really like to go—"

"No, she—"

"She *said* so," Betty insisted.

"Her husband is overseas, and she said he wants her to start going to church," Connie explained. "But I'm sure she's still asleep now. I mean, she doesn't want to go *today*." She frowned at Betty, and shook her head at her insistence.

"Maybe I can run up and see her a minute when we come back," the nurse suggested. "If you think she wouldn't mind."

"I'll go with you and tell her how good it was," Betty said.

The nurse looked again at Connie. "You're sure you won't come?"

She shook her head, wishing they would go. The restless feeling inside made her edgy and she was glad when she could finally shut the door and watch through the window as they walked up toward the car. She could tell Betty was talking, and wondered how the nurse could stand it, and why she bothered to listen and even act as though she enjoyed the one-sided conversation. Probably because she didn't have to listen all the time.

Connie sat looking out the window long after the car had disappeared from sight, thinking again how strange it was that in all her life she had never heard of God or Jesus, except as swear words and now in just—she frowned, counting back through the days—in just two weeks He was everywhere she turned. It was Mrs. Brewster's constant talk about her husband's letters that bothered her the most. She couldn't escape the thought that if someone like that believed it there must be something to it. The real trouble was she didn't know exactly what it was all about. What did it mean to "believe in Jesus Christ"? This was the latest thing Mike was writing.

On impulse she got up and went quietly into the bedroom. She was sure Betty still kept her book under her pillow. She got it and tiptoed out, closing the door softly behind her and curled up again on the couch. It was a book for children with pictures and large print. But stapled inside the back cover was a mimeographed sheet for parents.

"For God so loved the world, that he gave his only begotten Son, that whosoever believeth in him should not perish, but have everlasting life." This is what God says to you. You may have life that will never end just by believing that Jesus Christ died for you to take away your sin. Jesus Himself said that He is standing outside the door of your life waiting to come into your life. When He does He will be with you forever.

What will He do for you? He will take the cold darkness out of your life and give you light. He will take away the unhappiness and give you joy. He will fill the friendless, empty places in your life with His love and He will never leave you. He will always be with you to help you. This doesn't mean that you will never be sad or discouraged or afraid or lonely. But it means that Jesus Christ will help you through these times. He not only gives life, but He gives it abundantly.

Connie sat staring at the words, so strange sounding to her and their meaning so unclear. Maybe it wasn't just an escape after all.

Then the muffled sounds from behind the closed bedroom door made her look up, startled. Could that be Myrna crying? She jumped up and went to the door to listen. Then she opened it and looked in to see Myrna's shoulders shaking as she tried to muffle the strangled sobs.

"Myrna?"

"Close the door!"

"What's the matter?"

"I don't want Ma to hear."

"I know, but I mean—" Connie went closer to the bed and looked down at Myrna. Then she sat down on the foot, trying to see her in the dim light of the room. "Do you want me to pull up the shade? It's so dark—"

"No!"

The panic in her voice made Connie feel scared, and she asked again, "What-what's the matter? Are you really sick?"

Myrna didn't answer, and after a moment Connie stood

up. "OK, if you're going to be like that don't expect any sympathy from me. I was going to offer to get you some breakfast, but I'll leave you alone."

She started for the door, but stopped at the ragged sound of fear in Myrna's voice as she begged, "No, Connie, wait. Please!"

Connie turned around and watched as she turned over and sat up in bed slowly, drawing her knees up and putting her head down on them. Connie caught a glimpse of the expression on her face and came slowly back to sit down again on the edge of the bed. Something was terribly wrong with Myrna to look like that. Then she listened, horrified, to the words she blurted out. "I'm going to have a baby."

Connie covered her mouth with her hands to keep back the gasp as she heard Myrna's weak, tired, helpless voice explain.

"I've been so scared—so scared for a couple of weeks. I wasn't sure—and then I got to feeling so sick—feeling so awful. And I knew Ma would kill me if she found out—if it was true. And-and now it is! And I don't know what to do! Oh, Connie! What shall I do?"

She looked then at Connie who sat staring back at her white face, her wide and frightened eyes, a pleading appeal for help on her face instead of the usual arrogant I-don't-need-advice-from-anyone look.

"You-you'll have to tell Ma," Connie answered, though the thought of Ma's screaming anger made her shiver for Myrna. "You can't keep her from finding out. She'll know—won't she?"

"Not if I run away."

"Where? And how? You don't have any money."

Her ignorance of all that was involved made her feel helpless to know what to say. "Can't you—I mean, can you—get married? I mean, whoever—"

She stopped at the choked sound that came from Myrna. She couldn't tell if it was a laugh or a cry as

she shook her head, her eyes closed, and her hands
pressed tight over her trembling mouth.

In the silence they heard the other bedroom door
open, and Ma stood in the doorway before Myrna
could lie down.

"Aren't you two up yet—" Mrs. Hamilton broke
off and looked at them, at Myrna's pathetic figure, at
Connie's stricken face, and her lips tightened into a
thin, hard line. She crossed over and yanked up the
window shade and then turned to face them.

"What's going on here?" she demanded, and the
harshness of her voice made Connie stand up nervously.

"Nothing, Ma. We were just talking."

But Mrs. Hamilton looked at Myrna, and the anger
and contempt in her face made Connie feel sick with
fear.

"So! Just as I suspected."

"If you're so smart, why didn't you do something to
stop me?"

"What did I ever do to have a daughter who turns
out to be a tramp?"

"I guess you just didn't bring me up right."

The mockery in Myrna's voice made Connie gasp.
How could she be so foolish as to make Ma any madder
than she was?

Mrs. Hamilton reached over and gripped her shoulder
and shook her, and Myrna didn't resist. Her show of
defiance was ended, and she began to cry, not loudly,
but with silent tears that slipped down her cheeks,
and she made no effort to wipe them away. Connie
watched and listened as Ma's voice ranted on about
how hard she'd worked to bring them up decent, and
how Myrna had inherited weaknesses from her no-good
father, and since she had gotten herself into this
mess she could get herself out, and this was what
came from staying out till all hours every night. All
the time Myrna's tears fell. And Connie listened and

thought about God and love and had to fight back the things she wanted to shout at her mother.

Finally Mrs. Hamilton's anger was spent, and she stalked out of the room. Connie could hear her in the kitchen slamming dishes and cupboards as she got herself something to eat. She turned to look at the clock and realized that Betty would be home soon. She hoped Ma would not start yelling again. There was no sense in Betty's finding out. She wouldn't understand.

"And I don't understand either," she reminded herself soberly. *Why would Myrna do such a thing?*

Then, looking at her as she lay in bed, exhausted from her mother's anger and her own fear, and looking sick and scared, Connie felt pity for her. She was her sister. Myrna needed help from someone, and certainly Ma had made it clear she wasn't going to give it. *But what can I do?* she wondered desperately.

"Can I get you something to eat?" she offered timidly.

Myrna shook her head weakly. "Not now. I've got to think—make plans."

"You want me to stay?"

"No. You can't do anything for me. Nobody can." She pressed her hand against her mouth, and her shoulders heaved with the pent-up sobs she was holding back.

"You want the door closed?" Connie was so near tears herself she could hardly get words out.

Myrna nodded. "And, Connie—if you can, keep Ma out for a while. Please? Before you go—get me something to drink. Water."

Connie went out to the kitchen and hurried past her mother as she sat at the kitchen table with coffee and toast. She was afraid Ma would tell her not to do anything for Myrna. But all she did was glare at her as she went back with the glass of water. Then she pulled down the window shade and went out, reaching back to close the door.

She couldn't sit still but stood looking out the front room window not knowing what to do. What she wanted to do was run upstairs and pour out the whole miserable story to Mrs. Brewster and get help. But she couldn't. Not with Ma right here. And anyway, how could she reveal how deep their family problems were, even to Mrs. Brewster? And what could Mrs. Brewster do? What could anyone do? Even God couldn't help Myrna out of this. Looking down, she saw Betty's book where she had dropped it, and furtively shoved it under one of the cushions on the couch. Ma had enough to make her mad without adding anything else.

She jerked around as her mother came into the living room with her coffee and looked accusingly at Connie.

"How long have you known about her?" She jerked her head at the bedroom.

"I didn't. Honest."

"She never let on until today?"

Connie shook her head.

"You'd better not be lying to me!"

"Honest, Ma! I didn't know."

"Haven't I been checking on her? Haven't I been asking her if she's been going to school? Haven't I been yelling at her every time she came home late? Haven't I told her to quit smoking and not to get mixed up with dope? Haven't I?"

Connie nodded mutely as her mother stopped for breath.

"I've tried my best to bring her up right. What else could I do?"

Connie knew her mother wanted reassurance, wanted her to say she'd done everything right. But she was afraid to open her mouth for fear she would say all the other things that were in her mind—how she felt about her mother's neglect and selfishness and temper.

So she sat nervously on the edge of the couch, while her mother finished a cigarette and her coffee.

Then she put the cup down with a clatter and stood up abruptly.

"Well, she'd better get up. No use hiding in the bedroom. We've got to decide what to do."

"Why not let her sleep for a while? I mean, she really is sick," Connie pleaded. If Ma got Myrna up all they would do would be to sit around and yell at each other. Her stomach knotted at the thought of the terrible things they would say and keep saying.

But her mother stalked to the bedroom and shoved the door open. "Myrna!" Connie cringed at the hardness of the tone. "Myrna! Wake up! You can't hide in bed forever."

She walked over and let the shade fly up and then turned and leaned over the bed. "Myrna?"

The difference in her voice reached Connie, and she ran to the door to see her mother back away from the bed and stare down at Myrna. Connie looked too, puzzled at her mother's expression of horror.

"She's taken something," she heard her mother whisper. "It must be sleeping pills. Call an ambulance. Hurry! Get that number!"

"Which one?"

"The one I wrote down—for Betty—there, some-place—on that paper—no, over there. Hurry!"

The next fifteen minutes were a frenzied blur as Connie found the number, and her mother called the ambulance and then dressed with frantic haste. She didn't have time to even put on lipstick before the ambulance came, and two men hurried in. Connie hovered fearfully in the living room, not knowing what emergency treatment they gave Myrna before putting her on a stretcher and rushing her out. Mrs. Hamilton followed, nodding her head in answer to Connie's quick, "I'll stay here—for when Betty comes."

She turned when the outside door slammed shut to face Mrs. Brewster, who sat silently watching on the top step.

"Myrna?"

Connie nodded.

"I'm sorry. I won't butt in but if I can help I'm right here."

Connie nodded again, helpless to put words together that would make sense. She closed the apartment door and leaned against it, her eyes closed, feeling completely drained and too exhausted to think through what had happened. The abrupt shrill ring of the phone startled her. It couldn't possibly be Ma calling already, she knew, but she picked it up fearfully. "Hello?"

"Hi there, doll. You must be the cute kid I met the other night. I told your mother she shouldn't keep you a secret."

Connie didn't know what to answer, but he went on easily and confidently, "Put her on."

"She isn't here."

"She's not? Look, you tell her I want to talk to her. None of this playing-hard-to-get stuff. I don't go for that."

"Really, she's not. She had to go—out."

"When's she coming back?"

"I'm—not sure. Sometime this afternoon."

Then Connie wished she hadn't said that. Panic beat in her. What if he came over anyway? But to her relief he growled, "Tell her I called and that I'll call this afternoon."

Connie put down the phone and then realized that she was shaking. She took a deep breath and tried to relax. She had to make it seem that everything was all right when Betty came home.

10

The Way Out

IT DIDN'T WORK. She couldn't relax, but prowled through the house restlessly, too keyed up even to sit down. The damp cold in the house and her jittery nerves made her shiver as she walked from room to room, waiting for the phone to ring.

Her mind followed the ambulance to the hospital. It would be there by now of course. And they would have rushed Myrna in, wheeling her down the long hall quickly. Would they take time for all the tests they had given Betty and wait for Ma to sign papers?

Ma would go to the waiting room—but would she wait? Connie stopped her pacing and pressed her hands to her cheeks, her eyes closed, seeing Ma sitting there impatiently, her redtipped nails tapping her purse. Surely she wouldn't leave the way she did before. She'd been so scared when they left in the ambulance that she wouldn't leave until she knew what was going to happen to Myrna. But the uncertainty remained. *I should have gone along,* she scolded herself.

Connie opened her eyes and looked around. She had to get hold of herself before Betty came. Maybe if she did something it would help pass the time. The kitchen was a mess—the whole house was a mess. She would clean it. She went to her mother's room first and quickly pulled up the shade, made the bed, and hung up the clothes that were scattered around the room. Her nose wrinkled in disgust at the saucerful of cigarette butts on the dresser, and she flushed them down the toilet.

Then she walked slowly to the other bedroom and looked in. Trying not to think of Myrna, she quickly yanked off the blankets, pulled off both sheets and the pillowcases and rolled them into a bundle, her mind carefully planning each step. When Betty got home and after Ma phoned, she would take the sheets and pillowcases and Myrna's clothes to the laundromat. She didn't want to go out in the snow and cold and walk the four blocks with a heavy sack of clothes, but she would have to, if she wanted something clean to sleep on tonight. Ma would be mad at her for spending the extra money when she had just washed clothes during the week, but she'd just have to be mad.

After sweeping the bedroom floor, she turned to look back at the room and stopped. She walked slowly over to the dresser to stare at the creams and powders that were Myrna's life. And then the awfulness of what had happened overwhelmed her. Her wide, questioning eyes stared back at her from the mirror as she groped for some meaning to what had happened, some answers to the questions that wracked her.

Why had Myrna done it? How could a person be so desperate as to want to die? Myrna said she'd been scared for weeks—*and I didn't know, Ma didn't know.* How could they have gotten to the place where they lived under the same roof and yet went their separate ways, thinking only of their own problems?

Suddenly Connie was sure this was what Janet and Pat were hinting at when they talked about Myrna, and she wondered how many others knew more about Myrna than they did.

Her eyes went to the clock. Had they gotten Myrna in time? And then a worse thought came—what if Myrna didn't want to be saved? She had taken the pills on purpose, as a way out. *She must have had them already with her when she asked me for the drink of water.* Myrna didn't want to live. And if she lived through this, would she try it again later? Ma wouldn't let her forget what she had done, Connie was sure.

The sound of Betty's voice in the hall brought her out of her somber fears, and she went to open the door. Betty had had a wonderful time. Connie could see it in her sparkling eyes and eager voice.

They stood in the hall, with Betty holding onto the nurse's hand, looking up at her. "Will you ask her?" she was pleading. "I want to go *always* and maybe she'll say yes for you."

The nurse smiled down at her and nodded. Then she looked at Connie, and the smile slowly faded from her eyes. "Is something wrong?"

Connie forced a smile and shook her head stiffly, her voice sounding strange even to her as she said, "No."

The nurse hesitated, her eyes sliding around Connie to the part of the room she could see. "I don't want to bother your mother. But I do want to ask if she will change her mind and let Betty come again."

"Ma's—not here right now."

Betty interrupted with a quick, "I'm going to go up and show Mrs. Brewster my pictures and my paper and tell her how fun it is and ask if she'll go next time."

They listened to her feet pound up the stairs while the nurse looked at Connie with a little frown creasing between her eyes. "Are you sure you're all right?"

Connie nodded again, but backed slowly into the room and sat down on the couch, staring straight ahead of her. After a moment's hesitation, the nurse came in and closed the door and sat down across from her.

In the silence Connie swallowed and looked at her, and then blurted through trembling lips, "My sister— Myrna—took sleeping pills this morning—just a little while ago. Ma's at the hospital with her. I haven't heard—I'm waiting—" she stopped and gestured at the phone.

"I'm so sorry!" The warm concern in her voice made tears well up, and Connie forced them back. She couldn't cry. Not now. "Do you want to talk about it?"

Connie shook her head. Something inside kept her from telling Myrna's secret. It wasn't shame she felt most, though it was there too. But it was pity. She'd never had this feeling about Myrna before. She'd hated her at times and been mad at her and envious of her, but never protective and—caring as she did now.

"I don't want to stay if you would rather be alone, but I would like to help you if I could. It's pretty hard to carry a burden around without being able to ask help from someone. I found that out for myself, and I guess that's why I want to let everyone know there is a way out of any problem." The nurse's voice was warm and friendly sounding, not preachy, and Connie found herself listening even though she didn't really want to.

"I wanted to tell you this the other night when we had supper together," the nurse went on. "Nobody has to lug around all their problems and fears and heartaches alone when God is right here waiting to help."

"Oh—God!" Connie exclaimed. "I don't know anything about God."

The nurse nodded. "I thought that must be so when I first met you in the hospital and from hearing Betty talk. And I'm sorry. But He knows about you, Connie, and loves you the way He loves every person in the world. He showed His love by sending Jesus Christ to die for us to take away our sin."

This is what Mike has been writing, Connie thought. She wanted to ask what it meant but she didn't want to even act interested, so she just sat and stared at the floor.

The nurse was going on. "One of the wonderful

parts about it is that if we believe Him now, we will be with Him forever in heaven."

Connie raised her head. "That won't help me now with this!" she said scornfully, with an angry sweep of her arm around the dismal room.

"It can."

"How? Can God take me out of all this—this mess and give me a decent life? And a nice place to live? And friends? And a mother who doesn't—" she stopped with tears on the edge of her voice.

The nurse shook her head gently. "No, He won't take you out of it. He will do something better than that."

"What?" Connie asked suspiciously.

"He'll make you able to live in the middle of all the mess."

"I don't get you."

"When God comes into a person's life, He doesn't change their surroundings. He changes *them*. He doesn't take the problems away; He makes you able to stand the problems."

"You don't know what my problems are like or you wouldn't say that," Connie answered, her voice sulky.

"God does," the nurse replied gently with a smile.

But Connie shook her head stubbornly. If she could just explain how hard her life was, maybe the nurse would see that staying in it was impossible. She took a deep breath and started in.

"We haven't always lived like this," she said with a gesture around the room. "When my father was here he had a job. It wasn't a very good job but at least we weren't really poor, and we didn't have to have welfare like we do now. But then my father walked out when I was eight years old. He and Ma were always yelling at each other anyway, and he used to hit us when he was drunk." The story was just a recital of cold facts that happened long ago, and Connie told it without emotion.

"So, then my mother had to get a job. And we had to have welfare, I guess because he doesn't send enough money to Ma. And we keep moving, and each place gets worse than the one before. And my mother—drinks now too—and—and runs around—and doesn't care if we eat right or—or have decent clothes. And now Myrna is—Myrna is—" Her voice was ragged now as the fear about Myrna pressed in on her and she stopped.

In the silence the nurse said softly, "The poor thing! That explains a lot. And I was blaming your mother without knowing the whole story." Connie looked at her uncertainly as she went on. "She's had a hard time, hasn't she? And all the time God was waiting to help her and no one told her about Him."

Connie was mad. The nurse was trying to explain away her mother's neglect just the way Mrs. Brewster had. *I'm not going to fall for it*, she told herself bitterly. *I'm the one to feel sorry for. Me and Betty and Myrna*.

She tried to close her mind to what the nurse was saying, but she couldn't close her ears, and she heard the words unwillingly.

"You won't know what I'm talking about, Connje, until you try it. If you let God into your life, He'll make you able to live with your problems so they won't seem impossible."

She looked at Connie then with a faint smile. "May I tell you a story?"

Betty's words came back to Connie, and she asked, "Is this a fairy story? From the Bible?"

'It's from the Bible but it's not a fairy story. It may seem like it to you, but it's really true. All the stories in the Bible are. Want to hear it?"

"I guess so," Connie shrugged sullenly.

'Sometime you may read it for yourself. It's about three young men, older than you, but still young, who really had problems. They were supposed to worship a king, and they were told they would be thrown into a blazing hot furnace if they didn't. And they said, well, that was all right. They were going to worship only God, no matter what happened to them. They said their God was so great that He could easily keep them from being put into the furnace if He wanted to—"

"And did He?" Connie asked scornfully.

"No, He let them be thrown in. But then, you see, He went into the furnace with them and kept them from being burned. The king couldn't believe his eyes when he saw what was happening. He ordered them to walk out if they could—and they did, and weren't burned at all."

She smiled at Connie. "You find that hard to believe, don't you? But if you give God a chance in your life, He'll be with you in your problems and help you to stand them. This isn't escape from reality, Connie. It's escape *into* reality—into the most wonderful life there is."

"I don't want to live with my problems," Connie blurted desperately. "I want a way out now."

"Do you have one?"

Connie didn't answer, but sat staring at the worn places in the thin rug. She'd given up the daydreams as useless. She still could get a job and save her money, but that was a long way off yet.

Then the nurse said slowly, "Connie, you may be surprised at what God can do for your mother and your sister if you let Him take over your life."

"But my sister may not even live!" she cried in answer. And then, "And Ma—you don't know Ma! She'll never pay any attention to God."

"She might. If you helped her."

"I don't know enough about it. I don't understand all this stuff you've been talking about."

"Come with Betty next Sunday and find out."

But Connie threw out her hands in desperation. "Don't you see? That's just the trouble. Ma hates church. She isn't going to let Betty go again. Not ever."

"That's what Betty said. But she told me she was going to be as nice and helpful and kind to your mother as she could be this week—" She held up her hand as Connie moved impatiently. "No, not just to get to go again, but so your mother would see what a difference it made when a person went to Sunday school and learned about God."

Connie stared at the nurse. This was a picture of Betty she couldn't believe. It shook her that one Sunday would make that much change. Then Betty clattered down the stairs and burst through the door excitedly.

"Mrs. Brewster says if you haven't already gone and if you've got time would you come up and talk to her? She's got coffee and choc'late cake. Can you?"

The nurse got up. "I sure can." She hesitated, looking down at Connie's bent head.

Betty grabbed her hand. "Come on, I'll show you."

"You stay here," Connie ordered. "You'll just be in the way."

"Uh-uh, I'm *supposed* to come. I'm supposed to keep Kevin quiet. Mrs. Brewster *said.*"

The nurse laughed. "All right. You babysit while we talk." She looked down once more at Connie, who sat with her hands stuffed in her jeans' pockets.

"I go on duty at three this afternoon, and I'll go in and try to see Myrna," she said quietly.

Connie nodded, not trusting herself to speak, and watched as they walked to the door and out into the hall.

She listened as they went upstairs with Betty chattering eagerly. Then when it was quiet she thought back unwillingly over the months, even the years, of her bitter and angry thoughts about her mother. She'd seen only the harshness, never the reason for it—the bitterness and hurt her mother carried that caused the harshness. The thought was so blinding in what it showed her of her own selfishness, that she got up and walked around the room, resisting it. It was too hard to love Ma. And even if she could, what difference would it make now, especially when she would be meaner than ever to Myrna —if there was a tomorrow for Myrna.

The phone rang, and she jumped nervously even though she'd been listening for it every moment. It rang again insistently, and she answered to hear her mother say abruptly, "They got her in time. But just barely. She's going to be OK. But she was so sick she lost the baby. Thank goodness for that! At least we don't have to face *that* problem. And believe me, I'm going to see to it that she's learned her lesson!"

The familiar hard tone was in her voice, and Connie wanted to drop the phone and run upstairs and tell them how wrong they'd been to waste time being sorry for Ma.

Then she heard her mother say, "You and Betty find something to eat. I'm going to stay a while—at least until Myrna wakes up. She'll feel rotten. And I can get a good meal in the cafeteria here. I certainly deserve it after what Myrna put me through this morning."

"Ma. You got a phone call. From that—some man."

"Who?"

"I don't know. He's going to call again."

She could hear her mother breathing and waited for an answer, her mind pleading, *Please, Ma! Please tell him you've got a sick kid in the hospital and you can't go with him!*

Then her mother said, "When's he going to call?"

"He didn't say. Just sometime this afternoon."

"Well, I'll be there by four o'clock. Tell him that when he calls. And, Connie." Her voice was sharp. "Tell him not to come before then. Hear me?"

Connie nodded. "Yes," she whispered through the tears of despair that blurred her eyes and voice as she put the receiver down slowly and stared at it. *Nothing was going to be different,* she thought dully. *Myrna would go on as usual. Ma was the same.* Her relief over Myrna was clouded by her feeling of hopelessness.

She turned to look around. The bare mattress in the bedroom was a reminder of Myrna's desperation. The clutter in her mother's room stood as mute evidence of her neglect. The dismal living room, the odds and ends of furniture, the shabby clothes, the empty refrigerator—this was her life. There was no way of changing it. She was trapped.

Then she walked over slowly and stared down at the couch and finally leaned over to pull Betty's book from under the cushion. There were the gold-lettered words. *God is Love. Could* this be the answer? Mike seemed to think so. The nurse said it was. She stood, undecided. *I could at least go up and listen.* After a moment she went out into the hall to the foot of the stairway and looked up. Then she went up quickly, her eyes fixed on the open door at the top of the stairs.

Part II

THE LIGHT AT THE TOP
OF THE STAIRS

11

A Second Chance

MYRNA FOUGHT HER WAY out of the drugged sleep. Her skin felt clammy, her hair damp and limp, her throat tight with the fear that always came with this recurring dream. She had stood as usual halfway down the long black tunnel. Though she had tried desperately to turn and run back to the light glimmering faintly at the far end from which she had come, her feet were heavy and wouldn't move. Her mouth had formed words that called for help but no sound came. She groped for Connie and felt instead the unfamiliarity of sheets pulled taut and blankets tucked securely on each side of the bed.

She opened her eyes then and stared blankly around the white walls of the room, seeing the other bed, which was empty, the blankets neatly stretched across its smooth surface with an air of waiting expectancy. Her glance shifted to take in the nightstand beside the bed, the glass of water with its plastic straw, the thermometer in its glass case, and memory jarred.

This was a hospital. She'd taken sleeping pills—but she was still alive. That meant the pills hadn't worked—she was alive—the nightmare wasn't over. She hadn't escaped and—there was still the baby. She tried to turn over, to hide under the blankets, but her body refused to obey. Then exhaustion swirled again to carry her back to a confused darkness of dreams in which Ma's voice nagged harsh, loud, accusing words. During the hours she was dimly aware that her pulse was taken, that the doctor stood over her silently, that the nurses did necessary things.

Finally she woke again, knowing there was no escaping the despair of being alive. She lay with her eyes closed, her thoughts bumping tiredly against the walls of her mind. She could feel the trap she was in, the trap she'd gotten herself into. Then she recognized the sound of Ma's heels clicking along the bare floor, and she stiffened.

I'm not going to open my eyes. I won't let her know I'm awake. Then she can't yell.

Though her nerves protested at the effort, she forced herself to lie quietly and make her breath come softly in regular rhythm. She heard Ma come in and felt the bed jiggle as she leaned against it. After a moment there was a scraping sound as Ma pulled a chair close to the bed and sat down. Myrna listened as her mother tapped her fingers impatiently on her purse.

Which one is it? The red plastic or the black imitation leather?

She had to fight the impulse to look. If she did, if Ma saw her eyes open, she'd begin again. And Ma had said it all already, over and over again yesterday—or was it the day before that? She'd said the same things over and over, blaming her and pitying herself, excusing herself.

The chair legs rasped on the bare floor again, and she felt the bed shake with the weight of her mother's body.

"Myrna? Myrna, I'm going. I'll get back tomorrow maybe. Not tonight though. You hear? And just be thankful you're out of this mess with nothing to show for it."

Myrna couldn't control the involuntary jerk of her muscles, but she forced her eyelids to stay down and listened to her mother's heels click across the room and down the hall. When it was quiet, she opened her eyes slowly, a deep breath relaxing the tight control she'd held; and she felt herself trembling. Her heart pounded as Ma's words echoed. "You're out of this mess—nothing to show for it—nothing to show for it—"

Was it over? Was it true she had nothing to worry about? Surely Ma wouldn't have said that if it wasn't true. She'd been too mad before. She moved her hand cautiously to her stomach and pushed down, feeling its flatness. If Ma was right— A shudder of relief washed over her and she licked at her dry lips. She would stay flat. There would be no rounding out to show everyone what had happened. The panic that had closed her in for the past month and the fear that had driven her to the sleeping pills was over. She didn't understand how the pills had made her lose the baby without dying. But it didn't matter. Oh, it didn't matter! She was safe! She covered her mouth with her hands to stifle the shuddering sobs that filled her throat and closed her eyes again, weak with relief that she was safe, that she had a second chance.

Footsteps sounded in the room, and she held her breath. Was Ma back? She let her eyelids flicker just enough to glimpse the white uniform and opened her eyes to look at the nurse standing at the foot of the bed, her hands in her uniform pockets.

"Hi. How do you feel?"

"OK."

"I just passed your mother in the hall. She said you were asleep."

"I was. I just—" She looked at the nurse and frowned. "How'd you know she's my mother?"

"You look alike."

"Me look like Ma? I should hope not!"

The nurse didn't answer as she poured a glass of water and held it out. "Doctor's orders. You're supposed to drink a lot."

Myrna made a face as she accepted the glass and took a sip.

"Your temperature has been pretty steady since last night. That's a good sign. You'll feel pretty rocky for a few days, but then you'll be all right. Just put on some weight. Unless you're planning for a career as a model."

Myrna stared up at the nurse, ignoring the smile, her eyes narrowed and her mind busy. Did the nurse know what she was in for? Probably. There wouldn't be much that was private in a hospital. The nurses probably gossiped about all the patients, laughing at them all the time they pretended to be so sympathetic.

Well, just so nobody else found out. If she could keep it from everybody at school, the gang at work, Alec—

She wrenched her mind away from Alec, hating the thought of him. She wouldn't think of him, not now, not until she was stronger. She wouldn't think of how dumb she'd been. It hadn't been her fault, of course, stupid as she'd been. It was the party, the stuff Alec had kept at her to drink. It was the fight she'd had with Ma that day, the need to be daring, the nervousness of too many cigarettes and drink on a stomach that needed something more than a greasy hamburger and fries. It was being hemmed in by life, not having anyone to talk to, being trapped in a cold house, growing up with insecurities, no way out—

But now she had a second chance, a miraculous second chance and she wasn't going to blow it. "I'll never get in a fix like this again. Never!"

Her lips moved silently with the words. She opened her eyes again and saw the nurse still there, looking at her from the foot of the bed. Myrna shifted irritably, hating to be stared at, especially when she looked horrible with no makeup and her hair stringy against the pillow.

"Anything I can do for you?"

"Yeah. Get me my purse. Somewhere around here

I've got one. Anyway, I hope Ma brought it. It's got all my stuff in it."

She watched the nurse cross the room to a door and pull it open, reaching to grope on a shelf. She pulled a purse down by the long shoulder strap. "This it?"

Myrna nodded and reached for it. She clutched it against her and stared up at the nurse, seeing her short, straight, black hair and equally straight black eyebrows that cut a line across her forehead above her deepset gray eyes. Resentment grew in her as she imagined what the nurse was thinking. It was easy for her to sneer. People like her didn't know what it was like to get caught in a trap and not know what to do. Probably nurses were too smart anyway; they knew how to be careful.

She could feel words slipping through her mind and bit down on her lip to keep from screaming them out. It was funny that the thought of Ma kept her from saying the words out loud. With all her drinking and running around and yelling at them for being in her way and tying her down, Ma never cussed them. Ma had this thing about swearing. She could still remember the way Ma had slapped her across the mouth once when she'd sworn at Connie and had warned, "Don't give out with words like that around here if you know what's good for you."

But she knew the words. Everyone she knew used them as easy as talking. Myrna said them to herself now, wishing the nurse could read her mind and know what she thought of her.

Aloud she asked, "How long do I have to stay in here?"

"I don't know. I'm not on your case. I work the other end of the floor."

"Then how come you're here?"

"Umm—just thought I'd say hello."

Myrna looked up at her. "Are all nurses that friendly? Or don't you have anything else to do?"

The nurse laughed. "Sorry. I didn't mean to look as though I were just roaming around being curious. But a little friendship never hurt anyone, did it? They say it takes less energy to smile than to frown, Looks better, too. See you."

Myrna watched her leave, the scowl deepening between her eyes. What was that supposed to mean? "Sounds like a dirty dig to me," she muttered. She jerked the zipper of her purse and dug for her mirror, looking grimly at her reflection.

"I *do* look like Ma. Like Ma after she's stayed up all night and drunk too much."

She searched through the deep bag, hauling out the jars and hefting them suspiciously. They felt light. *That Connie has probably been helping herself to my stuff.* Myrna unscrewed the caps from the jars and looked in. Well, if she had, she'd been careful not to leave any trace. Which was like her. *Sneaky brat.*

But, unwillingly, memory drifted back, bringing into her mind Connie's scared white face and the sympathy that had been so plain on it when she heard the blurted secret. She remembered Connie's helpless concern and the timid, "Is there anything I can do to help?" and the attempt at protection she had reached for blindly when Ma came into the bedroom and lashed out. She'd been so scared and alone that even Connie's helpless pity had been a shield from Ma's anger. She looked down at the jars of cream and lip gloss through eyes blurred with a mist of tears. Then she shook off the moment. That didn't make Connie any less of a brat; and if she'd been snitching makeup, she was sure going to hear about it.

Smoothing on the cream mask, she lay back on the pillow with her eyes closed, willing her mind not to think about anything. As long as she was in the hospital and shut away, she was protected. She lay motionless, feeling the mask tighten her skin. After a while she groped for the button to raise the bed and pushed herself to a sitting position, looking around. *How does a person wash around here anyway?*

Finally she poured water from the pitcher on the night-stand onto some wadded tissue and got the cream off, inspecting her skin anxiously. Propping the small mirror against the purse, she put on the base and gels and worked on her eyes, studying her face. She'd been too scared the last few weeks to even think of her looks.

The memory made her suck in her breath again and she reached under the covers to press in on her stomach, relief washing her at its flatness. It was over, it really was. It would never happen again. She'd learned her lesson. Ma could be sure of that.

She smoothed on lip gloss and combed her hair and then lay back against the pillows. *I'm dying for a cigarette. Wonder if they've got rules in hospitals about smoking.* She rummaged through her purse. Nothing. She'd had a couple there but Ma must have found them. You could always count on Ma showing interest in her kids by searching through their stuff.

Suddenly she grabbed for the purse. "I'll bet she found that money—"

Her fingers explored along the bottom of the bag, finding the torn place she'd glued down, and felt the slight bulge of the five dollar bill. She leaned back against the pillows, smiling in relief and victory. She'd like to let Ma know she'd fooled her, but then she'd never be able to use that trick again and it was too good a hiding place to give away.

She stared across the room, wishing she knew what the time was. Kind of scary, being all alone in here. Was it visiting hours when Ma had come? She said she wouldn't be back tonight, so it must have been afternoon then. It had been dark out, but then the dark came early in winter. Nobody else would be coming. Nobody else knew she was here. Her eyes narrowed in concentration. What day was it anyway? She made her mind go back. It was Sunday she'd taken the pills. She knew that for sure. There had been the long week before, all those awful mornings when she'd felt so sick and couldn't eat and had been so afraid that she was— Her mind clamped shut, refusing to put the memory into words.

Anyway, it had been Sunday she'd done it. But that didn't tell her how long ago that was, how long she'd been in here. She'd ask the nurse when she came back. If she came in on Sunday, this could be only Monday. How long would it take to get over feeling rotten after—after what she'd done? If today *was* Monday nobody would have missed her at school yet. If it was Tuesday—or Wednesday—the school had probably called Ma to check on her. They were so fussy about someone missing a day of their dumb school. But Ma wouldn't tell 'em. Not about why she was absent.

Not that she'd care about me. She just wouldn't want anyone to know her daughter was dumb enough to get in a mess like this. She frowned. Now if Connie got asked, she might blab. She didn't have much sense about some things.

She stirred restlessly. What time was it anyway? Where was everyone? It was like a morgue. Might as well be dead— No! Her mind pushed the word away as perspiration beaded her forehead and upper lip.

A hum of sound came from somewhere down the hall and with it, voices and wisps of laughter. She sniffed. Umm—coffee. It was the first time in weeks the smell of it hadn't made her feel like throwing up. Must be time for supper. She watched the door and glimpsed a big cart as it was wheeled past her doorway. A woman in an orange smock came in and put a tray down on an adjustable table at the foot of the bed, pushing it within Myrna's reach.

"You want me to get you some water to wash?"

Myrna looked at her hands. "How can you get dirty just lying here?" She lifted the cover from the steaming plate. "What is it?"

"Ham. Green beans with cheese sauce. Sweet potatoes. Pineapple salad. Pie. Ok?"

Myrna ignored the question and picked up the fork. She tried a bite of ham, chewing it carefully, not sure she liked the strange taste. The green beans were better than they looked and the marshmallow topping on the sweet potatoes was good. Nice and sweet. She took a cautious sip of milk. It was too thick and white-looking. Tasted funny, too.

She twisted to see out into the hall and called, "Hey!"

The woman stopped in the doorway. "You want something?"

"Yeah. Can I have some coffee? This milk has a funny taste. Looks funny, too. It's so white and thick."

"I can get you a different glass if you like." The woman crossed the room and picked up the glass, sniffing the milk. "Doesn't smell sour."

"I don't like milk much anyhow. I always drink coffee. It fills you up better."

The coffee was strong and hot, and she sipped it slowly, feeling its warmth spread through her as she relaxed against the pillows. The thoughts that had crowded at her so insistently when she wakened now seemed hazy and unreal. She was safe, and that was all that mattered. Everything that had been so terribly wrong had turned out right.

She let the bed down and snuggled under the blanket, pulling the sheet up and feeling satisfied and drowsy, only half aware that someone came in and took away the tray. After a while noises floating in from the hall brought her awake. She could see people coming and going as she looked out through the half-open door. A young man with a plant in one hand and what looked like a box of candy stopped in the doorway of the room diagonally across the hall. Myrna heard the excited cry of welcome from the person in the bed. *His wife, probably.*

An elderly man walked by slowly, pushing a wheelchair and leaning around from behind it to hear what the woman in it was saying. A young couple walked along the hall and back again, the man in pajamas and robe, the girl leaning close to him, their arms around each other, oblivious to others in the hall.

Snatches of conversation mingled with the laughter from television programs gave warmth and gaity and life to the once-empty halls.

Myrna sat up straighter. "Hey! How dumb. I can watch television. That'll pass the time."

She looked around the room, not seeing the TV. Maybe they had shoved it into the closet out of the way. She craned her neck to see the instructions for calling the nurse: "Push button and release. When desk answers, speak into end of tube."

"Well, here goes," she muttered and pushed the button. When there was no answer, she pushed again and waited. Even though she was expecting it, she involuntarily jumped when a voice answered, "This is the desk. May I help you?"

"Yeah. I'm stuck here in this room all alone. How come I don't have a TV? They've got them in other rooms. I can hear them."

"Just a moment, please, and I'll check." After a moment of silence, the voice came back. "I'm sorry, but no TV was ordered for you."

"How come?"

"Well, you see, they cost extra."

"Oh."

She flopped back on the pillow. She might have known it would cost extra. Naturally she couldn't have one. She folded her arms and stared resentfully out into the hall, hating the sight of the girl with the man's arm securely around her as they strolled by, hating the sound of the laughter from the room across the hall, resenting even the tenderness of the old man pushing the wheelchair so carefully. She watched the halls fill with people at the close of visiting hours and then gradually empty. Finally only the nurses went silently and quickly by.

Myrna twisted and turned in the darkening room, the short hospital gown winding uncomfortably around her. Her head felt itchy and her skin dry. She knew she should get out the cream and take off the makeup, but it was just too much effort. Why should she care how she looked? Nobody cared about her. She lay tense and stared up at the ceiling, the room shadowy in the light coming from the hall.

"Hi. Are you still awake?"

Her again. For someone who isn't even supposed to be working this end of the floor, she sure is on it enough.

Aloud she answered, "Who could sleep with all the racket that's been going on out there."

"Well, everything is about settled now. We just shooed the last visitor out. I thought you might like a back rub."

"What good does that do?"

"Umm—relaxes you. Gets the kinks out of your muscles."

Myrna stared at the nurse as she leaned to tuck the blankets more securely at the bottom corners. Suspicion sharpened her voice.

"I thought you weren't supposed to be on this end of the floor."

"We're short of help. A couple of nurses are sick so we're all shifting around some." She helped Myrna roll over and began to knead her back. "You ever thought of being a nurse?"

"Are you kidding? Who wants to run around with stinking bedpans and all the other junk? And stick needles in people.''

"Someone has to. Bedpans are a pretty important part of a patient's life. You've been using them yourself for a couple of days.''

Myrna didn't answer but felt herself relaxing as the nurse worked on her back. Funny—it did feel good.

Her voice came muffled from where her face was buried in the curve of her arm. "You know what I'm in for?''

"Umm—hmm. Too many sleeping pills at one time.'' She finished the rub and gave Myrna's back a little thump before she pulled the gown straight. "There you are. I'll help you turn over.'' She looked down at her then, her head cocked and a questioning lift to her straight brows. "Want me to help you into the bathroom while I'm here? Since you hate bedpans so much.''

Myrna shook her head. "I can make it myself.'' She sat up abruptly and swung her legs over the side of the bed. But a wave of dizziness swept her, and she stared across at the bathroom which seemed miles away. The nurse came around and helped her stand. Her legs were weak, and she was glad for the solid feel of the nurse's arm as she clung to her and was helped across the room. She made a face at the hollow cheeks and stringy hair that stared back at her from the mirror over the washbasin.

The nurse helped her back to bed and pulled up the covers. "It's really warm in here, but it's so cold outside you just naturally feel as though you need all the covers you can pile on. Sleep well. Use the buzzer if you need anything in the night.''

The warm weight of the blankets was comforting, and Myrna stretched out gratefully. Nuts! She'd forgotten to find out what day it was. The nurse had said something about a couple of days—oh, well, she'd ask tomorrow. Tomorrow—how good to know there would be a tomorrow with its second chance.

12

A Persistent Nurse

THE MURMUR OF VOICES, the subdued clatter of dishes, and the coffee fragrance floating in from the hall roused Myrna, and she stretched under the warm covers. She heard the drapes swish back on the rods and opened her eyes to the nurse who stopped at the foot of the bed and smiled down at her. "Good morning. How do you feel?"

"Warm," Myrna answered drowsily.

"Too bad you can't stay in. It's really a cold one today. The sun is out and sparkles the snow like diamonds but it doesn't warm you any. I practically froze just coming in from the parking—"

Myrna raised herself on one elbow and demanded, "What do you mean I can't stay? They're sending me home?"

The nurse nodded. "The doctor will be in right after breakfast to give you a final check. But he said yesterday there was no reason you couldn't be dismissed today."

Myrna looked around. "What time is it?"

"Umm—seven-fifteen."

"Does my mother know? That I'm getting out today?"

"Why—I don't know—"

"I gotta get hold of her before she goes to work. She's got to bring me some clothes." She reached for the phone on the stand beside the bed and dialed jerkily.

"Ma—me. Look, they're sending me home today . . . When? I don't know. Wait a minute."

She looked over her shoulder as the nurse brought in the breakfast tray. "When do I go?"

Then, listening to her mother's voice pouring out impatient words, she said into the phone, "Well, OK, OK! Give me a chance to ask."

She held the receiver against her shoulder to stifle the sounds coming from it and looked up at the nurse. "Is it still the rule that we have to be out by noon or pay for a whole extra day?"

"By one o'clock," the nurse nodded, and Myrna said into the phone, "Yeah, it is," and listened to the rapid words on the other end.

"Well, it's not my fault," she snapped back finally. "What? . . . Yeah, yeah, sure, it *is* my fault. So I shouldn't have been here in the first place. Well, I am, and now I've got to get home. . . Sure I can come on the bus but I don't have any clothes . . . Can't you bring me some on your way to work? . . . Can't you take time off— . . . OK, forget I even mentioned it. What about Connie? She can miss one day of school . . . Well, she can give them to a nurse if she isn't allowed up. Then she can wait and go home with me. . . . It's not going to hurt her to take the bus over. . . . Well, I don't care if she wants to or not, she *has* to. And, look Ma, give her bus money for me, too. . . . No, I haven't got any money . . . No, I can't call someone to come get me. Connie's *got* to come."

She slammed the receiver down and leaned back against the pillow. *That Ma! Never thinks of anybody but herself. Can't give a person any help. I'm glad she can't come get me. I don't want her around me.* Aware then that she was biting her thumbnail, breathing in short gasps of anger, she looked up as the nurse stopped again in the doorway and then came toward the bed.

"Do you want to get up before you eat and wash in the bathroom, or do you want me to bring you water and a towel?"

"I'd better get up. Gotta get used to being on my feet." She threw back the covers and got up slowly, feeling shaky, not sure whether it was from weakness or anger. *That Ma!*

When she was back in bed, she stared at the tray. Breakfast wasn't a meal to get excited about, but since it was here she might as well eat it. She lifted the covers from the dishes indifferently. The scrambled eggs looked surprisingly good, and the puffy doughnut with its sugar glaze made her mouth water. Getting up even on bitterly cold days wouldn't be so bad if you had this waiting for you. She ate quickly, drinking the hot, strong coffee greedily.

Finishing, she leaned back, staring out at the white cold beyond the window. The tops of the buildings across the street were layered with snow on which the sun glinted with a blinding reflection that hurt her eyes. She looked around the room. It was warm and cheerful with the big, flower-splashed blue and gold drapes that framed the windows. The nurse had it right. It was too bad she had to leave. It would be easier to stay and not have to face Ma and the gang—

She cut off her thoughts abruptly, her mind scrabbling for something else to think about. Would Connie come? She'd have to. Ma would make her.

That Ma. Telling her to call one of her friends to come get her. You'd think Ma wouldn't want anyone to know she'd been in the hospital so they wouldn't ask what for. Ma hadn't thought about that. She just didn't want to bother coming herself.

Her mind circled the edges of the question she'd been avoiding until she finally forced herself to ask it. Did anyone know about her? Her eyes narrowed in thought as she stared across the room. How would anyone find out? She had hid the secret, she was sure of that. Someone else would have to blab. Like Connie. What day was this anyway? Must be at least Tuesday, maybe even Wednesday. Which meant Connie would have been in school a couple of days. But since none of her friends knew Connie—

Her thoughts stopped abruptly, fastening on a memory. Karen had a sister in junior high. Joyce? No, Janice—Jan something—Janet, that was it. And she and Connie knew each other. If Connie told Janet she was in the hospital and Karen found out, it would be all over school. You could trust Karen to make up whatever facts she couldn't guess. Her only hope was that Connie had had sense enough to keep her mouth shut.

She reached for the phone. Then she stopped and leaned back, trying to plan. There was no use in making Connie mad.

What can I give her to make her shut up? My green sweater. She's been bugging me for that for a long time. And I'm sick of it anyway.

Then she frowned. "Maybe I already gave her that for another promise," she muttered, trying to remember what had happened in those frightful, sick days that now could be just a forgotten memory. Well, she wouldn't offer anything unless she had to.

There were voices just outside her door, and the doctor loomed in the doorway. She looked at him warily as he came to the bed and reached to take her pulse.

"Well, young lady, I think we've got you fixed up so you can go home. We'll just take one final check."

Myrna tensed herself for his examination, closing her eyes and her mind until it was over.

Conscious that he was still standing beside the bed, she looked up into his face to see him staring soberly down at her, a slight frown creasing his forehead. When he spoke, his voice was serious and the words came slowly. "Don't try anything like this again, will you? It isn't worth it.

There's always some way out besides this, you know. There's always someone who will help.''

The resentment that flared in her instinctively was stilled by the compassion of his voice, and she caught her lower lip between her teeth, knowing only tears would come if she tried to answer.

She listened as he went on as though to himself. ''If only you girls would think of the future, keep yourselves for then, not let someone pressure you for the moment. If you could only see in time that it's *your* life you're messing up. Don't let it happen.''

He focused his eyes on her then. ''A pretty girl like you has a lot of temptation, I suppose. But you've got so much to live for. Life holds so much that is fine and beautiful—as well as exciting in the right way. Don't throw yourself and the future away on something—or someone—who isn't worth it. Will you remember?''

She nodded wordlessly, the seriousness of his voice cutting deep. He was old and the deep lines across his forehead and running the length of his cheeks gave him a sad look. He talked to her as though she were a person, as though she were important and not just a no-good tramp like Ma said she was. Her eyes slid away from his compassionate face to the nurse listening at the foot of the bed and then out the window. She closed her eyes to squeeze back tears and heard them leave.

But her mind argued back at him. It was easy for him to talk. His daughters probably had an easy life with a fancy house and neat clothes. And parents who cared. What chance did she have? In abrupt defiance of him she let her mind repeat the words that would bring Ma's hard anger if she heard them.

The lunch trays were just coming around when Connie appeared in the doorway, standing silently with a brown paper bag in one hand and a coat over her arm.

''Well, it's about time!''

"They wouldn't let me come up any sooner. They said I had to wait until it was nearer time for you to leave."

Connie glanced at her as she answered, her eyes shifting quickly away as she put the stuff on a chair and walked over to stare out the window. Myrna watched her, seeing the delicacy of her profile. Her shadowed cheeks were hollow, accentuating her high cheekbones and the little point of her chin. Myrna caught her breath as she realized that Connie was going to be very pretty. Someday the guys would be whistling at her and wanting dates and—She wrenched her mind away.

"You're so skinny you look like a broom. Can't you stand up straight instead of hunching over like that?"

Connie ignored her and stood silently while an aide brought the lunch tray and adjusted the swinging bedside table. Myrna lifted the cover and looked suspiciously at the bowl of soup. Then she crumbled crackers into it and began to eat quickly.

The woman came back to stand in the doorway and look across at Connie. "How about some lunch? I've got an extra tray. Somebody in the kitchen made a mistake and there's no sense taking it back. The one in charge down there today is on a tear and she'll probably just throw it out. The price of food today as it is that would be a crime. Want it?"

"Well—if you're sure—I mean, I haven't eaten—"

"Sit down. I'll get it."

Myrna waited until the woman left before asking, "Ma say anything about paying?"

"She already has a signed paper from the welfare office. You're supposed to give it to the cashier and get a receipt."

"Is she going to be home tonight?"

Connie lifted one thin shoulder. "I don't know."

"You tell anyone I was in the hospital?"

"Who's to tell?" Connie's voice was cold. "None of my friends know you."

"What about what's-her-name? Janet. That her name? You say anything to her?"

Connie shook her head. "I haven't talked to her lately. Besides, why should she care about you?"

"Maybe *she* doesn't, but her nosy sister would sure like to know all about my business."

"Probably the school called Ma to find out about you. They usually do if you miss a day. When can you go back?"

"Right away, I guess. Might as well. Nothing to do at home." She threw back the covers. "I'd better get dressed if you brought me anything decent to wear."

"You didn't tell Ma what you wanted. Or anyway she didn't tell me. All I could do was root around in your stuff, and I knew you'd be mad no matter what I brought so—"

"OK, OK! Don't get excited."

Myrna took the sack of clothes and went into the bathroom to dress. When she came out, Connie had finished eating and was standing at the window watching the people in the street below as they huddled in their coats against the biting wind blowing off the lake. Myrna walked over to stand beside her, hating the thought of going out into the bitterness of the cold and away from the security of the hospital.

"Well, let's go. Where's the paper Ma sent?"

Connie dug it out of her pocket and handed it over silently as she followed Myrna out into the hall. Myrna looked at her. "You know where to go with this?"

Connie nodded. "I came with Ma when she got Betty. It's on the first floor, down the hall from the main entrance."

They took the elevator to the first floor, standing silently among the crowd. As they walked along the hall past the waiting room, Connie glanced in, the memory of the long wait there during Betty's operation vivid before her. She stopped suddenly as a figure standing by the information desk turned and came toward them.

Myrna looked too, recognizing the nurse who had been in her room the night before. She watched the level gray eyes smile at Connie as the nurse asked, "How are you?"

Myrna saw Connie's shy smile in return and heard her breathless, "Hi. I'm OK. I—I was hoping I would see you."

"How do you know my sister?" Myrna blurted, resentment fresh in her at the way the nurse seemed to be hanging around.

"I was Betty's nurse—"

"She took us home from the hospital—"

They spoke together and stopped to smile at each other. Then the nurse surveyed Myrna. "How are you feeling?"

Myrna shrugged. "So-so."

"You're checking out?"

"Yeah."

"How about letting me give you a ride home? I don't go on duty until three so I have plenty of time."

Myrna studied her through narrowed eyes, seeing the scarlet wool jumper and the white wool long-sleeved sweater.

What's she angling for? Nobody is that nice for nothing. Still, it wouldn't hurt to get a free ride home plus not having to wait on the cold street corner for a lousy bus.

She shrugged again. "Ok by me. But I've got to see about the bill or they won't let me out of here."

She turned away and then stopped to half-turn, frowning at the nurse, her voice suspicious. "If you don't have to start work until three, how come you're here so early? You like this place that much?"

The nurse looked back at her silently. Then she answered, "No. I asked when you were going to be released and came early on purpose. I wanted to take you home so you wouldn't have to go by bus."

Myrna stared at her. Her belligerent, "How come?" was lost in Connie's breathless, "That's awfully nice of you. Ma—you see, Ma couldn't get off work to come so I stayed home from school. Ma knew we'd be all right on the bus. I mean, she knew Myrna wouldn't need help the way Betty did."

Myrna frowned as she listened to Connie's rush of words. *What's she making excuses for Ma for? Ma sure wouldn't appreciate it. She'd tell Connie to keep her mouth shut. And how come the nurse came on purpose to give her a ride? There's something funny going on here.*

Myrna turned and walked quickly to the cashier's window. She glanced back over her shoulder and watched them standing together, Connie's eyes wide with admiration as the nurse talked and Connie listened, her head giving quick, agreeing nods.

The cashier made out a slip and handed Myrna a duplicate. "Your mother will have to sign this and turn it in."

Myrna nodded impatiently. Naturally. There were always papers to sign when the welfare did anything for you.

She turned to Connie and the nurse who had followed her along the hall.

"Let's go out this way." The nurse nodded down the hall. "It will keep us from being out in the cold too long. I'm parked right out by the side door."

She led the way and they braced themselves as the wind pushed against the door, resisting their efforts to open it, and then swirled at them with a lunge as they stepped outside. They followed the nurse and stood shivering as she unlocked the door and went around to the driver's side.

"We'd better all sit in front and get the benefit of the heater as soon as possible."

The nurse manuevered past the banked snow in the parking lot before asking, "How's Betty'?"

"OK."

"And Mrs. Brewster?"

"I haven't talked to her much. Since Sunday, I mean. I—I went up and talked to her and she—helped me a lot. She explained Betty's book."

Myrna listened curiously, aware of something unspoken between them and noticed Connie's uneasiness as the nurse said, "When you have questions, talk them over with her. I left her quite a bunch of things to read. You can be a help to each other."

She pulled the car to the curb, in front of the house and stopped, leaving the engine running. "Would you remind her that I'll be around by nine on Sunday?"

Connie nodded with a quick laugh. "I'll remind her but she hasn't forgotten. She's got it marked with a red pencil on her kitchen calendar. That's where she marks everything important. She took Kevin shopping yesterday and bought him a new outfit so he'd look as nice as the other little kids in the nursery."

Myrna watched as Connie half glanced in her direction and then down at her hands squeezed tight in her lap. "Was—what Betty wore last Sunday all right?"

The nurse nodded. "Of course some of the girls wore fancier things, but others didn't."

"What about—about—older kids? My age?"

"A lot of them wear school clothes. Some dress up more but a school outfit is all right."

Myrna leaned forward across Connie to look at the nurse. "What *is* all this anyway?"

"I took Betty to Sunday school last week."

"How'd you get away with that? How come I didn't hear the fireworks—" She stopped abruptly, remembering. "Did Ma find out?"

"She knew about it. I wouldn't have done it behind her back," the nurse answered quietly. "I'm coming over on Saturday and ask if Betty can go again." She looked at Connie. "When would be best to come?"

Connie shifted uneasily, glancing at Myrna. "Ma said—I don't think she'll—I mean, she won't—"

"No time is best," Myrna broke in, her voice flat and hard. "Ma won't let her go. Church is one thing Ma really hates." She looked at Connie. "I should think you'd be smart enough by now not to give her anything to blow her top over. We all catch it when she does."

She pushed down on the door handle. "Thanks for the lift. It beat waiting for the bus. Come on, Connie. I don't have a key."

She got out and stood impatiently, her teeth chattering, while Connie said something to the nurse, her hands gesturing helplessly.

"Hurry it up! I'm freezing," Myrna snapped and Connie got out, slamming the car door behind her. Myrna picked her way carefully down the broken, ice-crusted steps and stood shivering in the cold hall while Connie unlocked the door. She stepped into the apartment, feeling its chill. "Yow! It's almost as cold in here as outside."

She hugged her arms around herself, not taking off her coat, and looked across the room at Connie. "Did I get any calls?"

Connie shook her head as she took off her jacket and dropped it on the couch.

"You're sure you didn't talk to anyone in school about me?"

"No."

"See that you don't. I've got my own story to tell and I

don't want you or Ma spoiling it for me. And keep Betty quiet too."

"Betty doesn't know anything!" Connie whirled to face Myrna, her eyes blazing and her voice shaking. "She's too young. If you think I'm going to let her know what you're like—"

She stopped, backing away, her face changing from angry to scared as Myrna came toward her.

"Listen, you little punk. Don't act so goody-goody around me. Don't you say anything about this to me again. Not ever. It's over and done with. You hear?"

She glared at Connie who stared back defiantly a moment until her eyes shifted and she groped behind her for the doorknob.

"I've got to go. I'm supposed to sit with Kevin."

"Wait a minute! When did Ma tell the school snoops I'd be back?"

"I don't know. They maybe didn't even call. If they did, Ma was probably at work. Anyway we don't go tomorrow or Friday. We're off. Because it's Thanksgiving."

"Oh, yeah. Good. Well, beat it. I've got some planning to do. But don't forget what I said. And don't go telling that busybody upstairs anything about me either."

She watched Connie slip through the door and close it behind her. Then she turned and went into the bedroom, rummaging through a dresser drawer until she found the cigarettes she'd hidden from Ma. She lit one and went back to the living room, crossing over to the couch to stare unseeing out the window, her mind running through the maze, looking for the exit.

After a while she turned and wandered through the house, rubbing her arms from the chill of the rooms she could feel even through her coat. What a dump Ma had found for them. And of course she never lifted a finger to keep it clean. Always claiming she had to work to earn the rent money. So she worked. So what? And what did Connie do after school? Nothing but babysit for the snoop upstairs.

"Lazy, sloppy people," she muttered and ground out the cigarette in the dregs in the coffee cup on the kitchen table. Ma always kept blaming them for the mess they lived in.

"As though we asked to be born in the first place," she muttered.

As the words echoed in the silence of the room, a chill started somewhere inside her and traveled in a long shudder over her whole body. Death had been so near—it had seemed so welcome a few short days ago. But now—

She stumbled into the bedroom and threw herself down on the bed, her hands clutching the blanket convulsively as her sobs rang loud in the empty house. She didn't want to die! The relief at having escaped was overwhelming. But could she be sure the desperation wouldn't come again? Could she ever be *really* sure?

13

Invitation for Thanksgiving

THE BANGING OF THE FRONT DOOR roused her and she sat up, shivering in the cold of the room, and clutched the blanket around her shoulders.

"Connie?" Betty's voice came shrill and penetrating from the kitchen and Myrna got up and stalked out.

"Can't you ever come in without making so much racket?" She looked around as the door slammed again and scowled at Connie. "It's about time you got back. You cooking supper?"

Connie ducked past into the kitchen. "Who else?"

"What is there?"

"Hamburger."

"Yeach!"

"You got a better idea?"

Myrna turned back toward the bedroom. "Ma coming home?"

"She didn't say she wasn't."

Myrna tensed. If Ma was going to be home, she might as well get set for a whole evening of being yelled at. Ma could think of more things to tell you that were wrong with you. She never left you in peace unless she was going out or there was something on TV she wanted to see.

She went back and stood in the kitchen doorway, watching Connie narrowly.

"Ma been going out much lately?"

Connie's hands were still for a moment before she lifted one shoulder in a shrug. "Some."

"Same guy every time?"

"She doesn't tell me her business."

Myrna studied Connie's back. There was something she wasn't telling. Must be Ma had a new boyfriend on the string.

"Have you seen him?" she asked abruptly.

"Who?"

"Ma's new steady."

Connie jerked around. "How did you know—" She stopped and bit her lip at Myrna's soft, triumphant laugh. "I don't know what you're talking about," she finished shortly and turned back to the stove.

Hearing the sound of someone at the door, Myrna moved further into the kitchen out of sight and listened as Mrs. Hamilton came in, stamping snow from her feet.

"All I can say is a person's got to be crazy to go on living in this climate. Connie, I hope you've got supper ready. I'm hungry and frozen." She came to the kitchen and stopped, looking at Myrna. "So you're home. I hope you've learned something from all this."

"Now, Ma—"

"Don't 'now, Ma' me. I've had enough trouble and expense with you. Anymore and you can find yourself another place to live." She shrugged out of her coat on the way to the bedroom. "Hurry it up, Connie. I need some hot coffee."

Betty came up to Myrna and stared at her.

"Myrna, when you were in the hospital, did you have 'pendicitis like I did?"

"None of your business."

"If you were smart, you'd be nice to us at least." Connie looked across the room at her. "You might need our help sometime." Though she didn't say the word *again,* it hung in the air unspoken and Myrna glared back at her angrily. Before she could answer, Mrs. Hamilton came out to the kitchen, tying the belt around her faded chenille robe.

Connie carried the frying pan to the table, setting it on a folded newspaper on the oil cloth.

Her mother looked at it. "What's this?"

"Just some hamburger fixed different. I saw Mrs. Brewster make it and it looked good. And it's cheap. It didn't take much stuff. I didn't have to buy anything—"

"That Mrs. Brewster," Mrs. Hamilton cut across the rush of Connie's explanation. "Always that Mrs. Brewster." She sat down and reached a big spoonful onto her plate, salting it vigorously, and ate without comment.

"It's good," Betty said. " 'Course *anything* Mrs. Brewster makes is good."

Myrna watched with amusement as Connie shook her head slightly at Betty, a warning frown creasing her forehead. She glanced at her mother and then away as she asked hesitantly, "Are you going to be home tomorrow? It's Thanksgiving."

"Me be home when everybody else goes out to eat? You think people will stay home so all the restaurants can close down and all us waitresses get to have the day off? No, I'm not going to be home."

"Can't you just stay home? Tell the boss you've got kids to take care of on Thanksgiving?" Myrna let her voice be as mocking as she dared, ready to shift quickly out of her mother's reach.

"And get fired?" she shot back. "Who pays the bills around here anyway? Me, that's who. And where does the money come from? From my job, that's where. The few lousy bucks your father sends—when he thinks of it—doesn't do it."

"Well, OK, I just asked."

Mrs. Hamilton shoved her plate back. "Fix me some more coffee, Connie. And this time make it so it'll taste like coffee."

"I was just trying to make it last. The jar's almost empty."

"Didn't you get some at the store this morning? I told you to."

"I didn't have enough money—"

"What do you mean? What'd you do with the five I gave you? What'd you blow it on?"

"Nothing, Ma. By the time I got the potatoes and bread and meat and—"

"What kind of meat did you get? Steak or lobster or something?"

"Just hamburger. And I got—a—half a dozen eggs—"

"What do we need eggs for? That's the trouble sending you to the store. You waste money on stuff we don't need."

"Connie does too need eggs. She's gonna make a pumpkin pie," Betty blurted happily.

"A what? What for?"

"Shut up!" Connie ordered, glaring at Betty. "I said maybe I would. Only maybe."

"And Mrs. Brewster said it's her favorite kind," Betty finished.

"You're making *her* a pie?" Mrs. Hamilton's voice was sharp. "With her stuff or ours?"

"Ours. But—but I'm not making it just for her. I'm only going to give her a piece. She's done a lot for us. She's had Betty come up lots of times and—"

"And why not?" her mother demanded. "She's home all day. She's got nothin' to do. Except spend money on those toys her kid rackets around with all day and half the night."

Myrna watched Connie get up without answering and carry her plate to the sink, and couldn't resist a scornful, "I'll bet it won't be worth eating. You've never made a pie in your life."

"I have too! We made one last week in school. A small one. And it turned out good. I've got the recipe. It doesn't take much stuff. All you need is a can of pumpkin and some eggs and some canned milk. And a little sugar. And we've got the milk and sugar. I just had to buy the eggs and—"

"All right, all right!" her mother snapped, getting up from the table. "Just see that you don't go giving away stuff you buy with my money."

Connie watched her go into the living room and then looked at Myrna. "How about helping with the dishes?"

"Me? I'm just out of the hospital, remember? I've got to save my strength." She smiled mockingly over her shoulder and went into the living room to flip on the TV. In the silence before the sound came on, she heard Betty's "I'll help you, Connie. I'll even wash."

What a dumb kid to offer when she didn't have to.

She shifted over to the far side of the couch when her mother came to watch the program. In the occasional silence between commercials she could hear snatches of the companionable conversation going on in the kitchen.

"What makes them so buddy-buddy?" she finally asked, jerking her head in the direction of the kitchen.

"Well, what's wrong with a little sisterly affection? You could show a little more of it yourself."

I might have known that would set her off on one of her tirades. She closed her mind to her mother's scolding words which poured out until she stopped to light a cigarette. Myrna got up and stalked to the crowded, cluttered bedroom, closing the door behind her. The clean, smooth sheets of the hospital bed and the soothing back rub were a tantalizing memory. Reality was the thin mattress and blanket, the gap along the windowsill through which particles of snow drifted, the fuzzy sound of the TV, and Ma's cigarette smoke. She undressed quickly and got into bed, hoping sleep would blot out reality.

The acrid smell she thought was cigarette smoke finally drifted through to be identifiable as the smell of burned toast and she opened her eyes reluctantly. Connie was curled in a tight, closed heap beside her, her back arched, and one hand tightly gripping the edge of the blanket. Myrna yawned and pulled the blanket higher around her shoulders against the icy feel of the room. She raised on one elbow to see that Betty's bed was empty. If she was the one burning toast, it meant Ma was probably gone and she could have the heater. She got up and padded out through the living room, her arms folded around her shivering body, and saw her mother's unmade bed through the open bedroom door. She went out to the kitchen where Betty sat at the table crunching toast.

"What a mess! Can't you even fix a piece of toast without getting crumbs all over?"

"I'm gonna clean them up. Don't worry."

"Ma gone?"

"Uh-huh. A long time ago."

"Good. I'm going to plug in the heater and go back to bed. Don't make a lot of noise, you hear?"

"You're the one talkin' loud."

"Don't get bratty around me!"

Myrna dug the heater out from under her mother's bed and took it back to the bedroom to plug it in. She pulled it close to her side of the bed and crawled back in, huddling close against Connie who shifted in her sleep and pulled away.

Myrna closed her eyes, willing sleep that wouldn't come. Her mind raced with questions that had no answers. They should have let her stay in the hospital a few more days. It was warm there and they brought you breakfast in bed. Her mouth watered as she remembered the scrambled eggs and the fat, glazed doughnut.

The soft knock on the front door carried through to her and she listened to Betty pound across the linoleum floor and open the door. Then she heard Mrs. Brewster's light voice.

"Hi. Are you the only one up at your house?"

"Just me and Ma. And she's gone to work."

"On Thanksgiving Day? Too bad. Are Connie and Myrna asleep?"

"Yeah. But I'll call them."

Myrna kicked Connie. "Hey, wake up. Your nosy friend from upstairs wants something as usual."

Betty pushed the bedroom door open and marched in as Connie sat up and looked around, groggy from sleep. "Connie, Mrs. Brewster's here and wants to know if you're up."

Connie cut short a yawn and threw back the blanket which Myrna caught and pulled around her.

"Tell her just a minute," and she wriggled her feet into

her shoes and pulled a sweater around her. She went out into the living room leaving the door open behind her. Myrna sniffed. *Something sure smells good. Must be something Mrs. Brewster is cooking.* She sat up in the slowly warming room and listened to the voices at the front door.

"Hi, Connie. Sorry to get you up but I've got a problem. Mike's folks were coming up today to stay overnight. But they just called that they're snowed in and can't make it. They can't even get their long driveway shoveled out because the snow is so deep and heavy. I'm sick about it. I wanted to show Mike's mother what a good cook I've become."

She laughed down at Betty who was licking her lips and rubbing her stomach as she said, "You sure are!"

"The thing is I've got a turkey in the oven and it's too much for Kevin and me. I thought maybe you would all come up and help us eat it."

Betty was wide-eyed. "A *turkey?* We've never had one. Is it a real live one?"

Mrs. Brewster laughed. "I hope not. I put it in the oven early enough so it wouldn't be live when it got to the table." She looked at Connie hesitantly. "Betty says your mother has already gone to work. I don't want to interfere with anything she has planned for you—"

"Ma plan something for us?" Myrna's mocking voice cut across the room from where she stood in the bedroom doorway. "Not her! She's not even going to be home after work. She's got a date. So we'd just end up with one of Connie's hamburger messes again. Sure we'll come."

"Good. Come up about five."

Connie followed her out to the hall. "I'm going to make a pumpkin pie. I'll bring it for dessert if you want me to."

"Good. I was planning to make one, but my oven won't hold turkey and pie at the same time."

Myrna lounged in the bedroom doorway and watched

in amusement as Connie dug eagerly in her purse for the recipe she had copied out of her home ec notebook, and then she followed her to the kitchen and listened to her worry.

"The crust is going to be the biggest problem. What if it doesn't bake right? The control knob on the oven doesn't work right so I can't tell exactly how hot it is."

"If it's that much trouble, why bother?"

"Because I want to," Connie snapped back as Myrna shrugged and went to watch the parade on TV.

Connie had just slid the pie carefully into the exact center of the oven and had closed the door gently when she heard the back door open and then close. She turned to glimpse Betty's face.

"What's the matter with you?"

Betty stood still, her hand gripping the doorknob, not looking at Connie. Her voice came small and thin. "We *are,* aren't we? Going to have turkey?"

"You heard Mrs. Brewster yourself."

"I told her that. Debbie. An' she said we weren't. She—she laughed."

"What difference does it make what she said if you know you're right?"

"Because she said—she said—she said we—we couldn't have turkey because it—it cost too much. She said her mother said we couldn't—buy a turkey because—because—Ma—because Ma drinks up all our money." Betty's face crumpled with the effort to hold back tears. "She doesn't, does she, Connie?"

Connie reached out toward the still figure, wanting to put a comforting arm around the bony shoulders. But her hand dropped uncertainly. The flood of hurt tears was too near the surface and a hug she had never before given Betty could release them.

But Myrna's amused laugh from the kitchen doorway broke the silence as she said flippantly, "Tell you what,

Betty. You ask Mrs. Brewster for a turkey leg tonight and when you've eaten the meat you just save the old bone and give it to your bratty, know-it-all friend tomorrow. How's that?''

Betty turned and blinked back the tears, a smile lighting her thin face. "OK. That'll show her, won't it?"

Myrna sat down at the kitchen table to do her nails and Connie looked at her suspiciously. "You set your hair."

"So? Any law against it?"

"You're not going out instead of—"

Myrna shook her head, her impatience making her spill the polish. "No, I'm not, and look what you made me do. Quit stewing. I'm not going to pass up a free meal even though I'm not crazy about the company." She looked at Connie critically. "It wouldn't hurt you to dress up a little. You sure look scruffy."

"I'm going to when the pie is done. I've got to stay here and watch it so the crust doesn't burn before the pumpkin part is cooked."

It was a relief when the knife she carefully slid into the middle of the pie came out clean the way the recipe said it should. "It's done!" she exclaimed and set it on the table to cool.

"It's beautiful, Connie!" Betty breathed.

"Yeah. It looks just like the ones you see in restaurants."

Connie flushed under Myrna's unexpected praise and said, "I just hope it tastes good."

"Button me in back, Connie," Betty demanded. "I'm gonna go up and watch Kevin so Mrs. Brewster can cook quicker. I'm so hungry."

"Just be sure you help and don't get in the way."

"Course not. Mrs. Brewster says I'm never in her way."

As Betty clattered up the stairs, Myrna followed Connie into the bedroom. "What are you wearing?"

"My dress."

"Want to borrow my green sweater?"

"No. I don't have anything that looks good with it. Besides—" Connie stopped and looked across from her side of the bed. "It's mine anyhow. You already gave it to me."

"Since when? I've been thinking about letting you have it but I haven't done it yet."

When Connie was silent, Myrna demanded again, "When did I give it to you?"

"Last week."

Myrna's mind jerked back, remembered, and pushed the memory away. "OK, so it's yours. But don't expect me to give you a skirt to go with it. Or either of my jumpers. I was earning money to buy my own clothes when I was your age. You can too."

Connie didn't answer as she stood in front of the mirror brushing her hair. Looking at her clear skin and wideset eyes, Myrna saw again the hint of beauty. *It would be better for her if she were homely.* The thought brought a rush of fear and anger.

They finished dressing in silence, and Connie went to the kitchen for the pie. The sudden knock at the door was loud in the silence between them, and Connie turned from the kitchen table to watch as Myrna crossed impatiently to yank the door open. She stared up at Alec lounging against the door frame and laughing down at her, his cigarette hanging moist from his lower lip.

"Baby! Where ya been all week?"

She stared up at him without answering, feeling the hammering of the pulse in her throat.

"Someone said you'd been sick. That so?"

Myrna moistened her lips and swallowed. "Me sick? Are you kidding? I'm never sick."

"Missed you at school this week."

She lifted one shoulder in contempt. "School? What's that?"

"You weren't at work either. I checked."

She laughed up at him. "I'm sick of that joint. I'm planning on getting a job that pays off in clothes instead of greasy hamburgers."

He looked her over. "I like what you've got on now. But—" His eyes narrowed down at her. "It kinda looks like you're all ready to step out. Been waiting for me to come?"

"No, I'm—" She hesitated and then finished with a laugh, "I'm babysitting tonight."

He looked across at Connie standing motionless in the kitchen doorway. "With her? Come on now, honey. I'll find someone who'll enjoy babysitting her more than you will."

Myrna glanced over her shoulder at Connie and saw her wide, scared look and felt a chill start inside her. Alec didn't take no lightly. She moved back a step involuntarily as he shifted his position carelessly and reached for her wrist. Then Betty's shoes were noisy on the steps as she clattered halfway down. "Hurry up, will you? Everything's almost ready."

Myrna watched Alec look over his shoulder at Betty as she hung over the bannister impatiently and then raise his eyes to Mrs. Brewster standing silently at the top of the stairs.

His lips parted in a thin smile as he glanced back at Myrna. "Well, well. I didn't know I was interrupting a family party. See you around, kid."

He turned and pulled open the outside door, letting in a blast of cold air that eddied around her legs to join the chill that knotted her stomach in fear. She listened to the door slam shut and after a moment the engine of his car roared as he raced down the street. Funny. She'd never been afraid of Alec in the past. He'd never before left her with this sense of dread.

She silently followed Connie upstairs where Betty waited importantly. Mrs. Brewster had set the table at one end of the kitchen with a bright green cloth and a basket of artificial fruit and flowers in the center. Myrna looked around, trying to figure out what made her kitchen look different from their dark one. It must be the row of little plants on a shelf over the sink and the sheer yellow curtains framing the window.

She watched Connie as she helped lift the browned turkey from the roasting pan and then carefully stirred flour into the juices for gravy. Myrna turned and wandered into the living room, feeling useless and restless. She stopped to look at Mike's picture on top of the TV. His blue eyes crinkled in laughter as he looked directly out of the picture frame. *How lucky can you get to snag a guy like that.*

There were other pictures scattered around the room of the three of them, of Mike holding Kevin, of Mike with his arms around his wife. And always his blue eyes were lighted with a smile that said plainly, "See how lucky I am?"

She turned as Mrs. Brewster came into the room, snapping on a lamp. "The dinner is as ready as it can be, I guess."

When they were seated, Mrs. Brewster looked around and then folded her fingers together. "I hope you don't mind. Mike wrote that he wants me to pray with Kevin before we eat. He's doing it and wants us to get in the habit too. It's kind of nice."

They watched as she helped Kevin fold his hands and then bow her head. Betty and Connie did too, but Myrna sat motionless as Mrs. Brewster said, "Thanks, God, for this food. Bless whatever Mike is doing today. Bring him back soon. Please. Amen."

"Can I have a leg to keep and is Mike eating turkey today too?" Betty asked as soon as she lifted her head.

"Yes you can, and I think he is."

Myrna sat aloof as they ate, one part of her listening to Betty's constant chatter and to the conversation between Connie and Mrs. Brewster. The other part of her mind studied Mrs. Brewster's slender figure in its dark green pantsuit, the long lashes shading her gray eyes and the short brushed hair swinging loosely just at the top of her collar.

Some people have everything going for them. The thought was bitterly envious. Mike would probably be one of those who came home without a scratch and stepped right into some high-paying job.

She shoved her plate back when she finished and looked across at Connie. "Your pie was good. It needs a cigarette though." She looked at Mrs. Brewster. "Got any? I left mine downstairs."

"Sorry. I've quit. The only way I can be sure not to start again is not to have any in the house." She smiled across the table at Myrna. "You'd better quit while you're just starting out. It's easier."

"Why quit? Everyone I run around with smokes. I'm not going to be the oddball."

"You might live longer."

The reminder was friendly but Myrna shook her head impatiently. "So who wants to live—" She cut off the words abruptly. Death had come too close for her to be flippant about it now.

In the silence Connie said, "Let us do the dishes in thanks for the meal."

Myrna scowled at her. Connie's offering for herself was one thing, but dragging her into the dishpan too was something else. But when the dish drainer was full, she picked up a towel. As she wiped at the plates she was filled suddenly with a fierce longing to be with the rest of the bunch in familiar security with someone's stereo blasting out rock that drowned all speech and thought in the oblivion of noise. She was an alien here in the quiet of the kitchen with Betty and Kevin laughing in the living room and Mrs. Brewster and Connie sharing each other's thoughts.

She escaped as soon as the dishes were done and went down to shut out memory with the late movie. She ignored Connie and Betty when they came down with the turkey leg wrapped carefully in waxed paper.

14

Looking for a Job

BY SLEEPING LATE and watching television most of the day, Myrna made it through Friday, but by Saturday she was ready to climb the wall. She wished for anything that would break the monotony of the four walls of the house.

I should have gone to work. Even that would be better than sitting around this freezing dump waiting for Ma to get up and blow her top. And watching Connie make like a housewife.

She turned on Connie irritably. "Why waste your time scrubbing the floor? It won't even dry in this cold house. Look, there's ice all along the wall over there under the front window."

"Well, at least it will be clean."

"Who cares?"

"I do!"

"Since when? Why all the sudden interest in being clean?"

"Well, it's something to do." Connie turned away from Myrna's scornful eyes and bent to scrub at black marks along the baseboard of the living room. Then her head lifted at the sound of a car door slamming outside.

"You expecting someone?" Connie shook her head. Myrna's eyes narrowed. "Ma's boyfriend coming over?"

"I don't know." Connie leaned over the sofa to pull the front curtain aside. Then she dropped it and turned away. "I don't know anything about Ma's business."

"You must be expecting someone," Myrna persisted.

"Quit pestering me, will you?"

Betty burst in the front door, her nose running from the cold and her cheeks red and chapped. "Has she come yet?"

Connie turned on her. "Keep still! And why can't you get rid of the snow outside? You're tracking all over my clean floor—"

"Has who come?" Myrna demanded.

"Nobody—"

"The nurse—" Betty clapped her hand over her mouth and turned to Connie pleadingly. "I forgot! I'm sorry, Connie! I forgot we weren't going to say anything. Did she—do you think *she* heard?" She looked anxiously at the closed bedroom door. "Do you think she heard?" she repeated, her voice a loud whisper.

Myrna sat down on the arm of the sofa, swinging her foot. "Oh, yeah. Miss Goody-goody said she was coming today to talk Ma into letting you go to church again. Why didn't you tell her she'd be wasting her time? Why get Betty's hopes up for nothing? And what's so great about dragging off to church?"

"It's fun!"

"Ma can find enough to yell about without you handing her something ready-made."

"She *might* say yes." Betty's voice was doubtful and her narrow shoulders slumped.

Mrs. Hamilton opened the bedroom door as she struggled into her robe, pulling the belt tight around her waist. "What's all the yelling about? Can't you let a person get a little sleep? What time is it—eleven already? Put some water on for coffee, somebody. And don't hand me that line about not having any."

"I saved some for you." Connie's voice was quick and placating.

"I'll fix some toast!" Betty's voice was eager, too. "I'll cut it fancy like they did in the hospit—"

"No! None of your burned toast for me. I'll fix my own so it will be fit to eat."

Connie followed to the kitchen while Betty knelt on the couch and pulled the curtain apart to stare out the window. "Here she comes," she exclaimed suddenly. She slid off the couch and darted to the door. She pulled it open and said breathlessly, "Hi! You're just in time. My mother just got up so you can ask her." She grabbed the nurse's hand and pulled her into the room.

"What's all the racket? Oh, it's you." Mrs. Hamilton scowled at the nurse standing just inside the room with Betty clinging to her hand. "What do you want?"

"I promised Betty—" There was a momentary hesitation and Myrna saw her eyes shift to Connie standing just behind her mother, and then back to Mrs. Hamilton. "I promised Betty I would stop in and ask if she could go to Sunday school again tomorrow. She enjoyed it so much last week. I thought perhaps Connie might want to go too."

"And if I say no, you'll stop for her anyway."

Mrs. Hamilton reached to grind out her cigarette in the saucer on the TV but stopped as the nurse answered, "No. I told Betty if you didn't want her to go, then she shouldn't."

"Yeah? How come? What's the catch?"

"There isn't any. Except that Betty should obey you.

If you don't want her to go to Sunday School, then she shouldn't.

"That's a new wrinkle!" Mrs. Hamilton's abrupt laugh ended in a cough. "I'll bet that's supposed to make me feel ashamed so I'll let her go."

The nurse shook her head. "No. If that's your decision, then that's what Betty should do."

"OK. So it's no. I don't want me or my kids to have anything to do with church. So don't bother coming around again and getting Betty all worked up over it. Or Connie either," she added with a threatening look over her shoulder.

Myrna watched Betty reach up to wipe away the tears running down her cheeks. Her mouth twisted in scorn. *What a dope! She's old enough to know that Ma never lets you do what you want to if she can help it.*

She watched the nurse cup Betty's chin in her hand and smile down at her. "I'm going to run up and see Mrs. Brewster a few minutes. Would you be able to watch Kevin while we talk?" She looked at Mrs. Hamilton. "May she?"

"Sure—if she gets paid for it."

"I don't *hafta* get paid for playing with him. Besides, she always gives me good stuff to eat."

Betty followed the nurse out, her busily talking voice fading as they went up the stairs.

Connie looked at her mother. "Ma?"

"Well?"

"Can't we go—just this once?"

"No."

"But why—"

"No, I said! If you want something to do so bad, clean the house. It looks like pigs live here."

"I just cleaned it—"

"Well, clean it again."

She stalked to the kitchen, and they could hear her

muttering as she ran water into a pan and slammed cupboard doors.

"You're sure dumb, Connie. Just get up tomorrow and go. You know Ma'll sleep all morning. She won't know if you're here or not. I won't even tell on you."

Connie shook her head. "You heard what the nurse said."

"You mean that stuff about obeying?" Myrna's lip curled in scorn. "Who's she to obey?" She glanced nervously toward the kitchen as she spoke and lowered her voice. Then she followed Connie into the bedroom. "How come you're hooked on this church business? Betty I can see. She's just a gullible kid and she's taken a liking to this nurse. But you're too old to be taken in by stuff like this."

"Mrs. Brewster says that Mike says—"

"Oh, I get it. Your snoopy friend's been taken, and you've gotten sucked into it too."

"No. It isn't that. That's not the reason. I read this book Betty got while she was in the hospital. It—it tells about God. About how He loves you—"

"Don't give me any of that line. That's a lot of baloney."

"That's what I thought too. But then I read this book last Sunday—"

Myrna whirled on her, keeping her voice low. "Last Sunday? Why last Sunday?" She reached out and grabbed Connie's arm. "What do you mean by that crack about last Sunday?"

"Nothing! I just meant I found out things. In that book. And then talking to Mrs. Brewster. I—I wasn't talking about you—"

Myrna shook her. "What's there to talk about me? Just don't get so smart-acting around me. You hear?"

"Yes. Let go! You're hurting me."

"I'll hurt you more if I ever find out you said anything

about me to anyone. What's done is done, and it's nobody's business. I'll do my own explaining when it's necessary."

Connie backed against the wall, rubbing her arm. When she was out of reach she said, "You ought to read the book too. Maybe it would make you nicer."

"Yeah? Let's see this church jazz work in you first if it's so great. Then maybe I'll believe it."

Myrna reached for the jar of face cream, her eyes lifting to catch Connie's in the mirror, and she stopped, startled at the pinched and stricken expression that came over Connie's face. She half turned to see her better, but as she did Connie turned abruptly and went out to the kitchen. Listening, Myrna could hear her clattering dishes. Finally she shrugged and massaged cold cream into her face.

No telling what's eating her. But Connie's words about Sunday brought a reminder of her problem. A line deepened between her eyebrows. On Monday she had to face everyone. She stared back at herself. One thing was certain. "No one is going to know anything for sure about me. No one!" She whispered the words aloud fiercely, her hands gripping the edge of the dresser.

But going back to school was worse than she had anticipated, not knowing for sure how much anyone knew or had guessed. She did a slow burn all Monday as she sat through one boring class after another, handing the pass slip to each teacher to be signed.

Just like a little kid, she thought in disgust. She shrugged off all the curious questions about where she'd been.

"Ever hear of appendicitis?" she finally snapped back at Karen's question.

"You caught it from your sister, I'll bet," Karen agreed with that slow, sly smile Myrna had always tried to copy and now hated, wanting to reach out and wipe it off her face.

The week dragged by. The heavy snows and icy winds off the lake made trudging back and forth to school bitter. All week she successfully fended off Alec's efforts to give her a lift home, a couple of times cutting the last hour to leave before he did. But on Friday as she slammed her locker shut and turned to leave, he blocked her way, putting a hand on the wall on either side of the locker and leaning toward her possessively.

"Anybody'd get the idea you didn't like me anymore." He looked down at her, and she felt unaccustomed panic grow in her. She'd never been afraid of him before. At least not until the other night. But then she'd never noticed how his lids hooded his eyes, making them narrow cold slits under his thin eyebrows. *Like–like a snake,* she thought suddenly, and felt trapped as he loomed over her.

"What's the matter, baby," he coaxed. "Come on, I'll take you home and stop for something to eat. You're kind of skinny these days. You know I like my girls to be an armful." He grinned down at her and she forced a smile back.

Her mind raced, looking for a way out as she gave him a provocative glance, her lips pouting. "Ok, I'll hitch a ride but you can drop me off downtown."

"Come on! This is Friday. We should celebrate."

"I can't. I'm going to look for a job. I've decided to quit this drag."

"Smart girl."

He took her elbow and steered her out to the car. She let him slide her in from the driver's side, sitting close to him. "How about it? Pick you up about eight tonight? Or are you babysitting again?" His voice was mocking, but his eyes were hard as he stared down at her.

She tilted her head back and smiled up at him, keeping

the pout on her lips while she scrabbled frantically for the right answer. Could she do it? Could she keep him at arm's length until he got tired and gave her up? She'd have to go out with him sooner or later. There would be no escaping him if he knew she was trying to. *Maybe—maybe if I act like I'm crazy about him it'll turn him off.*

"Eight o'clock. I'll be ready." She leaned forward to peer out the windshield. "Where are we? Here, let me out here. I want to try this place first."

"Here? It's a woman's store. What you want to work here for? No guys can hang around here."

"I've had it with greasy hamburgers." She made a face, laughing back at him over her shoulder as she slid across the seat and reached for the door handle. "Anyway, you can always wait for me out front."

Car horns blew impatiently behind them and she opened the door and got out, leaning down to look in at him. "See you tonight. Keep your fingers crossed for me."

She stepped through the crusty snow in the street, feeling some of it slide inside her shoe, and stood shivering on the sidewalk. Alec whipped the car through the yellow light, the exhaust from the tail pipe a white cloud in the cold air. She stood motionless. How could she have been so stupid to get involved with him? And how was she ever going to get away? There was no help anywhere, nobody she could talk to. Certainly not Ma. Her mind circled Mrs. Brewster's name, remembering the direct, level expression in her gray eyes, and a faint hope stirred. No—she was too nosy. The nurse? She would only purse her lips and preach, telling her she should go to church. This was something she would have to work out herself—somehow.

She turned slowly and pushed through the revolving doors into the warmth of the store. A clerk who was arranging scarves on a counter near the door looked at her.

"Yes?"

Myrna shifted her armload of books and smiled. "I'd like to apply for a job."

The woman looked her up and down and answered curtly, "We don't hire inexperienced help."

"But I can learn—"

"Not interested." The woman moved away, her hands busy with the scarves, but Myrna knew she was listening for her to leave. She stuck out her tongue at the stiff back and turned away, but stopped abruptly as she glimpsed herself in a mirror by the door.

No wonder she isn't impressed, she thought grimly, seeing her hair tangled by the wind, the smudged lipstick, the stack of books clutched against her thin jacket as though for protection. She walked down the street a block to the department store on the corner of the avenue and took the escalator up to the women's lounge. It was empty, and she dumped her notebook and books in a corner behind the tall wastebasket and went to work on her face. She carefully applied fresh base and gels and outlined her mouth with lipstick before adding extra gloss. Then she brushed her hair carefully, sweeping it back from her forehead and fastening it with a wide barrett.

She frowned at herself. Did she look older? She twisted to look at her reflection, straightening her shoulders and sucking in her stomach. Thank goodness she was thin and not slobby fat. Satisfied, she picked up her jacket, wishing it were a coat and less juvenile-looking. She debated wadding it up and leaving it in a corner with her books. But it would look funny to come in to apply for a job on a cold day like this without a coat. Besides, old as it was someone might take it before she got back, and if she didn't get a job she couldn't afford a new one.

She put the jacket on and twisted again to see herself. It didn't look too bad. Just bad enough to make it clear that she really needed a job. Maybe it would soften up whoever had charge of hiring people.

She took the escalator to the first floor, wondering where the employment office would be. Strolling over to the cosmetic counter, she sniffed the perfume fragrance that was advertised as the month's special, sizing up the two clerks behind the counter. One with piled, glazed hair looked like an imitation beauty queen; the other was younger and less sophisticated-looking.

Myrna picked up several bottles, sniffing them, until she caught the eye of the younger clerk. After pretending interest in the perfume, she asked casually, "By the way, who do I see about getting a job?"

"You have to go up on fourth floor. Go past the credit department to the desk by the door that's marked private." She looked at Myrna. "How old are you?"

"Sixteen."

"You're through school already?"

"No. If I get a job I'm going to quit."

The clerk shook her head, sympathy showing in her eyes. "They'll never hire you. Better try the dime store or look for a waitress job."

"Who wants to work in the dime store?"

The clerk shrugged. "It's one way to get experience. Believe me, you can't buck the we-only-hire-experienced-help line they give you in these places. I know. Go ahead and try if you want to but you'll find you're wasting your time."

Myrna took the escalator to the fourth floor and followed directions to the desk. The woman sitting at the typewriter looked up at her.

"Well?"

"I want to apply for a job."

"Your age?"

She started to say "eighteen" but stopped. It would be too easy for them to check that. She remembered how Ma had fumed at having to put her right age down for her social security card.

"Sixteen."

"Too young."

"But—"

The woman's voice was heavy with impatience as she interrupted. "Look, we have more people applying for work than we have openings. Some of them are women who are supporting families. We're not taking inexperienced help—especially kids who should be in school learning to amount to something."

She turned her back, rolled paper into the typewriter and began to pound out a letter, ignoring Myrna.

Myrna turned slowly and went back to the lounge and picked up her books. *I might have known it wouldn't work out. The dime store! Who wants to work in the dime store!*

The whole idea was to work in a place where she could earn good money and maybe get a discount on clothes. She went down to the first floor, circling behind the perfume counter to avoid the clerk there, and went out into the cold. She moved along with the shoppers who were huddled in coats and stopped reluctantly in front of the dime store.

"I might as well try it," she finally muttered. "No use wasting the time I spent on my face."

The manager gnawed at his lip as she talked to him. When she told him her age he asked, "Your folks know you're planning to quit school?"

"It's just my mother. My dad ran out on us and I need a job to help support my two younger sisters." She looked up at him, her eyes wide and pleading.

"I've heard that story before. Sometimes it's true, sometimes not." Then before she could protest that it was true, he said, "Well, we've got the Christmas rush coming on so we need help bad. If your mother says it's OK for you to quit school, we'll take you on. Temporarily, anyway. Start tomorrow. Be here at eight-thirty. Sharp."

"Oh, thank you," she breathed, but he had turned away and she made a face at his retreating back. Who did he think he was to be so bossy?

The smell of the food at the nearby lunch counter made her mouth water and she debated what to do. If she ate now to stop the gnawing feeling in her stomach, she wouldn't have enough money for bus fare. And if she took the bus, there wouldn't be much at home to eat. Well, she'd eat what there was and then make Alec buy her something later on.

She went out into the gathering darkness and ran for the bus that was pulling to the curb for other passengers. Crowding on, she pushed to the back. As she clung to the back of a seat on the swaying bus, she tried to decide what to wear tonight. Probably none of her stuff had been washed while she was in the hospital. If she didn't look after herself, no one else would. The bitterness of her thoughts obliterated the cold in the half-block dash from the bus stop to the house. She banged the door behind her, dumping her books on the couch on the way to the kitchen. Connie was bent over a notebook, chewing the end of a pencil.

"What are you doing now?"

"Trying to figure out how to fix this recipe when we don't have half the stuff it calls for," Connie answered without looking up.

"You've really gone domestic, haven't you?"

"Someone has to."

"Ma must not be home or you wouldn't talk so smart."

"She's not coming home 'till late. She called."

"You never did tell me who her new boyfriend is."

"I don't know him."

"You've seen him?"

Connie nodded. "He was here once. When Betty was in the hospital."

Myrna looked at her, caught by a sound in her voice. "Betty wasn't here, huh? And neither was I. That means—that means Ma probably didn't tell him about us. She wouldn't want him to know she had kids until she had him snared. You think she's angling for him?"

"She said—that night—she said she was trying to work things out. For all of us she said."

Myrna stood tapping her fingers on the kitchen table, concentrating on the thoughts that circled. "What's he like?"

"Awful!"

"What do you mean? Is he old?"

"No. I suppose he's Ma's age. But he looks—he looks—he acts like—" Connie stopped.

"Well, if he's someone who'll get us out of this dump, I'm all for him, no matter what he's like. Hurry up with whatever you're cooking," she threw back as she headed for the bedroom. "I'm going out tonight."

She stopped short in the bedroom doorway, looking at the clothes in neat piles on her side of the bed.

"What's all this?" She turned to look back at the profile view of Connie.

"I washed today so I wouldn't have to tomorrow. Your stuff was there so I threw it in too."

Connie didn't look around as she answered. Myrna turned slowly to walk over and stare down at the neatly folded and pressed clothes. What was Connie doing anyway, being so helpful? It made her mad. Then she shrugged. Whatever the reason, she might as well take advantage of it.

15

Acting Like Sisters

THE BEAT OF THE COMBO and the figures jerking in a dance ate into the headache that had been building all evening. The smoke curling up from cigarettes hung heavy in the air, making her eyes water. It was hot in the basement room and she was having trouble trying to be casual about fending off Alec's possessiveness. She knew it was useless to suggest leaving before he was ready to go, but finally about one o'clock he agreed to take her home on her plea that she had to get a couple of hours sleep before getting up for work.

He pulled to a stop in front of the house, slouching behind the wheel as she fumbled for the door handle.

"Maybe I'll come in and buy something from you."

She tried to match his light tone and pouted, "That only does the store some good. Buy something *for* me instead—like lunch."

She slammed the door and hurried down the steps to the porch, listening to the motor roar as his car pulled away from the curb. All the mothers on the block would be screaming tomorrow if the noise woke up their kids. She'd better get in before they knew who to blame. As she opened the outside door, she could hear Kevin crying and see the light shining in a thin line from beneath the door at the top of the stairs. "All I need is a crying kid to keep me awake the rest of the night," she muttered and slid quietly into the apartment.

Good! Ma's door was still open. *What luck to get in before she does. All that talk about making me stay in is a lot of baloney when Ma never stays home herself.*

She snapped on the light in the bedroom, ignoring Betty's whimper as she roused slightly and then flopped over on her stomach. She set the alarm and creamed her face and then undressed, pulling on pajamas quickly. Hauling the blankets from where they were both wrapped tightly around Connie, she crawled in and huddled shivering against Connie's back. Her mind refused to quiet, but circled with thoughts that whirled in a crescendo of anxiety. Kevin's persistent crying was a reminder of what she had been spared. . . Alec was going to be a problem. . . He wouldn't let her drop him. . . No one else would date her as long as they thought she was Alec's girl . . .

She turned restlessly but shifted back again quickly to lie close to Connie. It was easier to be young like Connie, or better yet, like Betty who didn't face any of these problems. But she would. Problems were unavoidable when you had to live the way they did. Nothing helped when you had no money.

As her mind slowed, drugged by the need for sleep, the unwelcome thought of church intruded. All Connie's talk about God . . . Was there escape that way? *Probably,* her mind jeered. *But that means losing the excitement and thrill of belonging to the group.*

She roused finally when Connie shook her saying crossly, "For crying out loud, when you set the alarm at least turn it off yourself!" Connie huddled down under the covers again while Myrna stared stupidly at the clock. It couldn't be seven already! She sat up groggily.

The job wasn't worth it. New clothes weren't worth getting up in a freezing house before it was light. She was crazy to do it. Somehow she dragged out and dressed, ignoring Connie's complaints when she pulled on the light to make up her face. She went out to fix coffee but found the jar empty and stared down at it grimly. The only good thing about going to work today was not being here to hear Ma yell when she had to go without coffee too.

The bus was crowded when she got on, and the driver stopped to pick up passengers at almost every corner. The door of the store was locked when she tried to push through, and she rattled the knob. Putting her face against the glass, she peered into the dim interior and could see a few figures moving around at the back of the store. Finally a woman came to the door. Myrna could see her lips move with the words, "Not open yet."

"I'm supposed to start work today," Myrna mouthed back. She watched as the woman called something over her shoulder to someone out of sight. After a moment the manager came to the door and unlocked it. "You're late. Don't make a habit of it or you won't last long."

Forcing back the angry retort that rose automatically to her lips, Myrna said apologetically, "I'm sorry. The bus was so crowded I couldn't get off at the right stop and had to go two extra blocks."

"Well, next time start earlier. Come back and I'll assign you to the section clerk who'll be telling you what to do. Today you'll just restock counters."

By ten o'clock Myrna didn't think she could possibly make it through the rest of the day. Her feet ached and her mind was fuzzy from lack of sleep. Nothing she did was right. When Alec loomed up suddenly beside her, she dropped the box of buttons she was holding, scattering them across the floor.

"Save your visiting for your break or lunch hour," the section clerk snapped. She frowned at Alec. "If you aren't here to buy something, take yourself someplace else."

Alec leaned against the counter, his hands in his pockets, a grin on his face. "OK, OK, don't get excited. I'm shoving off." He looked at Myrna. "See you tonight. Eight o'clock."

Myrna felt the command of his eyes and nodded weakly. She made herself wink back at him as he turned away, his hand lifted in a mocking salute to the clerk who only scowled at him.

Myrna gave a sidelong glance at her thin, ringless hand. *She probably thinks I've got an easy life with a boyfriend hanging around. If she only knew!* For a moment Myrna was swept by a longing to be old and safe and beyond the pressures and anxieties of life.

She dragged home at the end of the first week too tired to want to do anything but slump in a chair, grateful that Alec hadn't been around to command a date for the evening. Her feet were killing her and she just wanted to sit. Even the paycheck she had waited for so greedily to blow on the dress and shoes as a present for herself couldn't lift the exhaustion that weighed her down. She limped into the apartment, kicking the door shut behind her and sank onto the couch, letting her head fall back and closing her eyes.

After a few moments she looked across the room at Connie bent over a lap full of yarn, frowning down at a magazine. "What're you doing?"

"Making Ma a Christmas present. But don't tell her," Connie warned.

"You think she'll thank you? Especially for a home-made present? What is it anyway?"

"I got a couple of packages of these things that you make and then sew them together. You can make lots of different things like a long scarf or sort of a—I forget what it's called. An af-afghan or something like that—it's sort of like a shawl—"

"You think Ma's going to wear an old lady's shawl? You're nuts!"

"It's not to wear!" Connie's voice was defensive. "It's

to put over your lap to keep warm while you're sitting around watching television.''

"You're wasting your time. Be like me—I'm getting Ma a carton of cigarettes. What do you want to bet she'll like my present better than yours?''

"Mine will be better for her. She smokes too many cigarettes now.''

"Sure, but I dare you to tell her that.''

Connie didn't answer as she bent over her knitting, counting the stitches as she laboriously worked the needles.

"What are you getting me?'' Myrna shifted to the arm of the sofa as she asked, swinging her foot back and forth. Then, without waiting for an answer she gave a sudden short laugh. "Don't waste your time making *me* one of those whatever they are. I'm not about to sit around like a granny with something over my lap. That's what's such a laugh about making one for Ma. She never stays home if she gets a chance to go out on the town.'' She stared down at Connie's bent head and kept her voice casual as she asked, "By the way, how's her romance coming?''

"I don't know anything about it. And I don't want to.''

"You'd better care. You'll be right in the middle of it if Ma gets married again.''

"So will you.''

Myrna shook her head. "Not me. I'm getting out as soon as I can.''

Connie looked up, her eyes wide and questioning. "What do you mean? Where would you go?''

Myrna immediately regretted her spur-of-the-moment confidence when she had no plans and snapped back, "None of your business. And don't go blabbing to Ma either. Not that she'll care what I do as long as she doesn't have to pay out money to support me.''

But Connie's eyes were troubled as she looked across the room at her. "You can't just go someplace when you don't have any money. Ma—even Ma wouldn't want you to do that. She just sounds that way sometimes when she's tired or doesn't feel good. Her life isn't—well, easy, either.''

Watching her, Myrna felt her throat constrict as it had momentarily in the hospital when she had seen Connie's face silhouetted against the window. She saw the slender line of her cheek, almost gaunt in its thinness against the long hair shadowing her cheek. Her thick, stubby lashes hid her eyes as she looked down at the material in her lap, her hands still on the knitting needles. Someday soon the guys were going to discover her and then—

Myrna wrenched her thoughts away and her voice was harsh in its demand. ''Why all the sudden interest in my welfare? I've never known you to put on such a sisterly act before. And even making excuses for Ma! My, my, how good we are getting!''

Connie didn't look up as she answered, ''There's nothing wrong in trying to be nice, is there?''

''When you're being nice to me there's some catch. What skirt or sweater are you trying for this time?''

''None! I'm just—'' She stopped, biting her lip, still not looking up from the needles she twisted in her hands.

Myrna waited and then said impatiently, ''Well? You're just what?''

She could see Connie struggling for the words she finally blurted out. ''I'm just trying to act like a sister is supposed to. The Bible says we should be kind—''

''The Bible! Are you nuts? What are you fooling around with the Bible for? Wait'll Ma finds out. Anyway, where'd you get one?''

''I bought it. I got one out of the library first and then I bought one.''

''What a waste of money! If you've got it to throw away, give it to me.''

"It didn't cost much. Anyway, I earned the money babysitting Kevin. I saw Mrs. Brewster's and—"

"I might have known *she'd* be behind it. If you ask me, she's going nuts sitting up there all alone waiting for her husband to come home."

"He's the one who told her to get one. He wants her to read it all the time so they'll know the same things when he gets home."

"How come you know so much about them?"

"Mrs. Brewster talks to me lots. I like her." Connie's voice was defiant. "She's nice. She's like a sis—"

She bit off the word and gave a quick, upward glance from under her lashes. Myrna stared at her angrily, aware of the implied criticism, and heard Connie's anxious attempt to smooth over the moment. "I just mean we've talked a lot since I stay with Kevin. You'd like her too if you got to know her."

"You think I need advice from her? Sure, she can dish it out. She's got it made. She's free to do what she wants even if she is tied down with a kid. She gets money from him every month. She's got nothing to worry about—"

"Only her husband getting killed!" Connie's words were scornful as she broke in and Myrna whirled on her.

"I don't mean worries like that. Sure, that's rough. I'll admit it. But it probably won't happen. I'm talking about worries like you and I have. Living like this. With Ma like she is. I want to be a person, not just someone who's in the way. Mrs. Brewster can make her own decisions, do what she wants. What freedom have we got? None."

"It looks to me like you do what you want." The words came slowly and Myrna turned on her ominously.

"That sounds like a dirty crack to me. I told you to quit snooping in my business. What's past is past."

"I'm not snooping. I'm not!" Connie looked up, her eyes slowly welling with tears, her voice ragged as she spoke. "I just meant that you've got a job now. You're nearer to being on your own than Betty and me. We're stuck here for a long time yet. That's—that's why we want to go to church. We've got to have something to help us.'' Her voice was quietly stubborn as she added, ''Mrs. Brewster and the nurse both say God will help.''

Myrna looked down at Connie's narrow shoulders hunched over the heap of yarn and heard the yearning and misery in her voice, but she turned it off impatiently.

''That's your problem. If you and Betty can wrangle church out of Ma, go ahead. But don't expect any help from me. That's one place Ma and I agree. God and church?—that's a lot of soft soap and fake sweetness no matter what your precious Mrs. Brewster says. Wait'll she gets in a tough spot and see how much good it does her.''

Connie stood up, her face averted. ''I'd better put this stuff away. Ma'll be here pretty soon.''

Later, when Mrs. Hamilton went into the living room and reached for the television schedule, Connie followed and stood nervously in the doorway.

''Ma, next Sunday night the church is going to have a Christmas program and we—Betty and I—we—we—wondered if—''

''No, you can't go if that's what you're about to ask. How many times do I have to tell you that we're not having any church stuff around here?''

''What's the harm in them going one time?'' Myrna heard her words and saw Connie's startled, thankful look. *What am I doing getting in the middle of this argument,* she thought in disgust.

She watched her mother swing around to glare at her as she demanded, ''What are you butting in for? I don't need any help from you in running this family.'' She turned back to Connie. ''When is this thing?''

''Next Sunday. It's—Christmas Eve and they're having a program.''

"How'd *you* find out about it?"

Connie swallowed under her mother's suspicious look. "Mrs. Brewster told Betty she was taking Kevin."

Mrs. Hamilton adjusted the knobs and banged the sides of the TV while Connie stood with her hands gripped tightly together. Finally Mrs. Hamilton gave an impatient gesture. "OK, OK! Stop staring at me like a sick cow. All right, you can go. This once. Because it's Christmas Eve. Maybe Betty'll get some free candy and won't be everlastingly at me to buy her some." She turned abruptly. "How are you going to get there?"

"Mrs. Brewster said we could go with her—" Connie stopped, one hand going up to cover her mouth.

"Oh, so you already have all the plans figured out? I suppose if I'd said no you would have sneaked out anyway in spite of that nurse's fine words about obeying? I've a good mind to make you stay home after all."

"No, Ma. Really! We didn't plan anything. She just said *if* we went we could go with her. But I said we probably couldn't—"

"So now I find you talking everything over with her! Talking about me behind my back. After all the work I do for you! What kind of church business is that?"

"We didn't talk about you at all!" Connie was close to tears and her voice trembled. "But you always said we couldn't go to church so we didn't want to plan on it."

"Yeah, and then when I do let you go you don't even act grateful. That's the trouble with kids. You give in to them for every little thing they whine for, and then they're not satisfied."

She sat down on the sofa in front of the television set and Myrna followed Connie out to the kitchen, raising her shoulders in an exaggerated gesture. She waited until the water was running and laughed softly. "You should know by now that you can't win with Ma. You're wrong no matter which side you're on. Just don't argue with her

and slide along as best you can. In a couple of years
you'll be old enough to get a job. Then you can quit
school and be on your own.''

"I'm not going to quit. I'm going to college"

Myrna stared at her. "College! You're getting pretty
high up, aren't you? Where'd you get this big idea? Not
from Mrs. Brewster. I'll bet she barely made it through
high school. I suppose it's some of your nurse friend's
wise advice.''

She made her voice deliberately mocking, wanting to
slash and hurt. The lost, forlorn, left-out feeling that
gripped her suddenly made her mad, and she stalked from
the kitchen to pretend interest in the TV program Ma had
on.

When Betty clattered downstairs a few minutes later,
she went immediately to the kitchen. Myrna could hear
the murmur of voices and then Betty's excited gasp.
Apparently Connie has broken the big news to her, she
thought scornfully and stared across at Betty standing
shyly in the kitchen doorway. After a moment she darted
across the room and hugged her mother.

"Thanks for letting us go,'' she whispered and ran
back to the kitchen.

Mrs. Hamilton threw out her hands in a wide gesture.
"That's the trouble with kids. The only time they show
any gratitude is when they get their own way.''

The next Friday Myrna spent the day marking Christmas decorations down to half price. As she handled the
small, boxed, artificial Christmas trees, the memory was
vivid before her of Betty's wistful face the night before as
she had described Mrs. Brewster's tree. They'd had a
tree, she remembered, the year Betty was born. But not
since then. Not since Ma had to pay the bills. On impulse
she scrawled her name across a tree box and on a carton
of marked-down miniature lights to pay for when the
store closed. Ma would yell of course about how much

the electricity would cost to burn the things, but this time she could just yell.

When she got home, she looked around. "Betty here?"

"She's out playing."

Myrna tossed Connie the package. "Here. Find a place for this."

Connie pulled the tree out of the box and looked at it. Then she looked at Myrna, gratitude and delight lighting her face. "Myrna! It's beautiful! How did you know Betty's been praying for—" She stopped abruptly.

"For crying out loud! She's been praying for a Christmas tree? How nutty can you get?"

"It worked." Connie's voice was low but steady as she looked up from where she knelt on the floor. Then she went on quickly. "I'm going to put this together before Betty comes in. Ma has to work late, so is it all right if I put it on the kitchen table so she can see it real good while she eats?"

"Put it any place you want. As long as it's not in Ma's way when she gets home. She'll throw it out if she gets mad about it."

Connie shook her head. "No, she won't." She looked up at Myrna again, her voice quietly stubborn. "Betty prayed for two impossible things. That Ma would let us go to the Christmas program and that she'd have a tree of her own. And both things happened."

She stood up and looked at Myrna and then away quickly, and this time her voice was unsteady with emotion. "And the nicest thing is that *you* bought her the tree. We never thought God would do it that way."

"Well, if I did it, don't give God the credit," Myrna snapped back, her voice sharp even in her own ears.

But Connie stood unhearing, transfixed with another thought. Her voice was thin and breathless as she looked off across the room, not seeming to see Myrna. "I'm going to pray for something impossible too." Her eyes focused then on Myrna. "I'm going to pray that if Ma does marry that man, that he'll be—nice. That he'll—he'll say it's all right for us to go to church."

Anger swept Myrna at Connie's words, but with it came a feeling that she stood shivering on the outside of a room warm with happiness, wanting to enter but not knowing where to find the door.

16

Alec Cools Off

LIGHT FILTERED DIMLY along the frayed edges of the window shade, and Myrna lay staring at it, angry at herself for waking up a whole hour before she had to get up. She moved closer to Connie who was huddled on her side of the bed, and closed her eyes, trying to will herself not to think. But it was impossible, for pictures clicked off and on behind her shuttered eyes. . . Betty's face lighting when she saw the tree while tears ran down her cheeks . . . the way her hand reached out, not quite touching it for fear it would disappear. . . the blouse Connie had bought her for Christmas with money she'd saved from babysitting . . . the little packet of candy Betty had saved for her from the Christmas program at church. Then there were the darker images . . . the loneliness of sitting around the cold house Christmas day, wondering why Alec didn't call and yet dreading that he might . . . her mother's impatience at being stuck home all day and the bitterness of some of her words.

She turned restlessly again just as the alarm went off,

stridently loud in the quiet of the house, and she reached to silence it. Neither Connie nor Betty stirred, and Myrna looked enviously at Connie's back. *The only good thing about school is the decent vacation you get.*

She stumbled to the kitchen, yawning, and held her hands under the faucet, splashing water over her face and shivering in the chill of the house that made her ankles ache under the pajama legs. Ma was already gone, the ground-out cigarette in her empty coffee cup showing what she had had for breakfast. Myrna yanked open the refrigerator door, wrinkling her nose at the stale smell.

"That Connie! Nothing to do but sit around all day, and she can't even clean things once in a while!"

Her sleeve tipped over an open dish of canned peaches as she reached in for the margarine, and she dabbed futilely at the juice which dripped down to the next shelf. *Well, now maybe Connie will do some cleaning.* She backed against the door to close it and put water on to heat, staring out at the grayness of the day as she waited for it to boil.

Only the thought of the pay check at the end of each week kept her setting her alarm and forcing herself up each morning to make up her face and go out to the monotonous routine of each day. And there was Alec hanging around lately every day. There was the constant pressure of having to act crazy about him and cover her need to scream at him to keep away. And yet—she didn't want to get away completely. She craved the excitement, the thrill of being crazy and independent and free, of ignoring opinion, not worrying about what people thought. If she could just have the freedom without being trapped in the nightmare again.

There was no freedom when you were just sixteen and had no money. No matter how she added and multiplied, she ended up subtracting each week. There was nothing left of her salary by the time she bought the clothes and makeup she needed and gave Ma the ten dollars she insisted on every week for her room and board. It wasn't her place to support the family. It wasn't her fault Ma had to do it.

And now Connie and Betty were yapping about church and the Bible all the time. She thumped her coffee cup down on the table. That Betty—praying for two impossible things that came true. It *couldn't* happen that way —and yet it had. *Dumb kids!*

The weeks slowly marked off January with its bitter cold and short days and deep snows that left ice-crusted streets and sidewalks. February inched by just as slowly, though the days gradually lengthened. During the day the cold, brittle sunlight gave an illusion of warmth as it reflected on the store windows. But by quitting time as Myrna joined the crowds waiting for the bus, only the cold remained.

As March blew itself in with gusts that eddied through the cracks of the window in the bedroom, she realized that Alec wasn't coming in the store as often. She was partly relieved and partly jealous of whoever had caught his eye. *It's probably that sneak Karen.* If she had stayed in school she'd be in on the excitement of belonging to the crowd, on the heady thrill of knowing envious eyes followed her when Alec lounged at her locker or blared his horn for her to come running.

She caught her breath sharply at the danger of her regrets and turned abruptly. As she did, the box of dress patterns she'd been sorting, teetered on the edge of the counter and fell off, skidding patterns along the aisle.

She stooped impatiently for them, and an amused voice spoke from behind her. "Maybe if I help pick them up, I'll find the one I've been looking for for weeks."

Myrna looked around and scowled at the nurse.

"Every time I've been in lately, the clerk who is usually at this counter acts as though customers should be

barred from the store. She always says she doesn't have
the pattern you want—no matter which one it is. I know
because I've asked for a different one each time and she
always says, 'We don't carry that one.'" Her voice ran
on as she flipped through the pack and finished, "Aha!
Just as I thought. Here it is."

Myrna looked at the picture on the package. Flared
slacks with a matching fitted jacket. "You going to make
that?"

"Umm-hmm. I got material from myself for a Christmas present, but I couldn't find the right pattern. If I
don't get it made, winter will be over."

"Not in this place. Summer almost never comes
around here."

"Well, good. This can be a year-round outfit then."
She looked at Myrna, her head tilted. "Do you sew?"

"We don't have a machine," Myrna answered, not
adding that she didn't know how anyway.

"Too bad. You sure save a lot if you do. And have
more clothes too." She moved away with a friendly wave
and Myrna looked after her enviously. She had on a neat
outfit now, too.

She glanced at the clock and then began pulling the
long cloth over the counter, wondering as she did every
night whether any other store in the whole country followed this old-fashioned custom. Mr. Putnam's grand-
father had done it in the store he'd had, so now it was a
sacred custom. What a fussbudget the manager was.

At five-thirty Myrna pushed through the door into the
chill of the damp March day. The sound of a car horn
tooting at the curb made her look expectantly, hoping and
yet dreading that it would be Alec. It wasn't his car, and
she looked away until she heard her name called and
looked back over her shoulder.

"Can I give you a lift?" the nurse asked through the
rolled-down window.

The impatience that rose in her at being pursued was swallowed in relief at not having to wait for a bus.

She ducked in, shivering for a moment as the warmth of the car wrapped around her and then relaxing in it. She admired the ease with which the nurse slid the car smoothly into the flow of traffic, not talking until they were away from the stop and go of the downtown streets.

"How are your sisters?"

"Oh—like always. Betty's bugging Ma about Sunday school again." She was sorry the minute the words were out. She hadn't meant to give the preachy nurse that much of an opening.

But the nurse was frowning slightly. "She really shouldn't, you know. Your mother has enough to worry about without coping with that, too."

Myrna shrugged. "She doesn't let it worry her. She just yells no and that settles it. Ma doesn't waste words." But as she answered, her mind was busy with the nurse's words that implied pity for her mother. *What did she know about her mother? About their business. That Connie must be talking.*

They stopped in front of the house, and as Myrna reached for the door handle the nurse stopped her with a quick "Myrna—would you be interested in a skating party? Going to one, I mean?"

"Where? Who with?"

"With a bunch of kids your age. It's a church thing but not everyone who will be coming goes to—"

"No thanks."

"You don't skate?"

"Sure."

"Well, then, you can come and hold me up. I'm not much good at it."

"My skates don't fit anymore."

"We can find some that do."

"No. I don't like church kids."

"How do you know if you've never been around them?"

"I take after Ma." She pushed down on the door handle and shoved the door open, ignoring the nurse as she leaned across the seat to look up at her.

"If you change your mind let me know. It'll be next Saturday. I'll drop around the store Saturday morn—"

"Don't bother." Myrna slammed the door and ducked for the house to get out of the wind. She pushed through the apartment door feeling through the thin soles of her shoes the wetness of the puddles she'd stepped in. Connie looked around from where she sat hunched over a book at the kitchen table and then glanced at the clock.

"You're early."

"Thanks to your friend, the snoopy nurse. She's beginning to bug me. Every time I turn around, there she is."

"It got you a ride."

"The ride I can take. The preaching I can do without. What's to eat?"

"Spanish rice. Sort of."

"What do you mean, sort of? Is it or isn't it?"

"Well, we didn't have any bacon or green pepper so I just used rice and a can of tomatoes. And a little bit of cheese."

Myrna made a face. "If I'd known I was going to get a ride home, I could have used the bus money for a hamburger on my break. Instead I'm stuck with your cooking. Still, it's better than Ma's."

She gave a quick glance at her mother's door and Connie said, "It's a good thing for you she isn't home."

"That's OK. I'm paying my way around here. I deserve something decent to eat."

She went toward the bedroom, shrugging herself out of her jumper, and Connie followed to stand hesitantly in the doorway.

"What did she talk about? The nurse."

"Nothing. Invited me to a skating party."

"Me too?"

Myrna shook her head at the hope in Connie's voice. "She didn't even mention you. But don't worry. I turned her down. What a laugh! Me going to a church party."

"I could go in your place."

The hope was still there and Myrna faced her, hands on hips. "Look. I told her no and that's that. In the first place, she didn't ask you. In the second place, she asked me and I said no. In the third place, Ma would blow up if you asked her to go. So just quit bugging me about it. And quit talking to that nurse about our business."

"I haven't. She never asks personal questions. She's just interested in people. She never asks snoopy questions."

"Then how come she's always dripping with sympathy for Ma? Always feeling sorry for her?"

"Just because—well, because she's nice. *Some* people are, you know."

"Well, if she gets too interested, Ma'll fix her."

She almost regretted the refusal to the skating party when Alec came into the store Saturday noon and leaned close. She smiled up at him, her mouth pretending a welcome while her mind beat a frantic note of warning.

"I'd decided you'd forgotten all about me." She blinked her lashes as she looked up at him.

"Been busy."

His reply was almost absent-minded as he turned, his eyes following a girl who walked by. Myrna wondered what his return meant. Had he thrown Karen over too? She'd been pretending disinterest in him when kids stopped in the store after school and on Saturday, and no one had mentioned him lately.

He turned back to her. "There are a couple of parties going on we can take in tonight. I've got to get you back in the groove. I've been neglecting you lately. Pick you up around eight.''

She watched him walk off and then turned aimlessly to straighten items on the counter, not really seeing them. His words echoed in her ears all day and went home on the bus with her. Her throat was tight with the longing to have the thrills and excitement and the feel of belonging without the danger of being swept under as she so nearly had been. If she could just belong somewhere, to someone.

Running from the bus stop, Myrna felt salty tears mix with the driving March rain that pelted down in gray lines, washing away the final remnants of the winter snow.

The party was a drag, with Alec paying more attention to a couple of other girls than to her. She was relieved not to have his possessive attention centered on her, and yet mad too, wondering why he had brought her. *He must be trying to get even with someone.* His disinterest in her was plain when he pulled up in front of her house and left the ignition running as he stretched his arm across the back of the seat, his fingers drumming restlessly on the upholstery. Usually he pulled her to him for a kiss. Tonight he didn't, and she felt relief and regret, not sure which emotion was stronger. She didn't want his interest but she needed something. She couldn't stand the emptiness of being alone.

She turned toward him impulsively just as he reached to shift into drive. ''See you around, kid.''

The dismissal in his voice was too plain to be ignored, and Myrna slid across the seat, fumbling for the door handle to get out and away before the tears of hurt and anger spilled over. They would only amuse him, she was sure. He wasn't the kind to care for someone without demanding something in return. He had already proved that to her. Then why couldn't she be glad about his indifference? She stumbled blindly into the hall and fumbled for the apartment door.

"Myrna."

She jerked around and looked up at Mrs. Brewster sitting on the top step, her fingers laced together around her knees.

"What are you? My self-appointed spy?"

"I'd like to be your friend, if you'll let me."

"I've got friends."

"You could use another. Someone who'll be honest with you." She stood up and came down the stairs until she was on a level with Myrna. Her face was indistinct in the light shining out from the door she had left open upstairs.

"I know it's none of my business really. I'll admit that before I start. But I'm near enough your age to know or at least remember all the anxieties you're going through. I can't sit by and watch you ruin your life."

"I don't know what you're talking about." Myrna's voice was sulky.

"OK, let me give it to you straight. In case you haven't gotten around to admitting it yet, what you did was wrong. I know it probably happened so fast you didn't have a chance to think. And you've probably tried to push it out of your mind ever since. I don't blame you. But that's not the way to keep it from happening again."

"It won't! There won't be a next time."

"There will be if you keep on fooling around with this guy. He's no good the way he is now. Make a clean break with him. Get a new bunch of friends."

"How?"

"Find out which kids at school go to church—"

"You're trying to tell me church kids never do anything wrong?"

"No, I'm not saying that. It's not church that does it. It's God—"

"Save your preaching for Connie," Myrna exploded in a ragged voice. "She likes it, I don't. Just leave me alone!"

She shoved open the apartment door and closed it behind her, breathing hard as she leaned back against it. She listened to the sound of Mrs. Brewster's light steps going back upstairs and the tiny click of the door shutting. Her teeth clenched and her eyes squeezed shut to hold back the tears of anger and hopelessness.

17

An Unexpected Escape

HER ANGER AT MRS. BREWSTER made her side with Ma in alternately criticizing and ridiculing everything Connie did.

"What's this supposed to be?" Mrs. Hamilton poked at the noodles on her plate.

"Lasagna."

"What's that?"

"It's good!" Betty's words came muffled through the food that swelled her cheek.

"What's it got in it?"

"Just hamburger and tomato sauce and noodles—"

"What's the funny taste?"

"It's the sauce you make it with. You buy this little package of stuff and add it to the meat—"

"How much did that cost? I don't want you throwing money away on any fancy packages of stuff."

"Mrs. Brewster gave it to her—"

"Keep still!" Connie whirled on Betty, cutting off her words.

"Mrs. Brewster again, huh? I've a good mind to go up and tell her off, tell her to keep out of my business. Snoopin' around here to find out what we're eating. *I'm* the one buys the food around here, and we don't need her butting in acting like a fairy godmother."

Myrna watched her mother take another big serving of the casserole. Leaning forward to tap the ash off her cigarette into her saucer, she looked across at Connie. "What's all that stuff in the box under our bed?"

"What stuff?" Connie's defiance was only in her voice as her eyes flicked from Myrna to her mother and back again.

"You know what I mean. All that material."

"I'm—making something."

"Now what? Who for?" Her mother's demand cut across Connie's nervous gestures of gathering up the dishes, and she turned to face her mother desperately. "It's just—just something I'm making."

"What?"

"Something to wear."

"For yourself?"

Connie shook her head, looking away from the building anger in her mother's face.

"For your precious Mrs. Brewster, I suppose."

Myrna watched Connie look down at the dish she was gripping and shifted impatiently. "Let her alone, Ma. If she wants to waste her time with stuff like that, let her."

"I don't need advice from you." Myrna shrugged under the look her mother threw at her and sat back. "There are going to be some changes around here one of these days, so don't get too uppity if you know what's good for you."

In the silence Connie's voice was loud as she asked, "What k-kind of changes?"

Mrs. Hamilton stood up, tightening the belt of her robe as she turned away from their questioning eyes.

"Never mind. You'll find out when it happens." She half turned suddenly to look back at them and then gestured defensively, almost pleadingly. "It's something that will make things better for us all. You'll see."

"Are we gonna move away?" Betty's voice piped thin in their ears as they listened to the bedroom door close. "Are we?"

Connie looked across the table at her and shook her head. "I don't think so," she said, her voice uncertain. Then, "Aren't you going up to read Kevin a story while Mrs. Brewster does some sewing?"

They listened to Betty pound through the living room and bang the door behind her. Connie looked across at Myrna. "Ma's going to get married again for sure."

"So? What's so tragic about that?"

"It'll change everything."

"We can stand some changes. If he's got a job maybe we'll get out of this dump. Things couldn't be any worse."

Connie turned on her, her voice shaking. "Is he going to want to pay out money to take care of a whole family? And what if he isn't—isn't nice? What if he's mean to us—to Betty? What'll Ma do?"

"Stick Betty in a home and make us get out." Myrna's voice was expressionless.

Connie turned away, her eyes brimming with tears. Myrna sat at the table tapping her fingers restlessly on the oilcloth as she watched Connie scrape the dishes and run water into the kettle to heat. Then she stood up. "Well, there's no use worrying about it. If it's going to happen, it will. Anyway, there's always your magic that might work."

"What do you mean?"

"All that praying for the impossible you were talking

about. Remember?'' She looked at Connie's thin back held rigid against the sink and waited, but Connie didn't turn around or answer.

Mrs. Hamilton said nothing more about her plans as the days finally warmed, melting even the lingering piles of snow along the back of the house where the sun seldom reached. Alec had stopped coming into the store, and kids who came in after school to fill up the snack counter stools didn't seem to know who he was dating.

"Not Karen even though she wishes he were," Marcia reported. "He got tired of her hanging on him. He only runs after the ones who play hard to get. Then he drops them once he's gotten them hooked." There was silence as everyone looked at Myrna and then away.

Myrna looked back evenly. "Yeah, if you wait long enough he might even get around to you."

Marcia shrugged. "Who wants him? You never know what'll happen when you go out with him."

Myrna managed to keep an amused smile on her lips while the forbidden words crowded against them. The past was too far gone to be brought back by her anger which could be interpreted as guilt. No one knew anything for sure about her and never would.

She was unprepared to hear Alec's voice behind her in the aisle the next day.

"Hi, beautiful. Miss me?"

"Would it do me any good?" she asked pertly, glancing at him from under her lashes, while fear thudded in the hollow place in her throat.

"Maybe. I'm going to pick you up at seven tonight, and we'll make the rounds." He walked off with a careless wave and she stared after him, feeling the pounding of her heart. What had brought him around again just when she thought she was beginning to get free? And why hadn't she invented some excuse, *anything* to keep from going out with him? But what Marcia had said was true. If she acted as though she didn't want to go out with him, he'd never let her alone.

Her fear made her edgy the rest of the day and rode home with her on the bus. Betty banged into the house for supper and knocked into the ironing board Myrna had set up in the living room to press her long-sleeved blouse. Myrna grabbed for the iron as it fell over, burning her wrist, and turned to give Betty a swat.

"Watch where you're going, will you?"

Betty ducked out of reach, swung away, and skidded on the linoleum, the thin soles of her shoes sliding her across the floor. She lurched back but not in time to avoid hitting the wall with her shoulder. As she slumped to the floor she cried out in pain and Connie came to the kitchen doorway.

"What's the matter?" She looked from Myrna to Betty who was struggling to get up, and ran to kneel beside her, looking up at Myrna. "Can't you ever be nice to anybody?"

"Can I help it if she doesn't look where she's going? It would have hurt her worse if she'd run into the iron." Myrna rubbed at the burn on her wrist and stared back at Connie.

She watched as Betty stood up, rubbing her shoulder, tears streaking a clean path down each cheek.

"Are you all right?" Connie knelt in front of her, looking up anxiously, and Betty nodded as she wiped the tears away with the back of her hand.

"She's not hurt that bad," Myrna said scornfully. "You'd think I did it on purpose. It was her own fault."

Connie got up without answering and stalked out to the kitchen, and Myrna could hear her getting dishes out of the cupboard. Betty followed, her thin high voice floating back. "Want me to set the table for you, Connie?"

"Yes, but wash your hands first so we don't all get germs."

"What do germs look like?"

"I don't know. I've never seen any."

"Then how do you know I've got them?"

"Because your hands are dirty. Wherever there's dirt, there's germs."

Myrna leaned over to unplug the iron and carried it out to the kitchen. "If you don't quit the health lesson we'll never get supper. What is it anyway?" She lifted a lid from a kettle and sniffed suspiciously. "What did you do to the hamburger this time?"

"It's just a recipe I found in a magazine. I don't remember what it's called." Connie's voice was cool and distant, and she didn't bother looking at Myrna as she answered.

"And anyway, Connie's a *good* cook. *Whatever* she makes is good." Betty went over to stand close to Connie.

Myrna looked at them, a flare of jealousy stifling her. The two of them were joined together, leaving her outside the circle with no one to confide in, no one to tell how afraid she was of life, how much she dreaded the evening ahead with Alec and yet how she couldn't stand not having fun with someone.

Betty turned and began setting the table and Connie turned to reach into the refrigerator. Myrna wanted to cry, "Help me! Talk to me!" Instead she ran water into a kettle and slammed it onto the stove to heat. "I'm going out tonight so hurry it up. At least we don't have to wait for Ma."

When supper was ready she ate silently, listening to Betty's chatter and Connie's replies, and then went to dress, paying no attention to Connie's, "You *do* have time to do the dishes."

She was ready when she heard the blare of the horn and ran out to the car, swept up in the old excitement of having something to do and someplace to go. The fine drizzle that had been falling when she came home from work had cleared, leaving the air damp but mild with that indefinable but exciting hint of spring. She was glad to see that Alec hadn't put down the top of his convertible as he usually did as soon as the air warmed slightly. She knew he liked the feel of the wind and the sound of it whistling in his ears, adding to the illusion of speed and danger. But she hated it tangling her hair and blowing against her eyelids, making her squint against its pressure.

"Where we going?" she asked as she slid in next to him.

He gave his usual careless shrug. "Everyplace. No place. Just bumming around."

And they did, dropping in for ten or fifteen minutes on one party and then another, picking up several other couples along the way. From a party in a housing project north of the city, Alec drove up along the ridge road, circling above the lights of the city and the bay with the mournful sound of the foghorn wailing its warning in the damp grayness of the night. Then he swept the car around the eastern edge of the city and headed back to the bright lights of the downtown and then beyond to the psychedelic flashing lights over the entrance to the billiard parlor.

"Let's go shoot some pool." His voice was a flat statement which gave the others in the car no chance to express an opinion. Myrna followed him into the crowded, smoke-clogged room, loud with pulsating rhythm. Alec joined the group at the pool table and Myrna gave a swift glance around the room trying to assess who was there that she didn't feel too out of touch with. She finally drifted over to a table full of girls whose guys were also clustered shooting pool.

She sat on the fringe of conversations as she looked around the dirty room, the floor littered with cigarette butts and crushed, empty packs. She had no feel of belonging. She lit a cigarette, feeling the trembling of her hands as she went through the familiar motions, and realized that she was jumpy. She tapped her fingers on the table in time with the beat blasting through the room but tonight it grated her nerves, stretching them wire-tight.

The regular, casual disappearance of one or two through the door leading to a back room added to her nervousness. Their reappearance a little later heightened her suspicion that they were shooting dope and she kept a nervous eye on Alec. If he went back there, she would figure out some way to get home. She would not get mixed up in that. Drink she could handle now and then; dope, no. It was the end of the road from which there was no return.

But Alec didn't go back and after half an hour he sauntered over to her. "Let's go."

She followed obediently, hoping desperately he would take her home even though it was only nine-thirty. Maybe she could pretend to be sick—she certainly felt as though she were going to be with the headache that was building up to an intolerable pressure. This time Alec put the top down before getting in and wheeling out of the parking lot.

"The police are going to bust that place one of these days." His voice was matter of fact and she glanced at him quickly, seeing his lean profile and thin lips. An uncontrollable shiver shook her and he glanced at her and then pulled her close. "Cold?"

She nodded, holding herself rigid. She didn't dare let him guess that she was cold with a sudden, overpowering fear of him that made her skin clammy and the palms of her hands sweaty. If she got home safely this time she was never going out with him again. Never! But she had to keep the resolve safely hidden so she sat close to him and slitted her eyes against the rush of wind. He drove with a sure carelessness, one arm draped around her shoulders and the other resting loosely on the wheel. She had no idea where he planned to go, what he had planned for the rest of the evening. Mrs. Brewster's warning beat an insistent refrain in her mind. *He's no good – He's no good – Make a clean break.* She swallowed her panic as he headed back toward the business area again, flashing past the winking neon lights over hamburger joints, restaurants, and movie houses.

An abrupt blare of music and snatches of words in song reached their ears as they waited for a light to change. Myrna looked across Alec to see the group clustered outside the mission building on the corner of the avenue. Alec looked too until a horn blared behind him and he swung the car left up the avenue and then turned left again at the street.

"I'm going back to take another look at those creeps."

"Why bother?"

"I've seen them out there before singing religious stuff. Some of 'em hang around school too."

Alec turned down the hill at the next avenue as he answered and then along the street. This time he pulled up along the curb, moving the car slowly forward until he was almost even with the group. One of the guitarists was a slender blonde, her long hair pulled smoothly back from her forehead and caught at the back in a wide barrett. In spite of the wind, her blown hair was ruffled rather than tangled and her face was lighted with a smile as she strummed and sang words that Myrna couldn't quite hear. She looked at the others in the group, remembering some of them from school, and then back at the blonde and frowned. Ann something. A junior transfer from California after school had started. She'd been in chemistry and Myrna remembered how much she'd talked religion. Like the nurse. Craning her neck to see if the nurse was in

the group, Myrna looked up at Alec with a mocking,
"What a bunch of nuts!" Her eyes followed the direction
of his as he stared at the blonde. So it wasn't all the creeps
he wanted another look at but that one creep.

Well, well, the cool Alec interested in someone religi-
ous! Amusement choked her as she glanced up at him
again and then back at the group. They had finished singing and were handing out pieces of paper to the few people walking by. A couple of boys who looked like junior
high age began putting the papers under the windshield
wipers of cars parked along the curb until one of the older
men with the group shook his head at them, motioning
them to take the papers back. One of the boys walked by
and glanced at them. He came over to the car, holding out
a paper. "Want one?"

Alec looked at the folded paper the boy held out and
then reached for it. He flipped it over and the question
"Where are you going?" stared up at them. With a sudden violent motion Alec crumpled the paper and threw it
in the gutter. Then he pulled the car away from the curb
and swung up the avenue again. Myrna had seen him mad
with this white anger often enough to know that even an
attempt at humor now would bring a savage reply, so she
said nothing as she sat with her hands gripped together.
In this mood he was a dangerous driver as he drove fast,
taking the corners on squealing brakes. She was weak
with relief when he headed toward her house and pulled
to a stop in front of it, saying abruptly, "See you around
sometime."

She slid across the seat and out of the car and stood in
the quiet softness of the night, watching until the car
disappeared around the corner. There was an unreality to
standing alone in the darkness of the spring evening.
Alone and safe. She knew now that she hadn't felt safe all
evening. At the parties where there had been loud laughter and drinking, in the billiard parlor with the door to the

back room opening a few inches to admit those who slid through, Alec's thin lips and hooded eyes had given her the chilled feeling of a snake hypnotizing its victim before it struck. There had been reason for her to be afraid.

Then abruptly it had all changed. Alec's anger at the question on the paper had turned his thoughts and plans from her, and she had been delivered. She closed her eyes and swallowed hard, the fingers of both hands pressed against her mouth. Something—or someone—had delivered her.

She felt herself trembling in the chill of the night air and turned to walk slowly down the broken steps and along the path to the porch. She pushed the outside door open and stepped into the hall quietly. It was early yet, but habit made her close the door soundlessly behind her. The apartment door stood open a few inches and she heard voices inside. One of them, Connie's, was broken, almost incoherent, the other was soothing and murmuring.

"You said—you *said* so. You said it would work—that God would do it—and He hasn't! He hasn't! It doesn't work."

"Connie, Connie, dear. Listen to me—"

"But you said! You said God would do things in Ma and in Myrna—change them—if I believed Him. And I do. But He hasn't. They're just the same. And now Ma—Ma's going to get—m-married ag-g-gain."

"Connie, listen to me. God does work. He *does*. But not always the way we think He should. Or even the way we want Him to—or when we want Him to. I know you'll find this hard to believe, but He works in ways that are far better than we could plan for ourselves. Trust God, Connie. Don't try to make Him do what you think He should."

"But all I want is for Him to make things better here. So Ma will let us go to church. Both Betty and I try to be nice to them—at least most of the time—but they don't care. They only think about themselves. Myrna always says hateful things. And m-makes fun of us when we p-pray. And if Ma gets married—"

She broke off to cry again, and Myrna pushed in through the door, anger blazing as she saw the nurse sitting beside Connie, her arm around her shoulders.

"What's going on here anyway?"

Connie jerked around, her face swollen from the tears, but the nurse answered evenly. "Connie needed help and I stopped to give it to her."

"I'll bet Ma doesn't know you come sneaking around here when we're not home to know about it."

"She didn't sneak—"

"Hush." The nurse interrupted Connie's anger, her eyes still on Myrna. "I was visiting Mrs. Brewster at her invitation but I came down here because someone kept knocking on the door and wouldn't go away. Betty especially was frightened and afraid to go to bed."

"Well, I'm here now."

"Will you be of any help to Betty? Or to Connie?"

The question, asked quietly and with that direct look in the nurse's gray eyes, made Myrna angry. "I can do as much for them as you can telling them all that jazz about God."

The nurse glanced at her watch and stood up, looking down on Connie's bent head.

"I have to be on duty at eleven so I must go. But just trust God, Connie. Remember, you don't need a way out but just a way through your problems. Go back and read that story in the Bible about the young men who trusted God even when they went into the fire and it seemed as though God wasn't doing anything for them. He was. He was there with them. And He's with you, Connie, even when it doesn't seem like it."

She turned then to look at Myrna. "You can't get away

from Him either," she said gently. "Not with Connie and Mrs. Brewster and me praying for you. We prayed for you while you were out tonight. God loves you, Myrna, and wants you to love Him."

Myrna watched her go out the door and close it quietly behind her. She hugged her arms around herself, standing in the cold ragged room listening to Connie move around in the bedroom. She'd been thankful for her deliverance from Alec. Did she owe it to God? Was it because of the prayers? She shook her head, trying to clear her mind of its confused jumble of thankfulness and doubt and anger.

18

Mike Comes Home

SHE SPENT MOST OF SUNDAY loafing in bed, drifting in and out of sleep, refusing even to think of the anguish that had come through the tears in Connie's voice. "Bratty kid," she muttered. "Always blabs everything about us to that snoopy nurse."

She shuttered her mind against the quiet voice that intruded repeatedly through Monday's routine of work—"God loves you . . . He wants you to love Him." The words wouldn't go away. They stared at her from a downtown bookstore she had never noticed before, one that sold Bibles and other religious things. There was even a placard on the bus that mocked her with a quotation from some guy about God's love.

She got off the bus and walked the half block to the house, glad for the warming of the early April day. The air was shrill with the sound of children at play in the lengthening day after a long winter indoors. Mrs. Brewster was sitting on the front step watching Kevin struggle to make the wheels of his trike go.

"Sit down and join us."

Myrna shook her head stiffly but couldn't resist smiling back at the wide grin Kevin gave her.

"That's the thing he's been riding that's probably about driven you up the wall the last few weeks. I shouldn't have let him do it over your heads, but it's been too wet to take him out and he wants to know how to ride it when his dad comes home."

Kevin, sitting close on the trike, pushed at the pedals with his feet and gave his bashful smile. "Daddy come," he repeated.

Myrna turned back from the door to look down on Mrs. Brewster as she sat with her elbows propped on her knees, her chin in her hand. "Is he coming home? Discharged or just on furlough?"

Mrs. Brewster hesitated, biting her lip. "He's discharged apparently. I had a letter from him—only not really from him. He's been wounded but he didn't say how bad. Someone else wrote the letter for him. He—he kind of joked about whatever it is that's wrong with him. Said he was giving his hand a rest—" She stopped, her soft voice unsure and Myrna could see how white her knuckles were as she clasped her hands together around her knees. "It's probably nothing serious."

"Probably not."

Myrna pushed open the door and went into the hall, turning for another glimpse of the slender figure just as Mrs. Brewster reached suddenly to catch Kevin to her in a hug.

How do you get to be so lucky! Envy made her cheeks hot and her eyes burn. *To be independent and able to do what you wanted to. Not to have to listen to Ma's nag-*

ging. Not to have to drag out every morning and never have any fun and spend the day waiting on fussy old ladies who always complained that you sold them the wrong color thread.

Again regret at dropping out of school swept over her. School itself was a drag but at least you were in things, knew what was going on, knew people. The old hackneyed expression old Hanson used all the time in history last year came back—you had a chance to make something of yourself.

"But I am!" she told herself fiercely. "I'm doing what I want to do."

The living room was chilly after the warm outside. Connie wasn't home yet and Myrna turned to look out the window. Maybe it wouldn't hurt to go out and be a little friendly. As long as Mrs. Brewster didn't give advice on things that were none of her business—

As she went to the open door, she heard the murmur of voices from the porch. Connie's, young, unsteady, eager, as she said, "God won't *let* anything happen to him. He—He can't! He just can't!"

Mrs. Brewster's voice was low-pitched in reply. "I don't know, Connie. I don't know how things like this work. That's what I was asking the nurse about on Saturday."

"What did she say?"

"She didn't help much. She just said God always did what was best for those who love Him—"

"But how could Mike's being hurt be best for him? Or for you and Kevin?"

"I don't know. But—oh, Connie, I'm scared. I shouldn't be, but I am!"

Myrna heard the fear that colored Mrs. Brewster's voice and felt guilt at the memory of the times she had sneered at Mrs. Brewster's loyalty to her absent hus-

band. But then—maybe there wasn't anything wrong
with him after all.

She felt drained and decided to go to bed early, hoping
Ma wouldn't get going on the late movie. With the sound
acting up, the volume had to be turned on loud, and then
sometimes it blasted out unexpectedly. But Mrs. Hamilton went out right after supper, looking back over her
shoulder at them as though she had a secret she was
bursting to tell. She had been so pleasant at supper that
even Betty had watched her uneasily.

"I wonder what's going on," Connie worried. She
peeked out the side of the curtain at the living room window. "She's not getting a ride. There's no car out front.
Looks like she's walking to the bus stop."

"You're so nosy you should have asked her. And gotten a swat for butting in. You know Ma's going to do
what she's going to do no matter what."

Connie stood biting her lip and frowning, and suddenly
Myrna laughed. "Must be you've stopped praying for
God to make her sweet and loving." The words and tone
were mocking, and Connie whirled.

"Don't say things like that—not like that!"

"Why not? Don't you think He can?"

"Yes!"

"Well then?"

"Maybe—maybe He doesn't want to do it that way."

Myrna curled her lip in scorn. "What kind of a God
would let Ma go on acting the way she does? Or let that
guy upstairs get hurt after he talks about Him all the
time? Some God that is!"

"That's awful to say things like that." Betty came to
the bedroom door and looked at her, her hand clutching a
book and her lips quivering.

"You two are nuts. Just plain nuts!" Myrna went into
the bedroom, shoving Betty out of the way. "Read out in

the living room. I'm going to bed and I don't want the light on."

But the phone rang and she whirled to grab for it. "Hello? Who? . . . Ann—" Her voice flattened. "Yeah, I know who you are. . . Yeah, I saw you too. . . No, I'm not interested. . . No, I won't be interested next week either."

She slammed the receiver down. "Everybody's nuts!" she exploded and brushed past, ignoring the curiosity in Connie's face.

Ann's voice brought back into blurred focus Alec's evident interest in her and brought back too the memory of his violent anger at the paper he had been handed. She knew she would have felt the anger if he hadn't taken her home and then driven off so furiously.

She stood in the middle of the room, her thoughts nibbling at the edges of the strange puzzle. Was Alec really interested in the blonde? He couldn't be—Alec *couldn't* be seriously running after someone who stood on a street corner and sang religious songs. Sure he liked to chase a girl he thought was hard to get, but not one who went to church. Not Alec.

She undressed and slid into bed and lay staring into the shadowed corners of the room, the nagging uncertainty eating at her. When Betty came in and put on the light, Myrna threw one arm up over her eyes. "Turn that off! Leave the door open and you can see to undress by the living room light."

"OK!"

Myrna turned over, sighing loudly at the bumping, stumbling noises as Betty undressed. She had almost dozed off when Connie came in, moving quietly around the room. Myrna felt the bed shift but there was no feel of Connie getting in beside her. She half-opened her eyes and then raised her head to see Connie kneeling beside the bed, her hands folded on the blanket and her head bowed.

Connie felt her movement and raised her head, her eyes defiant in the moonlight shining in through the cracked windowshade.

"Well," she said in answer to Myrna's unasked question, "you said to pray. You said to ask God to change Ma. And to make Mike not be hurt bad. So I am."

"I suppose you expect an answer."

"Yes, I do. You'll see. I'll show you. Then maybe you won't think you know so much"

Myrna flopped over and listened to the silence on Connie's side of the bed and Betty's regular breathing deep in sleep. She thought of Ann's breathless "Wouldn't you like to come to one of our One-Way meetings?"

No, she wouldn't! She'd seen those posters with a finger pointing to the sky and thought they were dumb. She was not going to get mixed up in stuff like that. No matter who else did.

She was acutely conscious of Connie getting up and sliding into bed, turning her back and settling down against the pillow.

"Well, when the soldier boy comes walking home with both arms and legs in place, then you'll know your prayers got through." When Connie didn't answer, she asked, "What'd you pray for Ma for? That she'd sit in a rocking chair and knit?"

"You'd be surprised if that happened, wouldn't you?"

"I would. I sure would! But don't worry. I won't hold my breath. And you'd better not either."

It was just a lot of hocus-pocus. But if Alec– She shifted again irritably, mad at herself for getting worked up over nothing, and punched her pillow into a ball under her head.

The week was busy with the store full of customers

buying Easter baskets and candy and greeting cards. When she dropped down at the snack counter Saturday for her break, Karen slid onto the stool beside her.

"Hi." Her voice offered friendship and Myrna glanced at her, nodding her head in reply.

Karen ordered a hamburger and fries and spent time carefully extracting the straw for her coke from the paper casing. She stirred the drink aimlessly for a moment and then asked, "People—keep you up with the news, I suppose?"

Myrna shrugged. "Some. Whatever's important."

After a moment Karen said, "You know about Alec then."

"All I want to." Myrna kept her voice carefully noncommittal, ignoring the quick look she felt Karen give her.

"He's chasing the wrong one this time." Karen's voice was suddenly vicious and Myrna turned to look at her, surprised by the anger. "He won't get anywhere with this one. She's gone on religion and she won't have any part of him. Not unless he changes."

Myrna felt an unexpected surge of pity for her former best-friend-turned-rival and now a cast-off from Alec also. But she carefully restrained any impulse to confide. The renewed overture of friendship was too fragile to trust with confidences. She only hoped Karen hadn't— hadn't—*been as foolish as you were,* her mind chided and slid away from the reminder. They finished lunch in silence and Myrna got up from the counter stool.

"Have to get back to work. See you around."

"Myrna." Karen's hand fluttered out in a quick gesture. Then she looked away. "Never mind."

Myrna walked back toward her counter, glancing back once at Karen sitting hunched forlornly over her half-eaten hamburger, and wondered what she was thinking.

So there was something to the rumour of Alec's interest in the blonde. Her hands worked automatically all afternoon as her mind churned with the incredible thought. Would Ann go out with him? And where would they go? To church? Not Alec! She repeated the denial to herself angrily as the bus jolted her home, feeling as though this church business were hemming her in on all sides.

As she stepped into the dim hall, Betty was just clattering up the stairs, her face bright with excitement.

"Now what's going on with her?"

Connie looked up from the book she was reading. "She's amusing Kevin while Mrs. Brewster packs. She got word that her husband is in the hospital in Minneapolis, and she's flying down to bring him home."

"This is kind of sudden, isn't it? Did he write her?"

"No." Connie frowned as she answered. "She just got notified somehow—by the army, I guess. They said he was there for just another routine checkup or something before being discharged and would be released right away. Tomorrow, I guess."

"I suppose we're stuck with the kid until she gets back."

"No." Connie's voice was cold. "I *offered* to take care of him but she wants to take him along. Since she's flying it won't take long to get there and he's no trouble. And anyway, she wants his dad to see him as soon as possible."

"What's the matter with him? Her husband."

"I don't think they said. Anyway, if they did, Mrs. Brewster didn't tell me."

Betty hung over the bannister calling, "Connie, can you help me get Kevin's shoes on? He won't hold still for me."

"You'd better watch Betty or she'll tag along with them." Myrna pretended indifference but came to stand in the doorway as Mrs. Brewster came down the stairs carrying a small overnight case and a light coat draped over one arm.

She looked at them, tried for a smile, and then turned to Connie, biting her lip. "Pray for us, both of us," she said simply. "Mike has kept in such close touch but we've both changed in a lot of ways. For the better mostly. Anyway, I'm nervous even though I shouldn't be. It's been so long—and now, knowing he's wounded in some way—" she broke off as her voice caught.

"Here's the cab!" Betty tried to scoop up Kevin, his legs dangling, but he pulled away, squealing, and reached for his mother's hand.

"Take my case instead, Betty, and I'll carry him. We'll have to hurry. I don't want to miss the plane. We'll be back tomorrow in the late afternoon. Connie, would you sort of straighten up a little and maybe set the table with my good dishes? I cleaned real good but we've left things kind of messy-looking, and I don't want Mike to see it that way."

Connie nodded without speaking and watched as the driver helped them into the cab. Kevin scrambled up to wave out the back window, and they watched his face as the car pulled away from the curb and disappeared out of sight around the corner.

"Well, so at last we get to see the great Mike Brewster. I wonder if he's as good-looking in life as he is in his pictures."

Connie didn't answer as she turned and wandered into the house. She didn't seem to want to talk at all while Betty's mouth rattled all evening.

"Can I help you clean upstairs, Connie?"

"If you want to."

"Let's do it now—no, let's wait until tomorrow and then we won't have to wait so long until they come."

"What's it to you to get all excited over?" Myrna's

irritation at Betty's continual chattering finally spilled over. "He doesn't mean anything to you."

"He does, too! He's Mrs. Brewster's husband and Kevin's father, and I like them so I like him. And they like me, too. He told Mrs. Brewster to tell me he liked me because I was so good to Kevin. They're *always* nice. They're not just nice sometimes when they feel like being."

"OK, so I'm not. And this is one time I don't feel like being nice so just shut up for a while. Get something to do as long as it's away from me."

When Myrna finally woke Sunday morning, the sun streamed in through the torn shade and she could hear birds chirping along the ground outside the window. She stretched, feeling strangely relaxed and at peace. Connie and Betty were both up, and she could hear Betty trying to be quiet. She got up and wandered out to the living room, glancing at the clock. Noon already. Ma's door was still closed, which meant it had been another late night for her, one she was going to spend the day sleeping off.

Myrna put water on to boil, staring out absently at the patch of blue sky. If Ma did marry this guy, could they count on things being better? Connie didn't like him—but then, she'd only seen him once. And she had funny ideas—that Connie! Her and her prayers.

She drank her coffee while she flipped through a couple of magazines. Finally she went upstairs to see what was taking so long to do. Betty was carefully setting the table in the kitchen with Kevin's high chair pulled close to the table.

"She's got red steak meat in the 'frigerator," Betty exclaimed. "And she left me a note to put three potatoes in to bake at four o'clock 'cause they're Mike's favorite."

"Aren't you lucky." Myrna strolled through the

house, sniffing at the bottles of perfume on the dresser and listening to the chimes of the musical jewelry box.

A car stopped in front of the house and Betty ran to the window. "They're here! They're here! There's a cab out in front."

Connie hurried to the window. "Yes, it's them. We'd better go down and be out of their way. They got here early. It's not four o'clock yet."

"You mean I can't put in the potatoes?" Betty wailed.

"You'd better wait. Hurry up!"

Betty rushed down the stairs and reached to pull open the outside door, but Connie grabbed her. "No! Don't go out there! Let them come in first. We can watch out the window."

Betty pulled away and rushed to kneel on the couch, pulling the curtain aside. Connie sat down beside her and Myrna leaned over to look past Connie's head. They watched as the cab driver got out and came around to open the door and take out Mrs. Brewster's small case and then a larger one and carry them both down to the porch. He went back and as Mrs. Brewster got out, helping Kevin, the driver leaned inside the cab. They saw Mike's long legs first of all as he sat on the edge of the seat and swung them out of the cab. The driver gripped his arms and helped him stand before reaching into the cab to get something else. It was a cane, a white cane, which he carefully placed in Mike's hand and then took his arm to guide him slowly, stumblingly across the sidewalk and down the broken steps.

Betty's voice was ragged as she whispered, "He's blind—Mike's blind!"

19

Why Did God Let It Happen?

BETTY'S WHISPER shattered the silence that gripped them as they leaned forward to look through the curtains. They could hear the creak of the door as it was pulled open and the thump as a suitcase was put down on the floor.

"There you are. Just show me where this grip goes and I'll heft it for you." The cab driver's voice was falsely hearty.

"Right at the top of the stairs, please, and through the door." Mrs. Brewster's lilting voice drifted to them, sounding so usual, as though nothing were wrong.

"OK. Now you wait right there, and I'll give you a hand up."

They could hear his voice retreating as he went upstairs and then sounding louder as he came down again. "You want to go up first, Ma'am, with the little boy? We'll come on a little slower."

"Take Daddy's hand," Kevin's thin, piping voice insisted.

Then came the deep, firm voice. "Sure, son, take my hand. Hold tight and we'll all go up together."

The steps up were slow, stumbling, and as they listened, Connie began to cry silently, the tears running down her cheeks and dripping off her chin. She slumped down on the sofa and put her head down on her arm along the back of the cushions, her shoulders shaking with the storm of tears.

Betty began to cry then too, and Myrna watched them helplessly. The cab driver came down and went out, closing the door behind him. She watched as he walked slowly toward the broken steps, engrossed in something he was reading, stumbling a little over the bottom step where the cement had crumbled away. Then he folded the paper and shoved it into his pocket, turning to glance at the upstairs window before getting into the cab, shaking his head.

Myrna opened the apartment door quietly and listened. She could hear a murmur of voices through the open door at the top of the stairs and hear Kevin racing back and forth. She looked back over her shoulder at Connie and Betty still crumpled on the couch, Connie's face hidden in the curve of her arm.

"It's not going to help anything for you two to sit here and bawl your eyes out," she finally exclaimed. The sympathy she couldn't help feeling sharpened her voice.

"I—I—c-can't help it. Mike's b-blind! I p-prayed and God d-d-didn't k-keep him safe." The words came in gulps between the racking sobs, punctuated by Betty's tears. "I prayed for Mike, too, but he got hurted anyway."

"That ought to show you how much good it does to pray." But as she said the words she knew there was no satisfaction in them. It wasn't fair that Mike should be hurt when Connie had been so sure he would be kept safe. To be blind! Not to see again, ever! She closed her eyes and then opened them again quickly at the thought of being in darkness all the time.

"*Now* what's going on out here?" Ma's voice was querulous and Myrna turned to see her standing in the bedroom doorway, her hair tousled from sleep, her skin pale without its usual color of makeup. She looked at Connie and Betty and demanded, "What's the matter with them this time?"

"Mike came home an' he's blind an' we prayed but God let him get hurt anyway." Betty sobbed out the answer without looking up.

"He—he's blind? Oh. That's—that's tough." Mrs. Hamilton groped for a chair and sat down. "How do you know? Is he home?"

Myrna nodded. "We saw him come in. He had a cane, a white one like blind guys use, and the cab driver helped him upstairs."

Mrs. Hamilton shrugged. "Oh, well, if that's all you know about it, he may not be really blind. Maybe it's only something temporary." She looked across at Connie. "There's no sense in crying your eyes out until you know for sure."

Connie didn't move or indicate that she had even heard the words, and Mrs. Hamilton added, "You can go up later and find out what's wrong. Right now you'd better think about getting us something to eat. The whole world can't stop just because your Mrs. Brewster has problems."

"I'm never going up there again! Never!" Connie's words were blurred from tears.

"Well, if this will get you over that church craze, I'm glad it happened."

Betty looked around at her mother, her eyes wide and hurt and her lower lip trembling. "You're—you're glad Mike's blind?" Her chin wobbled and her eyes filled with tears.

Mrs. Hamilton gestured impatiently. "Of course I'm not glad he's blind—if he is. Nobody would be glad about something like that. But we've certainly had enough of this religious business. And maybe this will cure them, too. Connie, stop sniveling around and get something ready to eat. You're more interested in what happens to them than in doing something for your own flesh and blood."

Betty followed Connie to the kitchen, wiping her eyes with her sleeve, her voice floating back as she talked. "Connie, how can Mike see to eat that steak meat Mrs. Brewster has in her refrigerator? Can he cut it by himself? Won't it go all over the table? Can you find your mouth when you're blind?"

"Don't talk about it!" Connie's voice was sharp, anguished. "I don't want to talk about it. I don't even want to think about it!"

Myrna had followed to the kitchen in time to hear the broken cry.

"You'll have to. As long as you live in the same house with them, you'll have to see him. What are you going to do—duck out the back door every time?"

Connie turned on her. "It's easy for *you* to talk. You don't care anything about them. You never have. You've always laughed at Mrs. Brewster for everything. You've never liked her. But it's different with me. I—I—she's been my friend—" Her voice broke and she wiped angrily at the tears spilling down her cheeks.

"Well, here's your chance to be her friend. Honestly! The way you're carrying on, anybody'd think he was your husband. Quit thinking about yourself. How do you think she feels?"

Connie stood motionless for a moment and then turned away, wiping her eyes with the back of her hand and sniffing. When she didn't answer, Myrna shrugged and turned back into the living room. No sense in her getting worked up over someone else's problems. But she did feel sorry for them even if she didn't especially like them. It was tough to be blind; especially someone with eyes like Mike had.

All during supper Connie was sunk in a depressed mood that annoyed her mother. Finally she said impatiently, "Well, Connie, if you can concentrate on me for a few minutes instead of yourself, you might be interested in some news I have. I thought you might notice something I'm wearing." She held out her left hand and they stared at the diamond flashing on it. "This means you'll have a new father."

She stopped and looked around at them, her face flushed with excitement and her eyes bright. Myrna looked back, her face expressionless, and Connie didn't lift her eyes from her intent concentration on the crack in her plate. Only Betty's excited "A real father?" interrupted Mrs. Hamilton's rush of explanation.

"Yes, he gave me the ring last night though we picked it out last Monday. We're going to get a license tomorrow and go to the City Hall on Friday to be married."

"Does he know about us?"

Mrs. Hamilton looked back at Myrna. "Certainly!" she answered indignantly. "Connie met him. You remember, Connie? The night he came here?" Without waiting for an answer, she looked back at Myrna. "Of course he doesn't figure he'll have to support *you* for very long. He knows you have a job. I told him you want to be on your own as soon as possible. But he likes kids. He'll take good care of Betty. Connie too. He's got a good-paying job—construction. And I'll work for a while too. I'll have to because we'll lose those measly few bucks in alimony. And of course the welfare money will stop, too."

"Are we gonna move away? I don't want to leave Mrs. Brewster and Kevin," Betty begged.

"We'll stay here for now. After a while we'll move— get something bigger—and better. It'll be crowded but if we all try our best to get along—be nice—"

"What's his name?" Myrna asked abruptly, ignoring the plea in her mother's voice.

"Bert Radford." She looked at them again and this time reached her hands out toward them. "You'll like him. I know you will. Just give him—us—a chance."

They shifted uncomfortably under her unexpected softness, and in the silence the knock at the door was loud.

"I'll get it." Betty jumped up and darted through the living room and pulled open the door. "Hi, Mrs. Brewster. We—we saw Mike come home. We were watching you out the window."

"Were you?" Mrs. Brewster's voice came clear and fresh. "Then you'll want to see him up close. How about coming up and meeting him? You and Connie—" She stopped, her voice unsure as she looked across the room at Connie who came to stand in the kitchen doorway. "and—and anyone else who wants to meet him. He would come down here but it—it would be easier if you—came up." Her voice trembled slightly as she finished, and her smile faded as she looked around at them and felt their silence.

Mrs. Hamilton made an elaborate production out of digging in the pocket of her robe for a cigarette and lighting it before she spoke. "Well, uh, thanks—thanks, but uh—we—we wouldn't want to, you know—barge in—not when your husband is just home and all. I mean, you've got things to—to talk about and we'd—we'd just be in the way."

Mrs. Brewster looked around at them uncertainly.

"Maybe later—another time," Mrs. Hamilton added. Connie stood without speaking, staring at the floor.

"But I want to see him *now*!" Betty darted forward and grabbed Mrs. Brewster's hand, looking up into her face. "You've been talking and *talking* about when Mike comes home and the things he can explain to us. He can still do that, can't he? I mean, just 'cause he's blind doesn't change him any, does it?"

She looked up anxiously at Mrs. Brewster as Mrs. Hamilton said sharply, "Betty, keep still!" and Myrna added, "Shut up, you little dope!"

But Mrs. Brewster put her arm tightly around Betty's shoulder, hugging her close to her side, her eyes brimming with tears as she shook her head. "No, he hasn't changed any—not any—from the way he was in his letters." She answered Betty's question, but her eyes were fixed on Connie's white brooding face as she stood silent and withdrawn in the doorway. "Please come up and meet him."

She waited, and after a moment Connie moved slowly across the room as though walking in her sleep. Myrna watched, but shook her head when Mrs. Brewster turned to look at her.

"Later—maybe. Two are enough at one time."

She couldn't meet him. She didn't dare meet him. If it was true that he still found his religion gave him answers in spite of what had happened to him, then what defense did she have against it? She watched Connie's thin figure move through the open door and climb the stairs behind Mrs. Brewster and Betty. She was sure Connie was desperately in need of reassuring answers. And they couldn't both get the answers they wanted—Connie needing reassurance and she wanting a denial of the reality of Mike's faith.

She heard Ma's voice running on about what a shame it was and war did terrible things to people and what would Mrs. Brewster do with a blind husband and maybe this would cure them both of the crackpot ideas they'd been spouting off and maybe it would cure Connie too. That was certainly something Bert would put a stop to. She was sure he wouldn't put up with any foolishness about church. It was going to be good to have some help raising the kids after having to do it alone all these years.

Myrna only half-listened as she sat on the couch, her legs tucked under her and a cigarette hanging forgotten between her fingers. What was going on upstairs? *I should have gone up too.* But the part of her that was drawn to know what Mike was saying was at the same time repelled by his blindness. Finally she stood up with an abrupt movement.

"I'd better go up and make sure Betty and Connie don't stay too long. They don't have much sense sometimes."

She didn't wait to hear her mother's answer but went out, closed the apartment door behind her, and stood looking up through the darkness of the stairway. The door at the top was closed with only a thin line of light showing beneath it. She went up slowly, pulling herself up with one hand gripping the bannister. A sudden shout of laughter from Mike startled her as she stood listening outside the door. Kevin was laughing, too, in imitation of his father, and she could hear Betty's giggle. She knocked hesitantly and heard someone inside cross the floor and the door was opened.

"Myrna, come in." Mrs. Brewster was smiling though her red-rimmed eyes were evidence that she had been crying. She still had on the yellow suit she had worn to the hospital and Myrna remembered her laughing explanation the day before—"Mike always likes to see me wear yellow. It's his favorite color. I guess it's because he's always been an outdoor person and likes the sun."

Myrna slid into the living room, carefully not looking at Mike, and dropped down on a large puffy footstool next to the TV.

"Well, Myrna. I've been getting acquainted with Connie and Betty so it's good to meet you too. Tell me, do you look like your sisters?"

"She's prettier than Connie but Connie's nicer." Betty scraped the last of the ice cream out of the dish as she spoke.

Mike laughed. "That's a good example of trying to keep on the good side of everyone and not succeeding." He turned his head in his wife's direction as she sat on the arm of his chair and leaned against him. He groped for her hand and she turned hers over, curling her fingers around his.

Myrna looked away and then back from under her lowered lashes, fascinated by the dark good looks in spite of his sightless eyes. She was fascinated too by his seemingly lighthearted manner as though there were nothing wrong with him. She watched as Kevin came over, holding up a toy for his father's inspection.

Mike took it and ran his fingers over it, turning it around in his hands. "What is it?"

"It's really a dog but he calls it a kitty." Betty reached to put an arm around Kevin who pulled away and leaned against his father's knee.

"See kitty?" He looked up into his father's face as he asked.

Myrna heard Mrs. Brewster's quick intake of breath and saw her bite down on her lower lip. But Mike only said, "You tell me what it looks like and then I'll be able to see it."

He lifted Kevin to his lap and listened seriously to his shy jabbering. After a minute Kevin squirmed down and ran to his bedroom in search of another toy. Reaching for his wife's hand again, Mike turned his sightless eyes toward them.

"Maybe now is the best time to talk about my— accident, my disability, as they say in the hospital. Just remember that I'm no big hero type. I'm not going to pretend that I don't mind—that being blind is something I can just take in my stride. It—it was hard to face, knowing I'd never see my wife—Kevin—" He stopped and leaned forward, gripping his hands hard together between his knees. Mrs. Brewster wiped futilely at the tears sliding down her cheeks, and Connie didn't even try to stop hers.

"At first I tried telling myself that it could have been

worse. I could have been killed, or lost my legs and arms and been a helpless cripple, completely dependent on my wife. But it didn't work. I kept coming back to the fact that I was *blind*. Then one day when I was really low—really feeling sorry for myself, I remembered that story in the Bible. Maybe you don't know it. It's about a man who was born blind and Jesus healed him. And he kept saying, Once I was blind but now I see. Well, in a way it was the same with me. I'd been blind once too—not knowing God loved me, that Jesus Christ wanted to be my Saviour. God made me able to see that. And I had to admit God's goodness in bringing me back at all when a lot of the guys in my outfit didn't make it.''

"But God shouldn't have let you get hurt at all. Not—not when you believe in Him.'' It was Connie, her voice low, broken, as she stared down at her hands pleating and unpleating the edge of her skirt.

Mike turned his head in the direction of her voice. "Which one are you? Connie?''

She nodded and then, remembering, answered, "Yes.''

He waited a moment, his head bent in thought, and when his voice came it was remote, from some distant memory of pain. "I thought that too sometimes. Especially in the long nights when the—pain kept me awake and there was nothing to do but think, no one to talk to or joke with as an escape from the questions. And I asked them—Why, God? Lots of other guys got home with no scars, no marks. Why not me, too? He could just as easily have kept me safe. He's so powerful—there's nothing He can't do. So, finally, after a long time—after long nights of thinking—asking the questions—I got my answer. Since He could have done it—kept me safe—and didn't, it meant He didn't want to. And if He didn't want to, there had to be a reason for it even though I couldn't figure out what it was—and maybe never would figure it out. If God has a reason, it should be good enough for me, shouldn't it?"

"Even though God didn't—you still—you're not—I mean, you still—believe the same—" Myrna listened to Connie's halting words and found herself leaning forward, waiting tensely for the answer.

The answer was so positive she couldn't doubt his sincerity. "The only thing I had to hold on to those first weeks when the questions came so strong was that God *loves* me. Whatever He does is for my good even though I can't understand it or even see how it *can* be good for me. God is there back of it all and that's the thing I hang onto."

Myrna made herself sit still when everything in her was crying out to escape from the sadness. She needed to run from the disbelief in her that Mike's words could be true and the longing that filled her for them to be true. She stood up abruptly, hearing her voice loud in the quiet room.

"We'd better go."

Mike raised his head in her direction and then pushed himself erect to hold out his hand to her.

"Well, thanks for coming up and getting acquainted. We'll see you again."

He said the words easily with a smile and Myrna nodded wordlessly as she took his hand and felt his firm grip. "My wife has written me all about how good you girls were to take care of her and Kevin. I sure appreciate that."

"Did she tell you that I'm Kevin's best friend?"

He turned in the direction of Betty's voice and nodded. "She said you were a great baby sitter. And a good conversationalist."

"What's that?"

"It's a polite way of saying you like to talk." He laughed as he answered so that Betty did, too.

"I can understand what Kevin says better'n anybody else," she bragged.

Mike put out his hand, feeling for the big easy chair and moved to sit down, hitting first the arm and then easing himself onto the seat. The groping awkwardness made Myrna turn abruptly, reaching for the door knob.

"We'd better go," she said again, and stumbled through, plunging down the stairs to get away from all the questions and doubts and anxieties that the sight of Mike and all he had said had raised. Life was awful! No matter what Mike said, God was unfair to let something like this happen to him. There were so many awful people who deserved to be punished but nothing ever happened to them. How could he stand it? How could he be so nice about it? It wasn't natural to be like that. It had to be an act he was putting on. It just *had* to be.

She pushed out on to the porch, not wanting to face Ma's questions or listen to Betty's high-pitched chattering over how Mike looked and what he had said. Leaning against the porch railing in the darkness of the soft April night, she knew she wanted it to be real, wanted what Mike had said up there to be true.

20

Myrna Climbs the Stairs

THE MEMORY OF MIKE'S VOICE saying, "Now I see" while his sightless eyes looked at her, haunted her at work Monday. Her jumpy nerves made her skin feel dry and itchy. Going home, she wanted to lash out at the other riders who shoved their way on to the crowded bus. Even the shrill laughter of the girls playing hopscotch on the sidewalk in front of the next-door house was irritating.

As she came in the house, Mrs. Hamilton came out of the kitchen with an ash tray and set it on top of the TV, wiping her hand across the top of the set.

She looked around at Myrna. "Don't dump your purse down in here. Betty, straighten that stack of magazines. And take your junk out of here. Can't you put things away instead of dropping them wherever you happen to stand? Put those jacks away you left scattered on the floor. And fix the blanket on your bed so it doesn't look so lumpy."

Myrna followed Betty into the bedroom. "What's with her?"

"We're having company."

"Who?"

"I don't know. I'll ask—"

"No, wait!" She caught Betty's arm and hauled her back. "I can guess."

She went out to the living room. "Is someone coming?"

She tried to make her voice sound sweet and innocent and knew she hadn't succeeded when her mother turned on her sharply.

"Yes. Bert is coming. He wants to meet you all. See to it that you don't act smart and give out with any sassy remarks, if you know what's good for you." She stopped and looked at Myrna critically. "And don't wear that outfit. Put on pants or something."

"What's the matter with what I'm wearing? Isn't it good enough for him?"

"It's too short. Put on something that covers you up more."

"For crying out loud, Ma! I don't want to change! All kinds of people saw me in this today. I've worn it lots of times. It's not too short. You never said it was too short before!"

"Well, I'm saying it now. Go put on something else. And quit yapping about it."

"Now I've heard everything!" Myrna stalked to the bedroom and yanked off the skirt, her mouth grim and tight. If this was going to be the way things would be from now on, she sure wasn't going to hang around here very long. Too short! What was the matter with Ma anyway?

She went out to the living room, yanking up the zipper on the side of her pant suit and wishing it would break so she'd have a good excuse not to wear it.

"Go help Connie so we can get through eating quick. You too, Betty. And I don't want to hear any unnecessary words out of any of you as long as he's here, see? Or now either."

Her sharp voice sliced off the muttering Myrna had begun as she slammed plates down on the table and dumped the knives and forks in a jumble. Mrs. Hamilton kept giving stacatto orders through her quick bites of food. She shoved her plate back and stood up. "Get the kitchen cleaned up good and don't leave stuff around."

Myrna's lips curved scornfully as she watched Ma cross the living room and listened to the bedroom door slam. "She acts like she's on her first date."

"Well—I guess this is pretty important to her. It's making her nervous." Connie scraped the plates and stacked them as she answered.

"So she takes it out on us as usual. I'll bet *he* doesn't know she yells like this. She's probably been as sweet as sugar to him while she's been trying to snag him."

"What's snag mean?" Betty propped her elbows on the table as she stood beside it, one thin leg twisted around the other, and looked at Myrna.

"It means to catch something—or someone."

"Why did Ma have to catch him? Were they running?"

"He'll wish he *had* run," Myrna muttered, and Connie glanced uneasily toward the closed bedroom door. "You'd better be careful or *you'll* catch it," she warned.

Betty looked from one to the other and said plaintively, "I wish I knew what you were talking about."

"As usual, it's none of your business."

Betty pushed out her lower lip and straightened up. "OK! I'll go read my book if you're gonna be mean."

She marched out of the room holding her bony shoulders stiff, and Myrna ignored her as she asked, "Have you seen them today?" She jerked her head toward the ceiling and watched Connie shake her head. "They went someplace. They've been gone all day."

Myrna sat frowning, drumming her fingers on the table, watching Connie at the sink. "You believe all that stuff he said last night?"

"I believed it before. Now I know it's true."

"I suppose that means you'll go on praying that this guy will let you do what you want."

Connie faced her, her eyes clear and untroubled. "No, I'm not. I mean, yes I am praying still but not in the same way." She struggled for words to explain, frowning slightly with the effort to say it clearly. "I'm trying to pray for him for *himself,* and not just so he'll be good to us. The nurse said once—"

"Oh, the nurse—"

"She said once," Connie went on as though Myrna had not spoken, "that God didn't always take us out of problems. Sometimes we have to go on living with them but He helps us do it—live in them I mean. So—maybe, maybe that's the way this will be. But maybe not," she finished hopefully.

Myrna listened, slumped in her chair, thinking of the desperate wish she'd had last night for Mike's words to be true. The wish was still there but it was mixed with fear—the fear that believing all this stuff about God and

His love would be a new trap worse than the one she'd been in because it would bring a different life, one she wasn't sure she wanted. Would there be any fun, any excitement in it?

Then she heard Connie's shy, hesitant, half-fearful, "I've been praying for you too."

Myrna stared across at her through a haze of anger and longing, seeing Connie's thin white face as she stood like a bird poised for flight, ready to slip out from under a threatening hand. As she stared, holding back words that wanted to lash out, Mrs. Hamilton came to the doorway, adjusting an earring and looking at them with a frown creasing her forehead.

"It's about time you got those dishes done. He'll be here any minute. Now remember to answer any questions he asks and do it politely. No smart remarks from any of you. And Betty, don't talk too much, and for goodness sake don't yak about that blind guy upstairs. They'll meet soon enough."

She crossed the living room to straighten the curtain and pull a chair farther out to cover a worn place in the linoleum. When a car door slammed in front of the house, she moistened her lips and patted her hair with quick, fluttering motions. Then she looked at them again as they clustered silently at the end of the room, and her eyes pleaded, "Be nice now."

They watched her open the door and smile up at the man who stood there, his hands in his pockets jiggling loose change. She put both hands on his arm, pulling him into the room, her voice falsely gay as she hung onto his arm and gestured. "Here they are—your new daughters. Myrna, Connie, and Betty. And this is Bert."

"Hey, *three* dolls! I might have known you'd have good-looking kids." He reached to tweak Betty's braid. "How about it? You think you'll like having a new Dad?"

"You'll be my first one 'cause I don't remember my real one."

"Well, then, that means I gotta try to be a real one."

Myrna looked at him as he sat on the couch, his legs crossed. His broad shoulders leaned forward slightly as he twisted the loop of one shoelace around his finger. She listened to the bursts of loud laughter that punctuated his sentences, and thought, *Why, he's nervous!* She frowned slightly watching him, trying to figure out why Connie had said he was awful. *He probably winked at her and she thought he was trying to flirt with her.*

She looked at Ma sitting close beside him, a smile fastened to her lips as she darted anxious glances from him to them and back again. *She's nervous too.* For the first time she noticed the softness of her mother's mouth and eyes as she looked up at the man, her face lighted with admiration. As she watched them, Myrna heard again the warm sympathy that colored the nurse's voice when she spoke of her mother. She looked at her uncertainly, feeling a reluctant stirring of another emotion than the usual dislike. *I guess—maybe—maybe she has had a hard life.*

Bert had been looking around the room as he talked. He got up and walked toward the kitchen, glancing back at them over his shoulder. "Just want to see what the place is like where I'll be hanging my hat."

He sauntered over to the bedroom, whistling under his breath, and Betty escaped her mother's restraining hand to jump up and stand beside him.

"That's the bed I sleep in and that one's Connie's and Myrna's."

"Yeah? Kinda crowded, ain't it?" He lounged against the doorframe, looking around the room. Then he straightened up and walked across to the dresser. "You need that drawer fixed. Got a screwdriver?"

"I don't know. **What is it?**"

Mrs. Hamilton jumped up. "I'll get one. There's one in the kitchen cabinet."

He took it and pulled the dresser drawer out, whistling softly as he tightened the screws on the knobs.

Betty hung over him. "That looks easy."

"It is when you know how." He moved around the room and stopped to swing the door back and forth. "Shouldn't scrape that way. It needs the hinge screws tightened too."

"You know a lot, don't you?"

Myrna looked across at her mother, wondering if she was glad for once for Betty's continual chatter to keep some conversation going.

Bert had laughed at Betty's admiring question and answered, "Well, kid, as far as I'm concerned, fixing something soon's it's broke ought to be one of the Ten Commandments."

"What are they?"

He looked down at her, surprise showing in his face. "You don't know what the Ten Commandments are? How're you gonna break 'em if you don't know what they are?" He laughed, his teeth white and strong in his sunburned face, and winked at Mrs. Hamilton.

"Where do you learn about them?"

"Betty, quit pestering—" Mrs. Hamilton began.

"Leave her alone. Me and her are getting acquainted." Then he said, "I learned 'em in church."

"You go to church?" Delight widened Betty's eyes and her mouth hung open as she looked from him to her mother and back again.

"Naw! Not now. But I did when I was a kid. Every kid oughta go to church a coupla years anyway."

Myrna heard the little sigh, the uneven catch of breath that escaped Connie. Her mind traveled back to Connie's words—"I'm going to pray for something impossible. That he'll let us go to church." She had mocked and called it magic, but Connie had kept on praying anyway. And now the impossible was happening. Even though Ma was so dead set against church, anyone could see by looking at her watch him that she wouldn't argue if he let Connie and Betty go.

She felt as though the room had tilted crazily. There was no defense left to her, no place she could run to and be safe from prayer. Mike's faith was intact in spite of the terrible blow of being blind, Connie's prayers were all being answered, Betty would yak about church all the time now. Alec—even Alec was interested in religion though it was in the shape of a pretty girl.

Alec—the thought of him jolted her. What about Alec and—and herself? That was a problem she'd buried deep out of thought, refusing to think of it ever since it happened. Now—if she turned to God—she knew instinctively she was going to have to drag it out and look at it. *And I can't! I can't!*

"Myrna!"

She looked across at her mother, almost in a daze, roused out of the walls of panic that were closing in on her.

"We're going for a ride and stop to get ice cream. Do you want to come?"

Betty was hopping up and down, her braids flopping, her thin face alive with excitement. Even Connie was standing, smiling shyly, ready to go.

"N-no. No, I'm beat. I'll stay home."

"You're not going out someplace?"

Her voice was suspicious, and Myrna felt the usual flare of anger when Ma questioned her like that. She shook her head.

"Well, kid, be good. This time next week I'll be your old man. I'll have to get busy and fatten you all up some. You sure could stand it." He grinned and then the smile flickered and died, and he looked around at them soberly.

"I sure hope we get along. I'll do what I can. I've never had kids so maybe I'll be kinda slow learning." He looked down at Betty and suddenly grinned again. "Maybe getting ice cream is a good place to start."

The door shut behind them, chopping off Betty's "*I'm* gonna get choc—"

Myrna stood up and walked around the room restlessly, feeling a trembling along her bare arms, staring down at the worn, scuffed linoleum, the frayed couch. It sounded like things were going to be better—he sounded OK. But there was this other thing—this thing that loomed so frighteningly—

She lifted her head at the sound of the outside door opening and closing and light, quick footsteps going up the stairs. The knock carried clearly in the quiet of the house. When no footsteps sounded overhead in answer, she opened the apartment door and stood at the bottom of the stairs looking up.

The nurse looked down at her. "Hi, Myrna. The Brewsters aren't back yet apparently."

Myrna shook her head. "Connie said they went someplace."

"I know. But Mrs. Brewster thought they would be back by now. I'm working the night shift, and she asked me to stop by on my way to the hospital to meet her husband. She said to go in and wait if I got here before they got back."

She stood on the landing, looking down, her face a pale oval in the shadows. Myrna retreated to the apartment doorway and took hold of the doorknob, watching the nurse open the upstairs door and go in, leaving it open. A lamp clicked on, and the light streamed out to lie in a pool on the landing, reflecting up the wall. Almost against her will Myrna moved forward and planted her feet slowly one after the other up each step until she reached the top and stood hesitantly at the open door. The nurse looked up from where she sat curled in a chair and jumped up.

"Come in. How nice of you to come help me pass the time. Isn't there anyone home at your house either?"

Myrna shook her head. She sank down on the puffy footstool where she'd sat the night before and had listened to Mike talk. The memory brought a flood of words. Gripping her hands together she looked across at the nurse. "I don't know what to do! Connie's having all her prayers answered and now she's praying for me and it scares me. It makes me scared not to believe in God but I don't know how to. And if I do—what about—what about—" She stopped, not able to push the frightened words past the dryness in her throat.

"The baby you were going to have and lost?"

Myrna raised startled eyes, and the nurse nodded. "Yes, I know about it. But not from Connie. You see, it was on your record at the hospital. You may think I was snooping but that wasn't my reason for asking about you. I've been really interested in Betty and Connie—and in you. I've been wanting to talk to you about this but I didn't want you to think I was—oh, blaming you or—or thought I was better than you."

Myrna shut her lips tight to stop their trembling and stared down at her clenched hands through a blur of tears, listening to the soft voice.

"God forgives any sin, Myrna, every sin, when we ask for His forgiveness. This—experience will leave a scar. You will never be able to completely forget what happened. But it is something God can forgive, and He will, if you want Him to. Even though the scar of memory will always be with you, it needn't keep you from accepting God's love and forgiveness."

"What—do I—have to do?" She forced the words out, not able to meet the nurse's eyes.

"Simply believe that God loves you and that the Lord Jesus died for you, to take away your sin. You've seen

Connie's Bible even though you've probably not read any of it. The main theme of the whole Bible is put in one verse. 'For God so loved the world, that He gave His only begotten Son, that whosoever believeth in Him should not perish, but have everlasting life.' There's a lot more than that to know about God, but that's all you need to begin with. Can you believe that He loves you?"

Pictures glimmered through the mist of tears—Mike's sightless eyes in his shining face—Connie's lips trembling as she said, "I'm praying for you too"—Betty's quick delight at the thought of church. She nodded, whispering the words past the lump in her throat, "Yes—yes, I can, I do. But is that all?"

"Accepting God's love and becoming His child is very easy. But then comes the hard part." The nurse stopped, waiting until Myrna lifted her head questioningly, and then went on. "Now you have to live what you believe."

"How do I do that?"

"You begin by letting people know that you believe in the Lord Jesus—Connie and Betty, and they'll be glad of course—your mother—your friends—"

Myrna swallowed. "They'll laugh." She thought of Karen. Marcia. Alec.

"I said it would be hard."

"I—I won't know what to say—how to explain—"

"The best way is by how you act. There are certain things you can't do any more, certain words you can't say—"

Myrna's head jerked up and she looked at the nurse, thinking of the words she had said silently while she stared at her from the hospital bed. But the nurse went on thoughtfully, "—certain places you can't go. Others may but you can't because you are God's child now and you have to live like one."

"I don't know how."

"Of course you don't, not yet. A baby has to learn to

walk and talk. You'll have to learn to walk and talk like one of God's children. You do this by studying—the Bible especially, because that's where God tells you how He wants you to live. Then you'll want to go to church—'' She stopped, frowning slightly. "If your mother won't let you go, there are books you can read. Find friends at school who are Christians. And you can pray. You and Connie can help each other. And Betty too. Help her to grow along with you.''

She stopped and looked at Myrna, a smile lighting her face. "I told Connie only a few months ago that there was no telling what God could do for you and your mother if *she* would believe God and trust the Lord Jesus. Well—look what He has done for you! And now you and Connie and Betty working together—'' She stopped and threw out her hands expressively. "Think what He can do for your mother!''

Myrna felt a lilting pulse of hope beat inside her. The nurse didn't know that God had already started. Connie had dreaded Bert and prayed for him, and here God was already using him to soften Ma about church and he didn't even know it. And Alec—maybe she and Ann together—

She lifted her head and smiled back at the nurse. This life wasn't a trap at all. There was fun and excitement and satisfaction in it even though sorrow and regret would cast a shadow to the end of her days.